Heaven's Fire

Sandra Balzo

ISBN: 1475143001
ISBN-13: 978-1475143003

DEDICATION

To Sam Bartolotta,
heaven's artist-in-residence

ONE

June 29, 2001

"What I remember was being on my feet--all of a sudden on my feet, but I didn't know how I got there. And everyone around me, they were on their feet, too, and I could see their hands slapping together and I could see their mouths moving, but I couldn't hear them. Couldn't hear anything because I was standing in this place of pure light and noise, a place like nowhere I'd ever been before. And I thought, right then: This must be what heaven is."
--Pasquale Firenze

Heaven?

To TV8 producer Wendy "Jake" Jacobus, the video on the monitor in front of her looked more like hell.

But hell sure made for great TV.

A fireworks shell had just burst low over the northernmost of three barges anchored on Lake Michigan for the show. And now, as Jake watched, burning debris from the errant shell was falling into a plywood box the size of a truck bed.

Since the box in question contained all the fireworks shells that hadn't been launched yet, that seemed like a very bad thing.

"Luis!" Jake called to her camera operator on the barge. "Talk to me. What's going on?"

Confined to the TV8 production van for the duration of the broadcast, Jake had only the eight video monitors in front of her to serve as her eyes, and a radio connection to serve as her ears. Most of the time she was just as happy to be the impartial observer. All of a sudden, though, being stuck on the inside looking out was near intolerable.

On Luis Burns' monitor, Pat Firenze--son of fireworks patriarch Pasquale Firenze, the man who had been speaking on the voiceover—was levering himself up onto the edge of the box. As Jake held her breath, Pat lunged, grabbing at the flaming cardboard and looping it up and over the side and onto the deck of the barge, before he landed hard, himself, on top of the shells.

Jake, who had been hovering about two inches above her chair, sank back down as Luis's camera followed the debris, staying with the shot until the fire burned itself harmlessly out. Then the camera slid back over to Pat, already climbing out of the box. In the background, other men scarcely missed a beat as they hustled to pull shells out and get them loaded into the cardboard mortars.

"Luis!" Jake tried the radio again.

Still nothing. She turned to her technical director. "Archie, ready Camera One."

It was Jake's job to choose which shot from the eight cameras to use and then call it out to Archie, who made it all happen. He was very good at his job.

"Take Camera One," she told Archie now, sending a wide shot from the top of the Waverly Apartments out onto the airwaves...or through the cables, more accurately these days.

On the monitor, anchor George Eagleton was deep into "happy talk": "Wow, Martha, I think we here at the Lake Days Fireworks in Liberty, Wisconsin, were just treated to one of Pasquale Firenze's very special fireworks shells."

"A very special misfire," more likely, Jake thought. But then, George loved everyone and everything, even the awful "George and Martha: The First Couple of News" ad campaign TV8 launched when George teamed up with co-anchor Martha Malone. Martha had flatly refused to wear the Martha Washington costume, but George had bounded around the station spouting, "I cannot tell a lie," for days.

As Martha had put it then, "He reminds me of an over-enthusiastic puppy in a tri-corner hat. I'm afraid he's going to piddle on my foot."

But then Jake had more to worry about than her on-air talent piddling on each other.

Like finding out if everybody was okay out there. In addition to Luis and Pat, Pasquale Firenze's best friend Tudy and the rest of his crew were on the barge, along with a thousand pounds or so of explosives. And a TV8 microwave truck. A very *special* TV8 microwave truck. Or at least a very expensive one.

"Luis, talk to me," Jake pleaded, all the while scanning the bank of monitors in front of her for the next shot.

One screen showed the crowd that packed Shore Park. Another, the barges on the lake. Then there was the wide shot of the fireworks Jake was taking currently. And a tight shot of same. George, still talking. Martha Malone frowning at the notes on the desk in front of her. Reporter Neal Cravens prepping for a post-fireworks interview with an unnaturally blonde family of four.

Nothing, though, from Luis's camera, and that worried Jake. Luis Burns had a tendency to be a cowboy, even under the most innocuous of circumstances.

And these weren't the most innocuous of circumstances.

"Luis!" she yelled into the radio.

Silence.

Jake groaned and, with much reluctance, added: "Over."

She hadn't figured out whether Luis was a closet ham-radio operator or he had simply watched too many old war movies. Either way, his radio interaction was always sprinkled with "roger"s, "over"s and even the occasional "wilco."

"You're going to love this, Jake," Luis's voice finally crackled over the radio.

What Jake would love was to ring his disembodied neck.

"I got it all," he was saying. "This big ass fireworks shell explodes low. A mussel burst, the old guy, Tudy, said--I didn't know we had mussels in Lake Michigan, did you?" Luis was talking so fast, his words were even more tangled up in themselves than usual.

"I think he meant 'muzzle,' Luis," Jake offered, "not 'mussel.' But is everyone--"

"So, anyway, part of the burning shit fell into the box with all the unfired shells. 'Fire in the box,' they call it. The thing was so close I could have reached down and touched it. Junior--I mean, 'Pat' dove in and pulled it out before the whole mess blew. It was so cool. Over."

Jake closed her eyes and counted to three. She usually counted to five, but she was short on time today. Ten had fallen by the wayside years ago.

"Luis." She opened her eyes. "Is everyone okay?"

"Roger. Over."

"In *English*, please." Jake ran her hand over her face. "Hold on a sec." She checked the monitors again. "Archie, ready Camera Three."

Camera Three appeared on the preview monitor. Luis's monitor was back on now, but it was showing only the dark lake, with a sprinkling of lights from the spectator boats that dotted the water.

"Listen, Luis, I want the camera pointing up, okay? Fireworks? Sky? And I used your shot of Pat and the 'fire in the box,' but we didn't understand what we were seeing."

She thought for a second, chewing on her thumbnail. "I'll get hold of Gwen and find out if she wants it for news." Gwen Sonntag was TV8's news director and Jake's direct boss.

"That's cool, Jake, just make sure I get credit."

"Yeah, okay." She flipped off the radio and turned to the tech director. "Take Camera Three, Archie, and then let's see if we can get hold of Gwen..."

Unlike the TV8 on-air talent, Simon Aamot of the ATF understood exactly what he had just seen on his television screen.

The federal Bureau of Alcohol, Tobacco and Firearms had jurisdiction over the fireworks industry, and Simon was an explosives specialist out of the Milwaukee office, just north of Liberty.

What he didn't understand was how the camera operator--who was obviously right there--could have stood and filmed it all without doing anything.

You know, something simple like bending down and pulling the burning garbage away from the shells, so they weren't all blown to hell and back. Or just nudging it unobtrusively with his foot to Pat Firenze, so *he* could dispose of it. Or just getting the hell out of there, though that was one of the problems with shooting fireworks from a barge: Where do you go if something goes wrong?

Even assuming the crew had loaded the first group of shells in the mortars, there would be hundreds more in the box, waiting to be reloaded by hand as the initial ones were fired. If all of them had gone up, it would have been one hell of a mess *and* the end of Simon's night off.

He looked at the beer in his hand, the Oreo cookies on his chair and the Irish setter on his couch. The dog was working at getting a cracker and peanut butter off the roof of her mouth and didn't look up.

Okay, admittedly, the night wouldn't have been a huge loss, but the Firenzes would have been.

Simon had been in charge of an investigation of an explosion at the Firenze's fireworks factory two years earlier--one that had killed Pasquale's brother, Francesco. Since then, the ATF agent had spoken at the safety seminars the Firenzes held for their guys, eaten at the Firenze dinner table with the family, and talked late into the night sipping homemade wine on the Firenze porch.

To paraphrase Dickens, it had been the best of times as well as the worst of times. For Simon, anyway.

Pasquale Firenze reached around to peel the Lake Days T-shirt away from his sweat-sticky back and gave a sniff.

His new deodorant had failed, like those TV ads warned. Not that it mattered anyway--he was alone on the barge. No one to smell him or to see him. Nobody to nag, no cameras to play to. All peaceful-like. Just a man and his fireworks, like it should be here in the first year of a new millennium.

Let his son Pat do the publicity bullcrap for Bryan Williams, who was in charge of Lake Days. Who in hell wanted to watch fireworks on the television anyway, that's what Pasquale wanted to know.

Pasquale had been a natural showman from his birth nearly seventy years before. A show-off his mother had called him. Show-off or not, he knew instinctively what people wanted from his fireworks, and it wasn't something they could get through a TV screen.

They wanted to be afraid.

Just a little afraid, but enough. That's what made his fireworks different. They scared people. They were big and they were noisy and they were lighted by men with torches, not computers with wires.

So what if a shell broke low? You made it work, like Pat had just done. You *made* it perfect, even if it wasn't.

To Pasquale, fireworks weren't just something you watched, they were something you felt and smelled and tasted. They thumped you hard in the chest when they went up, and rained black powder and fire when they came back down. In the shower, hours after a show, he would suck in the smell of them, taste the grit in his mouth, and be happy.

Pasquale chewed on his lip now and looked out over the water toward the boats pressing in. The fireworks barges were set in a triangle inside the breakwater, with the north and south barges forming the base of the triangle closest to the shore. Pat was on the north barge with the fireworks for the body of the show, and Pasquale's daughter Angela and her husband Ray-- Tudy's son--were on the south barge with the shells for the grand finale. The center barge, Pasquale's barge, carried the big twelve- and sixteen-inchers, and formed the peak of the triangle, pointing east out across the lake.

Pasquale had done it that way so the big shells would be farthest away from the crowd on shore, just in case something went wrong. There was a crowd on the lake, too, though, and the Coast Guard had been running back and forth all night, herding the pleasure boats back a good two, three football fields away from the barges.

A muffled thud sounded just then, and a rocket went up from one of the spectator boats. Pasquale spat into the water and eyed the shell as it angled toward Angela and Ray's barge, then splashed into the lake, well short, thanks be to God.

Stonatos, he thought. We're sitting on two, three tons of powder out here, and it's like they're lighting giant matches and tossing them at us.

A Coast Guard boat motored past, looking for the *stonatos*, as Pasquale eyed the shells now breaking again over his son's barge. Too slow, he thought. He'd told Pat a million times: It's like music, Little Pat. We're building to a "crescendo."

5

Shaking his head, Pasquale pulled out his radio.

Angela Firenze Guida listened, shaken, as her father gave Pat instructions over the radio. When she'd heard the explosion, she'd worried that--

Ray whistled for his wife from the mortars. "Hey, Angie. Get your gorgeous butt over here. We go in three."

She stumbled to her husband. "But did you see what happened? Fire in the box. Your father and Pat could have been killed."

"Yeah?" Ray looked up from the sandbag he was adjusting at the base of the first finale mortar. "Makes you wonder who packed the shell, doesn't it?"

Getting no answer, Ray fished in his shirt pocket and pulled out a plastic sandwich bag. In it was a battered pack of cigarettes with a silver lighter tucked between the pack and the cellophane. "You got a flare or we going to use my lighter?"

"I have a flare, and you know you shouldn't smoke around the shells."

"You don't want me to smoke anywhere."

It was true. Angela hated that Ray smoked cigarettes. The smell clung to everything.

She just shrugged and Ray, watching her, slipped the smudged lighter out and, with one smooth movement, flipped open the lid and flicked the wheel, sending sparks and an orange flame up into the night. "See? Fireworks? Oohh-ahh..."

He smiled at her, and she caught a glimpse of the charming clown he had been back in high school. "It's almost time, Ray."

He blew out the flame and snapped the lighter closed, setting it down with the cigarettes before moving toward the end of the quickmatch. "You have to lighten up, Angie, you know? Things can't always be perfect."

He was right, of course. Angela did want everything to be right. And so little in life was. She picked up the red flare, twisted off the end, and struck it on the floor of the barge like a giant match. "It's just--"

"Don't jump the cue now. They'll count us down," Ray interrupted. His face looked yellow in the light from the torch.

Angela nodded and waited, flare burning at her side. Her father's voice crackled over the radio. "Finale in five, four, three, two, one."

She touched the flare to the end of the quickmatch and the flame raced down the fuse to the shells. Quickmatch was cotton string, coated in black powder and then encased in paper tubing. The tubing contained the gases from combustion, causing the fuse to burn very quickly--sixty feet per second. Without the tubing, the same fuse would burn closer to one inch per second.

The quickmatch flashed down the mortars set out on the south barge like giant explosive dominos--one row dividing into two, two into four, four into sixteen--sending up shell after shell, faster and faster, to create a spectacular tangle of light and color in the sky.

"Heaven's Fire," her father called it, and Angela treasured that verbal poetry from the man who had devoted his life to creating the visual and the aural.

To creating perfection, because nothing else would do.

As the titanium salutes started up, Angela Firenze Guida took a step away from her husband and lifted her face to the sky.

Pasquale was watching the lighted windows of the Waverly Apartments as he waited his turn, flare in hand. The white titanium salutes were thundering overhead, building momentum, and Pasquale could feel the crowd holding its collective breath, wondering whether this time, this year, the windows of that building would all come tumbling down. And they'd be here to see it.

Every year, the Monday morning after Lake Days, Mrs. Fetcher from the apartments would call and complain to Pasquale that her scrawny dog "Coco" was afraid to go out to do its business.

The way Pasquale figured it, *he* hadn't done *his* business right if that call didn't come.

"You ready, little dog?" Pasquale called out across the water. He waved the flare in the direction of the Waverly. His felt almost giddy now, like a young man with his whole life in front of him. "You already do your business for the night, Kooky? I sure hope so."

The salutes cut off then, and Pasquale, blocking the wind with his body, steadied his hand and touched the flare to the quickmatch. The quickmatch would light the time fuses on each sixteen-inch shell and send them up three seconds apart, just like clockwork.

The fireworks man felt good, focused, like he always did during a big show. Acutely aware of just himself and the job at hand. He heard only the whoosh of the quickmatch. Then the "whump," when the first lift charge ignited. And a whistle as the red shell rose. A sizzle now as the flame marched down the time fuse to the white shell. Pasquale stood back and counted. One one-thousand, two one-thousand, three one-thousand--

Whump. The white lift charge, right on time. Pasquale counted again, for the blue shell this time. One one-thousand, two one-thousand, three one-thousand, four-one thousand, five...

Something was wrong. Pasquale was already moving forward, fearing the time fuse had failed and knowing he would have to re-light the blue shell by hand. Nobody would even notice, though, if he worked fast enough. If he got there quick enough.

The hot wind died just then, without warning, and in the utter stillness, time seemed to downshift too, like slow motion.

Pasquale was almost at the blue's mortar with his flare, feeling like he was wading through water, when he heard the first shell, the red one, break overhead. He looked up--had to look even now, with time so precious--and watched the burst unfold so beautiful he just wanted to stop and savor it.

But the seconds were ticking away, and as Pasquale reached the mortar, he heard the white shell burst above him, too. The silver strobes cascading from the center--dangling, floating impossibly long in the sky--giving off just enough light for Pasquale to see the third mortar clearly.

It was just three seconds later--time enough for Pasquale to lean down to the mortar, time enough for the strobes to reach the lake, hissing as they touched--when there was yet another explosion of sound and light. A third explosion--louder and brighter than anything Pasquale had ever known. So much sound and so much light, so pure, so overpowering, that suddenly there was no sound or light at all. Just him. Pasquale.

And the sky.

The noise of the blast was deafening, followed by the stunned hush of a quarter of a million voices temporarily silenced. Then came the low whine of a small plane overhead, the light-bulb message dancing across its wings:

"Thank you for coming. Drive home safely."

.

TWO

Simon Aamot was on his feet in front of the TV screen. Irish, agitated by both the noise of the explosion and Simon's reaction to it, had jumped off the couch and was alternately barking and snarfling at the open package of Oreos that had fallen on the floor when Simon stood up.

"Quiet, Irish." Simon put his hand on the dog's head.

Martha Malone was speaking. "...trying to get more information here for you, but I think we can be fairly certain that something has gone horribly wrong at this year's Refresh Yourself Lake Days Fireworks."

The male anchor, George Eagleton, picked up from there. "Let's recap what we know so far. Apparently, there has been an explosion on the center barge. That's where Pasquale Firenze is, and also where the three sixteen-inch fireworks shells--that's sixteen inches in diameter--are. The shells: one red, one white and one blue, were billed as the largest ever fired in the state. We saw two of those three shells, the red and the white, go up. The blue shell did not. I should note, however, that the explosion we saw on the barge was not blue, meaning, perhaps, that it was not the third shell that exploded, but something else."

Or that the shell exploded deep in the mortar, Simon thought.

Eagleton's voice again. "I understand we have a closer look at what happened. Is that tape ready?" A hesitation, then a wide shot of three barges, a mass of white flickering lights suspended over the one on the right. The titanium salutes of the finale.

Then the promised close-up of the center barge. A barrel-shaped figure with a torch--Pasquale--moving toward the middle of the barge. Stopping. Then backing away from the mortars.

A flash in the first mortar as the lift charge ignited and the red shell went up. The time fuse on the shell would have been ignited at the same time the

9

lift charge was, Simon knew. The slow-burning time fuse was designed to give the shell enough time--probably ten seconds on a shell this size--to climb to the appropriate height before it actually broke.

Simon hunkered down, keeping his eyes on the screen. Irish turned and licked his face. She smelled like peanut butter and chocolate. Simon snagged the torn cellophane package of Oreos and tossed it onto the chair. As the cookies landed, a second mortar flashed on his screen and the white shell went up.

Simon waited.

He could see Pasquale moving back toward the center of the barge with the flare. The view was so close-in that he felt like it all was happening in the same room with him.

"Jesus, Pasquale, don't be a fool," he muttered under his breath. Pasquale and the flare stopped dead center of the barge.

Fireworks on TV generally sucked.

Still, standing there in his living room twenty miles away from Liberty, Simon Aamot could practically feel the concussion as the third mortar on the barge exploded, and fire engulfed the place where Pasquale Firenze had been.

The close-up made Jake sick to her stomach.

And if she felt that way, how would the Firenze family feel when they saw it?

It was her own fault. In Jake's haste to get the story to air, she hadn't previewed all of the footage Luis had fed her, and it proved far more graphic than she had expected. She'd had no idea Pasquale had returned to the mortar, that he'd been right there, leaning down, when...

"Jake!" Martha's insistent voice came over the radio. "Do you have that background?"

"Sorry, Martha." Jake looked down at the scribbled notes in front of her. "Two years ago, Pasquale's brother, Francesco Firenze, was killed in an explosion at the factory. ATF investigators ruled that lightning was the cause."

"Were there any *other* lightning strikes in the area at the time?" Martha's image on the monitor asked.

"Not that were reported," Jake was still sorting through the papers on her console. "Oh," she said, remembering Luis's 'mussel-burst.' "That shell that exploded low about half-way through tonight's show wasn't 'very special.' It broke too low, and debris from it landed in a box of unexploded fireworks. Pat Firenze managed to pull it out before it set the whole thing off. We have tape."

"Good, good." Jake could hear Martha scribbling notes. "Who's the source on that?"

"Luis Burns," Jake said, her stomach doing another flip. Luis's link had gone down again right after he'd fed her the close-up of Pasquale.

On cue, the radio squawked. "This is Luis. Come in, Jake. Over."

Jake stabbed at the switch so quickly she'd have broken a nail if she had any left. "Luis? Are you okay? What happened to your signal?"

"Jake?" Martha again, talking over the top of her. "For God's sake, is that it? Is that all you have to give me?"

In truth, Jake was dying to give her something else, but settled for, "That's it, Martha. We're out of the break in one minute."

Now, back to Luis.

"I'm okay, Jake," his voice was saying, "but we were rocked pretty good, and..." He let it trail off.

"And what?" There went her stomach again. "Is everybody else on that barge all right?"

"Sure, we're okay, but the microwave truck sort of..."

"The truck was hit?" Jake imagined the battered truck, all four tires blown, being towed off the barge. Competing local stations would be covering it along with, in her imagination, all the national and cable news--

"Actually, Jake," Luis cleared his throat. "It's gone."

"Gone?"

"Yeah. That corner of the barge was swamped, and it went over."

"The truck went...?"

"...over."

And out.

"Jesus Christ, is anybody out there? Dad? Ray? Angela?"

Pat Firenze tried to switch frequencies from "1" to "2", but his hand was shaking so badly the toggle switch on the side of the radio kept landing back on "1."

Tudy took the radio from him, pushed the switch to "2" and handed it back to him. "Take a deep breath, son. Getting yourself all worked up isn't going to help anybody."

Well then what was? Pat tried the radio again, this time on the alternate frequency. "This is Pat Firenze. Can anybody tell me what happened?"

His message was interrupted by another voice: "Hey, Manny? Is it okay to lift Gate Four? That way we'll empty the structure faster."

Manny? Structure? He had Manny's fuckin' Parking Garage on the radio. Pat winged the radio into the lake.

"That probably wasn't so smart," Tudy said as the radio disappeared into the dark water.

Pat knew the old man was right, but he sure wasn't going to admit it. "Fat lot of good the radios are. We're closer to Dad's barge than anyone, and we don't even know what happened." He waved at TV8's lights on shore. "They

11

probably know if my father's okay, the whole fuckin' world probably knows, except us."

Pat stopped and looked around. "Hey, where's that camera man? He'll have a radio."

Tudy shrugged. "Haven't seen him since he unplugged himself from that truck of theirs as it went down. Couldn't have gone far though."

"Next time," Pat said, "we get radios from TV8 so we can communicate with them, not just with each other. Next time..." He let it go, realizing there might not *be* a next time.

"Ray!" Tudy called out to his son across the water. "Ray, you hear me?"

Why hadn't Pat thought of that? Maybe now that the boat horns and sirens had quieted down some, Ray could hear them.

Pat gave it a try: "Angela? Dad?"

"Pat? Is that--" His sister Angela's voice wafted across the water, but was drowned out by the motor of a small Coast Guard boat streaking by.

Half the crowd had already left by the time Simon Aamot arrived at Shore Park. Or they were trying to leave, clogging every street leading from the lakefront. The other 125,000 people milled around talking and gawking.

Most times in situations like this, local agencies were just as happy to have ATF take the mess off their hands. Simon didn't figure this one would be any different, once everyone was done marking his territory. Like a bunch of dogs, himself included. Piss on it, it's yours. Even though you didn't really want it in the first place.

Because the fireworks show was on the lakefront, it was considered a marine event. That meant the Coast Guard had primary jurisdiction. The park land, though, was probably city or county. Depending on which, Simon would also be working with either the Liberty police or the County Sheriff.

Nobody paid Simon much attention as he wound his way through the crowd. He approached a uniformed city officer who was talking to a motorcycle cop by his bike. "Went up like a Roman candle," the officer was saying.

Simon identified himself to the two, then asked for the command post.

The cop eyed him. "You guys taking over?"

Simon shrugged. "Maybe. I'm just trying to get the lay of the land right now. Who's in charge?"

"Coast Guard, but I'm not sure who exactly. There's a command center set up just over the bluff." The cop nodded toward the south. "Check with them."

Simon thanked him and headed off in the direction indicated.

The command center was a white aluminum motor home with the words "County Sheriff's Department" stenciled in black and gold on the side.

Well, one question answered, anyway.

As Simon approached the door of the command center, a burly figure stepped out. Simon recognized Thomas Watson, the Liberty County Sheriff. "Thomas."

Watson was a little shorter than Simon's 6'4" but looked bigger, probably due to the extra forty or so pounds he had on him. The forty had been muscle at one time, but as the sheriff approached middle-age and settled into an administrative position, the muscle was softening to fat.

The sheriff turned toward Simon, extending a pudgy right hand. "Figured you'd be here. Your RAC was on the line to me before the barge stopped rocking. Quite the eager beaver."

Simon shook with him. "Collins is new," Simon said, referring to his RAC, or the Regional Agent in Charge of the ATF office.

"Yeah? Give him a couple more years. He'll burn out, too."

None of them was getting any younger, Simon thought, watching Watson hitch up his pants. "I saw what happened on TV. It looked like Pasquale took the full blast."

Watson shook his head sadly. "Likely blown to kingdom come. The Coast Guard and our boats are out there looking, but so far they haven't found any sign of Firenze. To make matters worse, his son-in-law," he checked his notes, "a Guida, Raymond, is missing off the barge to the south."

Watson looked back up. "You know, I've known Pasquale Firenze since he started doing shows here seventeen years ago. I've never seen him do anything outright dangerous."

Besides routinely firing a ton of explosives, Simon thought.

Watson read the look on his face. "You know what I mean, man. Firenze was careful. He didn't take chances. Shit, he drove his people crazy with all his rules. I just don't get why he went out there all by himself with those big-ass shells."

Simon shrugged. "Knowing Pasquale, he didn't trust anyone else with them."

But Watson was looking past Simon's right shoulder. "Well, look who's coming."

Simon turned and saw TV8's Martha Malone and a camera man bearing down on them.

Simon turned back to the sheriff. "Who's in charge for the Coast Guard?"

"Jeff Longenecker. He's inside." Watson was still watching Malone's approach. "She's got great hooters, you ever notice that?"

Simon shook his head, spared from answering by Malone's arrival. The reporter ignored Simon and grabbed Watson's hand, pumping it professional-to-professional. "Sheriff, Martha Malone, TV8."

Simon watched Watson assume his public persona, meaning he sucked in his gut, rendering the earlier pants-hitching moot. "Good to see you again, Ms. Malone," the sheriff said. "What can I do for you?"

Her camera man already had his light on and was shooting from the shoulder. Simon cracked open the door of the motor home as Malone pulled out her notebook. "We understand that two men are missing from the barges," she was saying. "Can you tell us..."

Inside the command center, two men and a woman were gathered around a table, studying a map of the harbor. One of the men looked up as Simon entered and the ATF agent was struck, not for the first time, by how uncannily Lieutenant Jeff Longenecker resembled his name. Though not as tall as Simon, Longenecker had an unusually lanky neck and a protruding Adam's apple that made him look like a caricature of himself.

"Aamot. Glad you're here." The lieutenant turned to the other two. "Simon Aamot, with ATF."

"I assume you'll want to get out to the barge as soon as you can?" Longenecker continued, not bothering with further social niceties, liked the names of the petty officers he had been talking to.

Simon nodded. "It's still afloat, then?"

The lieutenant pointed at three rectangles penciled on the map. "Steel-topped river barges--it takes a lot to sink them. We're assuming that Pasquale Firenze was blown into the water by the force of the blast on his own barge and that Ray Guida was swept off the south barge by the wash. We need to talk to Guida's wife, who was out there with him."

"No sign of either Firenze or Guida?"

Longenecker didn't look up from his map. "Not yet. We'll keep looking, but I'm doubtful we'll find any body until morning."

Longenecker had a disjointed way of speaking. Doubtful became "doubt full." Anybody became "any body." Appropriate in this case, if macabre.

The young male petty officer next to Longenecker spoke up. "I hate to ask this, sir, but can you give us any idea how far out we should be looking?"

Simon drew a finger circle around the center barge. "In theory, a sixteen-inch shell would have a sixteen-hundred foot bursting diameter."

The young officer rubbed his chin. "A third of a mile."

Simon nodded. "Yes, but I said in theory. If the shell never left the mortar, the burst would have been more contained."

Longenecker's Adam's apple quivered. "So, what is your best guess here?"

"I'd say Pasquale would have been thrown in the immediate vicinity of the barge, probably well within 500 feet. If Guida was washed off, he'd be closer in. But that's just a guess. You guys probably have a better idea of the currents than I do, which might affect their locations more by now, anyway. Can you get me out there?"

Longenecker nodded. "Kutchera here is heading back," he said, pointing to the petty officer. You can go with him."

The way Jake figured it, it was Martha's own fault the ATF guy, who she'd apparently ignored in favor of the sheriff, had gotten away. So why was she taking it out on Jake's crew?

Because she could, apparently. Dragging a camera man in her wake, the anchor was still searching for this Simon-Whoever. When she found him, she planned to shoot tape and then have the cassette run back to Jake at the production truck.

Meanwhile, George Eagleton was calmly continuing the live coverage from the set, and Neal Cravens was about to do a remote with the young family he had interviewed earlier. It was what Jake thought of as a "Howdy," or "How-do-you..." interview:

How do you...feel?

How do you...go on living?

Whatever Howdy fits the occasion. Jake hated Howdys. But they were broadcast staples. Especially a live disaster broadcast.

"Neal, you're on in thirty seconds."

The reporter nodded solemnly into the camera lens. Neal didn't like Howdys any more than Jake did, but he knew that this kind of exposure could win him an anchor job somewhere. And Neal was making the most of the opportunity.

A countdown and Neal and his guests were into the interview, pretty Mrs. Jenson recounting how she felt at the moment of the explosion.

Jake mentally turned down the volume, just as Luis called in from the main barge.

"I'm going to interview Pat Firenze," Luis said without preface. "And then I'll get the tape to you." The cameraman was so excited he forgot to say "over."

"And how are you going to do that? Walk on water?" Jake asked, not sure she wanted to know the answer. If the camera was waterproof, the kid would probably try it, climaxing his act by scaling the ladder that ran twenty rickety feet up the seawall from lake level. Taping all the while, of course. "Just do the interview and stay put for now. Do you need some questions for Pat?"

"Got it covered. What does he think happened, how could it have happened, how does it feel knowing that your fireworks may have killed two people. The usual."

"Try to use a little tact, Luis. One of those 'people' is Pat's father, the other his brother-in-law. And they're missing at this point, not dead."

"Faith, Jake. Trust me. How much of my stuff did you get before the van went down?"

Jake had to admit Luis had gotten some great shots up to the time of the explosion. She told him as much.

"Thanks. Did you get the old man going back to the mortar?"

Jake cringed.

But Luis wasn't waiting for an answer. "I started running tape when I lost the link. I think you'll like it. I may even have the van going glub, glub, glub--"

The sound of her career going under, Jake thought, practical concerns overriding the philosophical. Just how much would a microwave van cost to replace, did you suppose?

Jake could see Neal wrapping up. "Okay, Luis," she said. "Do the interview and get your butt back over here somehow. Safely."

"Roger and out."

Surreal, Simon thought, as Kutchera's 41-footer--what the Coast Guard considered "a small boat"--approached the center barge. The immediate area around all three barges was a mass of red strobes and searchlights, making the center barge's deck look like a half-scale model of an aircraft carrier.

"Where are the fireworks people now?" Simon asked.

"Mostly on the north barge." Kutchera nodded toward it as they passed. "We have a boat transporting Mrs. Guida there, too. She was on the south barge with her husband."

"No casualties on the north?"

"Just the TV truck, sir."

Simon looked over at Kutchera, who the rest of the four-man crew referred to as "Boats," short for "Boatswains Mate." He was busy threading their vessel through a maze of official craft. "TV truck?"

Kutchera kept his eyes on the water, but the corners of his mouth twitched. "One of those vans with the big antennae things on top. Reportedly, it's in the drink."

That struck Simon as perversely funny, too. "What a damn shame. Where was it?"

Now Kutchera grinned full out. "On the corner closest to the center barge. The swell from the blast swept it right off from the sounds of it."

Maybe not so funny. What had happened to the TV truck was a mirror image of what probably had happened to Ray Guida on the opposite barge.

"Why don't you drop me at the scene of the explosion so I can take a look around," Simon suggested. "Then I'd like to talk to Pat Firenze and his sister."

Kutchera, sober again, too, nodded.

Simon surveyed the center barge as they motored slowly toward it. It seemed to have a small list to one side, but he couldn't see any other damage. Nor anything else, except for two figures. "Fire department?" he asked.

"Just our people now. There wasn't much in the way of flames, but the fire boat took care of what there was."

Not much left to burn, Simon thought. The blue shell had been the last one of the night.

He stepped off onto the barge's deck, loaded down with the digital, 35mm and video cameras he had retrieved from his truck before heading out. Simon turned back to Kutchera. "You going to wait?"

"We're at your disposal. You need help with that stuff?"

Simon shook his head and approached the two petty officers. "Simon Aamot, ATF. I'll be looking around."

They checked his credentials and waved him on.

By definition born of necessity, a river barge is long and narrow. This particular one was a hundred feet by about forty, probably used to carry oil or paper down the Wisconsin River. Simon moved toward the middle of the barge, his footsteps rasping on the steel floor strewn with sand. When he got there, he stood stock still and looked around.

The mortars for the sixteen-inch shells would have been heavy cardboard and the size of garbage cans. Sandbags would have been stacked against them for stability. But now in the white glare of the floodlights, only burnt remnants, black scorch marks and the scattering of glistening sand marked where any of it had been.

As for Pasquale Firenze, there was no sign that he had ever been there at all.

THREE

Luis Burns was stoked.

He'd been on his belly at the edge of the barge trying to get a shot of the microwave van under water, when Pat Firenze tracked him down.

It turned out Junior didn't have any idea that his dad was blown up on one barge and another guy was missing from the other. Talk about a communications problem. Luis filled him in and then, striking while the iron was in the fire, got the guy to agree to an interview.

Luis wished he'd had the camera up and taping when he broke the news but, hey, sometimes a little restraint was in order. He would probably get a better interview, anyway, because he was being sensitive.

"So Junior...I mean, Pat," he said, raising his voice to be heard over the sound of a boat motoring toward them, "what would you do different next time?"

He asked the question over the top of the camera, thinking if only he'd brought a tripod for the camera he could step into the frame next to Junior. The question was good, though. It was one Luis'd heard Martha Malone use a lot.

Junior blinked into the camera light. "Well, I don't know. I think maybe we'd--"

"Excuse me, you'll have to do this later. I need to talk to Mr. Firenze."

Luis looked up from the eyepiece at the big dude that was blocking his shot. "Who are you?"

"Simon Aamot. I'm with ATF."

Cool. And come to think of it, the guy did look like a Fed. Sort of like Tommy Lee Jones, only taller and younger, thinner and better-looking. "Great. I'll talk to you instead." Luis tilted the camera up and leveled it on Aamot.

"No, you won't. You'll stay out of my way." The Fed stepped closer and put his hand up to block Luis's lens. *Nobody* touched Luis's lens. "Hey!" Luis lowered the camera and backed away. "You heard of freedom of the press? I got a right to be here."

"This is a crime scene. You don't have any rights here at all. Maybe you should go look for your TV truck."

Luis had already done that. But he didn't think that's what the Fed meant. This sounded more like a threat.

Luis thought about what Jake had told him once about getting more with piss than with vinegar. "Listen man, I'm stuck here. And you'll want to talk to me anyway, right? I mean, I shot the whole thing."

He could see Aamot was thinking about it. "You're right," the Fed finally said. "I'll need to see everything you filmed. Wait at the boat, and we'll take you back."

Luis wasn't good at waiting. Besides, he had to get his tapes back before the Fed or anybody else got their hands on them.

"I don't want to hurry you, man. Maybe he," Luis gestured at the Coast Guard guy on the boat, "could take me back to shore on the cutter and come back for you. I could have the tape all queued and ready for you in the production truck."

"What's your name?"

"Luis Burns. So listen, I'll--"

The Fed put his hand on Luis's shoulder and turned him and his camera around. "Well, Luis, that's a boat, Petty Officer Kutchera is piloting, not a cutter. Cutters are 65-feet or longer. But don't you worry. I'll be done here soon, and then we'll go back together and you can learn all about boats and the Coast Guard, before we look at the film. *Also* together. Understand?"

Luis shrugged away. He liked his personal space. "Yeah. Okay. Sure."

Aamot turned to talk to Junior, and Luis subtly edged back toward them.

"He kept asking questions," he heard Junior say. "What happened, what my father had done wrong, were the shells too big to be safely fired--"

The Fed asked something so quiet, Luis couldn't hear him. Whatever it was, Junior didn't like it. He pulled his cap off and ran his hand through his hair. "Damn it, Simon, what do you want me to say? That we shouldn't have done the sixteen-inch shells the customer wanted? Who knew? Other companies are doing bigger shells without a problem."

Simon, huh? Aamot and Junior must know each other. Pretty cozy, the investigator and investigatee being tight.

"But maybe not on barges," the Fed said, giving Junior the same kind of stare he'd given Luis. "And not fired by hand."

So maybe they weren't so tight. Junior looked like he was going to cry. "My dad...Dad wouldn't fire electronically. He said the drama was in the torches."

Aamot shook his head. "Your father didn't usually cut corners, Pat. I've seen him refuse to fire a show when the crowd was too close or he didn't think the site was safe."

Ahh, so the site wasn't safe.

"And you're wondering why he didn't do that this time?" Junior was getting mad all over again. "This is our biggest show next to the Fourth of July, Simon. Dad didn't want to lose it. Me, Angela and Ray, my mother and father, Tudy, our employees and their families, we all depend on Firenze Fireworks. We don't shoot fireworks, we don't eat."

The Fed started to say something, but Junior kept going. He was sticking his finger in Aamot's face for emphasis, something that struck Luis as not such a hot idea. "But big show or not," Junior said, "my father wouldn't risk hurting someone. Why aren't you looking for him, instead of trying to blame him?"

Sure enough, Aamot told Junior to drop the finger. Then he turned to Luis. "And you? You go to the boat or I'm going to drop *you* in your tracks. Got it?"

Luis got it.

Simon steered Pat away from Luis Burns and anybody else who might be able to hear them.

"Listen, Pat, the Coast Guard is doing everything they can to find your father and Ray. You have to know, though, that the chances of Pasquale having survived a blast that close are not good. As for Ray, let's hope that one of the spectator boats picked him up."

Pat hesitated, started to say something, then just nodded.

"You also know that I have to do my job and that means finding out what happened. But I'm not like that camera guy, I'm not looking for some talking point or sound bite. I just want to determine what happened. And so do you, I think."

"Pat?" Tudy Guida's voice behind them. "Another Coast Guard boat is bringing Angela."

Simon flinched and turned to face the little man. "Tudy, I'm sorry."

Tudy wouldn't meet his eyes. "You've found them then?"

"No, not yet. I didn't mean to make you think otherwise."

Tudy had a tooth missing in front and a habit of poking his tongue through the open space when he thought. He was thinking hard now, the tongue darting in and out. "This is terrible, just terrible," he said, looking beyond Simon toward the water.

"Why don't you tell me about the shells?" Simon suggested, wanting the old man to focus on something concrete. "How they were made, how they were fired."

Tudy tried to answer, but Pat interrupted. He seemed to be back in control of himself. "Three sixteen-inch round shells with two-pound black powder lift charges. They each had a ten-second time fuse."

It jibed with what Simon had seen on the vivid replay of the explosion. "The three shells were on one quickmatch?"

"Quickmatch up to the first shell, then a three-second time fuse between the first and second, and between the second and third. Dad wanted them to break individually, but be fired close enough so they'd overlap in the air. It should have worked."

"Who made the shells?"

"My father. He wouldn't let anyone else touch them." Pat looked over at Simon. "I saw him build them, Simon. Everything was right."

In the ATF man's mind, fireworks shells were a lot like parachutes. You didn't know they were packed wrong until it was too late to do anything about it.

Simon nodded toward Luis Burns, who was standing by the Coast Guard boat, chatting up Kutchera. "The media will be on you thicker than flies. Decide what you want to say now and just stick with it. They'll keep asking the same questions in every way they can think of. You just keep feeding them back the same answer. Don't let them rattle you."

But Pat had caught sight of a figure being helped off a second Coast Guard boat that had just pulled alongside. "I need to see my sister."

As if she had heard him, the figure turned and crossed the barge toward them. Angela Firenze Guida was tall and slim, the opposite of her fireplug brother and father. She slipped into their group, hugging first Pat and then Tudy, before turning to Simon.

She held out both hands. "Simon."

Simon hesitated and then took her hands, not quite knowing what to say. The Firenze daughter had always seemed more European, more "Italy" Italian, than either her father or mother, both of whom had been born in the country. Angela had an exotic grace about her, perhaps the result of going to school abroad.

"I'm sorry to be bothering you now, Angela," he ventured.

She ignored his apology, just staring up into his eyes. "Have you found Ray? My father?"

She seemed almost somnambular, like things weren't registering. In Simon's experience that meant she was in for a big fall later. Still it made the woman easier for him to deal with now, heartless as that might seem. He let go of Angela's hands. "I'm sorry. No. You were on the south barge with Ray?"

"That's right." She backed up a little half-step, and her eyes filled. "We fired the finale."

"Where was Ray at the moment of the explosion?"

"On the side closest to my father's barge."

"Was your husband near the edge?" His words sounded formal, even to his own ears.

Angela didn't react. "Yes, but I'm not certain how close. I had moved away to watch the finale." She looked down at her hands. "Ray liked to smoke after a show, and I hated his cigarettes."

Simon wasn't surprised. A lot of fireworks technicians smoked. Yet another warning from the Surgeon General for the side of the cigarette pack. "Warning: Smoking can blow you to smithereens."

"Did you see what happened to Ray?" he persisted.

Angela shook her head. "The blast...I looked over for him after the explosion. I was screaming for him to help my father. But Ray, he couldn't-- he wasn't there..." Her voice trailed off disbelievingly as she stared across the lake again. Tudy put one thin arm around her and gave Simon the eye.

Simon, already treading carefully, backed off. "Thank you, Angela. I won't bother you any more tonight." He turned to Pat. "Will you be at the factory tomorrow?"

Tomorrow was Saturday, but in Simon's experience, the Firenze family worked seven days a week. That was only partly because Pasquale and his wife, Sadie, lived in a house just up the private road from the fireworks factory.

Pat nodded, but didn't say anything.

Simon touched his arm. "Why don't we take you all back? There's no need for you to stay out here."

Pat was watching the boats still combing the lake. "I think we'll stay for a while. Thanks."

Simon nodded and returned to the boat. Kutchera was onboard, but Burns was still on the barge, his camera leveled at the triangle that Pat, Tudy and Angela now formed as they gazed out over the lake.

The kid just couldn't leave them alone. Then again, in his own way, Simon would be just as bad. Maybe worse.

George: *"Speaking of the three sixteen-inch shells, the last one of which, the blue one, evidently exploded too low, plunging Pasquale Firenze, president of Firenze Fireworks, and his son-in-law, Ray Guida, into the waters of Lake Michigan, we have tape of those shells being made . . ."*

Jake rolled the tape, wondering if George Eagleton could have made that sentence any longer. Still, this was one time it really paid off to have an anchor who loved to hear himself talk.

Martha Malone was back on the set now, too, apparently having given up on both tracking down the ATF guy and convincing the Coast Guard to take her out to the barge. It was probably the first time she'd been turned down by a sailor.

Yikes, Jake thought, where did *that* come from? She must be getting punchy. Nearly midnight and they had been on the air live for three hours, the last two of those hours unscripted, a producer's nightmare. At least if that producer was Jake.

She had taken a swig of cold coffee and was swishing it around in her mouth like mouthwash, when the door of the van burst open.

"Jake, I've got the ATF guy with me." It was Luis, back from the barge.

Jake swallowed the coffee, and swiveled to see a tall man, late thirties or so, duck his head into the van behind Luis.

Hot dog. Jake would have someone hustle him right over to the set for an interview and get Martha off her back. She stuck her hand out. "I'm Wendy Jacobus, producer of the show tonight. How do you spell your name?"

Aamot spelled it for her.

"Two a's, huh? And you pronounce that, how?"

"Ahh-mott, accent on the first syllable." He watched her write it down phonetically before adding, "I'm not doing an interview."

She blinked. "You're not?"

Aamot smiled at her. "No."

Jake tried to think of something persuasive to say, but she was out of practice with finessing reluctant guests. Or guests of any kind, now that she was no longer on-air herself. "Well, don't you want to get the facts out? Reassure the public?" Lame, but it was the best Jake could do at midnight.

"No." The smile again.

The immovable, if pleasant, object. Unfortunately, Jake wasn't feeling much like an irresistible force. Time to call for reinforcements.

"Hang on, we're coming out of a roll-in." Jake spoke into her mouthpiece. "Martha, can you do a recap when we come back to you? We'll show the tape of the explosion again and then break." She lowered her voice. "Then can you come to the production van? I've got something for you."

She felt Aamot, who had been checking out the bank of monitors, glance over at her. As Martha started her recap, Jake turned back to him. "So if you're not going to do an interview, why are you here?"

He nodded toward Luis. "I need to see his tape before you air it. I also need a copy of everything else your people shot tonight, including what Jimmy Olson here got at the moment of the explosion."

"He was a reporter," she said automatically.

That stopped Aamot. "What?"

Jake could feel herself flush. "Jimmy Olson. He was a cub reporter, not a photographer."

The ATF man stared at her for a second, then shook his head. "You're living in the past. In the old comic books, he was primarily a reporter--in the modern stuff, he's a photographer."

"Oh," was the best reply Jake could muster.

Aamot began pointing. "I also need a list of your personnel and a rundown of your camera positions. Oh, and I understand you shot some footage of the sixteen-inch shells being built. I'll need that, too."

At least she had slowed him down a bit with her incisive Jimmy Olson observation. Swift. The radio squawked, and Jake flipped the switch.

It was Neal. "Jake, I'm going to hang out at the command center, see if I can pick up anything."

"Good, Neal, keep an eye on the Coast Guard guys, especially. They're the ones who are going to know first if the boats find anyone."

She flipped the switch back and, thinking of both impudent cub reporters-cum-photographers and radios, turned to Luis. She had finally digested something he'd said to her from the barge. "Tape? Why were you running tape out there?"

Luis pulled the videocassette out of his camera and handed it to her. "I figured you never know. Good thing, huh?"

Never know what? When the microwave truck you're hard-wired to is going to be swept off a barge and land on the bottom of Lake Michigan?

But Jake didn't have time to think about it right then. "We'll discuss this later. Hang on." She turned to her tech director. "Archie, roll the explosion under Martha's voice-over."

As the long view of the blast replayed on the screen, she swiveled back to Aamot. "Listen, I'm not going to be able to give you all this tonight. How about tomorrow?"

Aamot tried to straighten up, but the low doorway of the truck defeated him. "What time?"

With what had happened, TV8 would likely keep the production truck down here. Even so, Jake would have to go to the station to duplicate the tapes. "I'll dupe them at the station tomorrow morning. You can either pick them up there or here. I'll probably be back down by twelve."

Aamot pulled a card out of his jacket pocket and handed it to her. "I'll meet you here at noon sharp. Call me if you have a problem." He hooked a finger at Luis, who was sitting cross-legged on the floor of the truck digging through his bag. "I need to see the tape he just gave you, though."

Luis looked up guiltily and closed the case. Jake's eyes narrowed, wondering what the kid was up to.

"Now," Aamot insisted.

My, thought Jake, aren't *we* a little pushy? Much as she wanted Aamot out of her already cramped van, Jake felt a responsibility to keep him there for Martha. "Okay, but it'll take me a minute or two."

She took her time setting the tape up on one of the VTR monitors. Martha was still on the air, leading into the break. Once in, she could make it here in no time. "I'd like to wait so our on-air talent can see it, too," Jake ventured.

Aamot shook his head. "I need to see it as soon as it's ready."

He needs this, he needs that. Jake sighed and pushed the play button. She'd done her best. "Fine, here we go."

Aamot crowded in behind Jake's seat to watch. As Luis had said, the tape began immediately after the explosion. The barge was still rocking as the camera was lifted and swung wide to focus on Pasquale's barge. The combined effect made Jake feel queasy.

The center of the barge was shakily lit by what burned there. The fire was flat, like it had spilled on the floor of the barge. Somewhere close by, someone was screaming. Then, as if on cue, sirens joined in and just seconds after that, air horns from the surrounding boats.

The boaters probably meant it as a signal for help, but the noise reminded Jake of the boat horns that were sounded after every fireworks display she'd ever seen on Lake Michigan. They were the nautical equivalent of applause for a good show. The thought made her shiver.

On the tape the red strobes of the Coast Guard boats were converging on the barge from all sides. One of the boats was the county fireboat, which Jake had seen spraying water only to entertain the crowds at summertime festivals.

Now as the little red fireboat's cannons shot fountains of water at the fire, the flames slid off the barge and into the water before finally extinguishing. Along with the fire, Luis's ambient light died and the screen went black. The screaming had stopped, but the air horns and sirens went on and on and on and on...

"It looks almost..." Jake couldn't come up with the word. "Fake or..."

"Surreal," Aamot supplied. "That was my reaction anyway." Then a change of tone, "What's next?"

Luis answered, disappointment coloring his voice. "I thought I got more than that. The interview with Pat Firenze is next. At least what I was able to do of it." He gave Aamot a resentful glance.

Jake looked at Aamot and decided not to ask what that was all about. Instead, she checked the program monitor--they were into the break. She twisted around to see Aamot. "You want to see that interview, don't you?"

Aamot looked up at the monitor, too. "Thanks, but I was in the studio audience for that. Tomorrow I'll need a copy of what you just showed me along with the other footage."

"If you can wait, I can dupe this one right now," Jake offered. Duplicating it in real time should give Martha enough time--

"No."

No. Of course. No. Aamot's cell phone rang then, just as Neal's voice came over the radio. "Jake, I think we've got some action here. It looks like they found something. They're all heading over to the old ferry dock."

"Good, Neal, you get over there. I'll ask if our camera on the breakwater can see anything."

She turned to speak to Aamot, but he was already gone.

Simon was waiting with Longenecker when Kutchera's boat docked. The pier hadn't been used since ferry service across the lake to Michigan had been abandoned. Tonight the pier provided a private place to dock where the media--including Wendy Jacobus's "Neal"--could be kept back.

Kutchera helped Angela, Pat and Tudy off the boat and then came over to where Longenecker and Simon stood. The body bag was next off.

"Where was he?" Longenecker asked Kutchera.

"Snagged underneath the barge itself." He glanced over at Simon. "You were right, he was closer than we thought."

"How the hell did you miss him?" Longenecker demanded.

Kutchera shrugged. "We looked there, but the divers were having trouble seeing."

Lake Michigan, even on a good day, was cold, dark and treacherous. This wasn't a good day.

Simon crossed the dock to the gurney. "Let me see him."

He looked away as they unzipped the body bag and then turned back. What he saw surprised him. Despite the horror of the fireball that had engulfed him, despite the burns that already had reddened and blistered the flesh on the rest of his body, Pasquale's face was untouched. In fact, he looked almost peaceful.

Simon moved in closer. No, peaceful wasn't the word. The old man looked like he was in awe, like he'd just seen God.

In Pasquale Firenze's case, maybe he had.

FOUR

Jake was cranky.

Not that she had anyone but her own obsessive-compulsive self to blame.

Barely lucid with less than three hours of fitful sleep, an explosion, and a five-hour live broadcast under her belt, here she was. Drawn to the YMCA pool like the swallows to Capistrano. Or something. To somewhere.

What was truly maddening, though, was despite the fact she had wrenched herself out of bed and been waiting when the Y doors opened at six-thirty, despite the fact she had arrived wearing only her swimsuit and a pair of gym shorts (the better for a quick change), and despite the fact she had flouted authority and *not* showered before "entering the pool"--despite all that, she *still* had to share a lane.

The guy was someone Jake had never seen there before. He'd hopped into the lane unannounced while she was swimming and nearly collided head-on with her. Luckily, she'd heard him coming: the interloper had a lazy right hand that thwacked the water, palm flat, on each stroke.

Stroke/kersplat...stroke/kersplat...stroke/kersplat...

For the first ten laps of the thirty-six that made up her daily mile, the sound was merely irritating. By lap thirty-five, she was ready to throttle the guy.

Stroke/kersplat...stroke/kersplat...stroke/kersplat...

Jake grabbed the end wall to turn and was nearly swamped by the swimmer's wash as he made a flip turn next to her and headed back. The fact he could do a flip turn only compounded her irritation.

Choking, she kept going.

So did he.

Stroke/kersplat...stroke/kersplat...stroke/kersplat...

36.

Finished.

Jake pulled herself up and out of the pool, aware that her lane partner had paused on the other end to watch her leave. Probably as glad to be rid of her as she was to be rid of him.

Jake picked up her towel and locker key and headed to the showers. A man two lanes over pulled off his goggles and hailed her as she passed by.

"You're dragging a little today, Jake."

She stopped and squatted down to answer. Doug was a firefighter on disability for a hearing loss caused by years of riding in a fire truck with a siren reverberating overhead, making the metal cab into a bell chamber. Doug's head was the clapper. Today, sirens on fire trucks were regulated, but it had come too late to save this firefighter's hearing.

"I worked late last night," she answered, "and have to go back this morning. I couldn't see over here--were you blowing me out of the water?" Because Jake's pace seldom varied from her first lap to her last, Doug had taken to using her as a sort of human metronome, pacing himself with her.

"Slow down, I didn't get all that."

The former firefighter wasn't talking about Jake's swimming speed. Jake talked in short, fast bursts, something she attributed to trying to fit a lot of information into the hurried radio exchanges with her crew. Or, perhaps, her fear of running out of time in general.

Whatever, Doug's hearing loss, combined with the echo-y indoor swimming pool, made it tough for him to catch every word. "I said I worked late last night."

Doug pulled himself up on his elbows. "I was watching the broadcast. Really sorry to hear about Pasquale. He was a good guy. Always insisted on having a truck standing by at a show, even if the municipality didn't require it. Had us wet down the ground before, too, if it was a dry year." Doug shook his head. "Of course, there's not much the fire department can do when the show's on a barge."

"I'm not sure there was much anyone could do, period."

"Do they know what happened?" Doug already was repositioning his goggles, ready to get back to his workout.

Jake stood up, her calves and thighs thanking her. She noticed her lane partner was still standing, but now on this end of the pool, and still staring. But she'd been stared at before. "ATF is investigating. A Simon Aamot--you know him?"

Doug nodded, but Jake wasn't sure if he had understood her. "Okay," he said, "I've got miles to swim before I sleep. Or have my coffee, more accurately." And off he went with a smile and a wave.

Jake waved back--to herself, really, since Doug was already under water-- and headed to the showers. When she first started swimming, she'd been proud that she was faster than Doug. That was before she looked over and realized he didn't use his legs. At all. Kicking aggravated an old back injury, he told her. Oh, and by the way, he was usually on his third or fourth *mile* by the time she arrived to do her first lap. Sort of took the wind out of one's sails.

Still, she liked Doug a lot. She saw him three times a week, speaking for maybe five minutes at a time, before they happily went their separate ways. What more could one want in a friend?

Simon caught the news the next morning before leaving for the fireworks factory. Although local coverage usually was pretty sparse on Saturday mornings, Channel 8 was sandwiching newsbreaks between cartoons.

The station opened with an aerial shot of the now-deserted lakefront. Clean-up crews could be seen picking up the trash left behind by the fireworks crowd. Despite the tragedy, Lake Days would open at ten a.m., a little more than three hours from now.

Neal Cravens was talking. "...last night's tragedy. Here's what we know: One person, Firenze Fireworks patriarch Pasquale Firenze, is confirmed dead. Another, Ray Guida, who is married to Firenze's daughter Angela, is missing. What we don't know, though, is why. Why did the shell--"

Simon switched over to CNN, then Fox News Channel, the Today Show and CBS Early Show. Liberty had made the big time. The Lake Days explosion was featured on all of them.

When Simon turned back to TV8, Cravens was talking to camera man Luis Burns, the two of them speculating endlessly and ignorantly on the possible cause of the blast. Behind them, a sanitation truck pumped out toilets.

Made for two loads of crap.

It took Simon about thirty minutes to get from home to the fireworks factory due west of Liberty. He was driving his government-issued Ford Explorer--a good thing, because the long drive that led up to the Firenze place was thick with coarse gravel that kicked up as he drove. The combination of spring rains and the heavy semi-trailers that trucked in raw materials used to build the shells and trucked out the finished fireworks, resulted in deep ruts that Pasquale spackled with more and more layers of gravel in an attempt to keep the drive level for the dangerous cargo.

Simon's Explorer made the final bend and the Firenzes' two shepherd-mix guard dogs, apparently lying in wait, sprang up to give chase. The dogs, Bela and Lugosi, loved to play chicken with cars. Bela was better at it than Lugosi, as evidenced by the fact that Lugosi now raced alongside the Explorer on just two legs--both of them on the right side of his body. The legs on the left had been lost to a 1990 Mercury Cougar.

As Simon turned into the unpaved parking lot, being careful to avoid the dogs, he saw that six or seven other dusty vehicles were already parked there.

Not unexpected. Fireworks was a family business and the Firenze family, both immediate and extended, was rallying around the homestead.

Simon parked the Explorer and got out, pausing to pat the dogs. Since the ATF agent had legs instead of wheels, Bela sniffed and lost interest, running off after some imagined quarry.

Lugosi, though, trailed after Simon unsteadily. The dog had gotten along amazingly well on two legs up till now, but it seemed to be like riding a bike. Lugosi needed to keep moving in order to stay upright and balanced. As he got older and slower, he'd get less and less mobile.

As Simon reached the red single-story building that served as the fireworks company's office, Lugosi stopped to catch his breath, sidling in close to prop himself up against the red exterior wall. Not for the first time, Simon wondered how the dog managed to pee.

As if Lugosi had read his thoughts, a long wet stain dribbled down the wall, which looked freshly painted. Huh, Simon thought, it's actually damned efficient. Didn't even have to lift a leg.

Simon waited for the dog to finish and gave him a sympathy scratch behind the right ear. Sated, Lugosi sprang to life, pushing himself up and away from the building with a full-body wag and bounded into the corn field as if to prove he, for one, didn't need the pity.

Simon walked--but did not bound--to the fireworks office, which looked more like a chicken coop than an office. In fact, surrounded by acres of open field for safety reasons, the entire fireworks factory resembled a working farm. Behind the office, an abandoned playground was half hidden. Probably where Pat and Angela had played as kids while their dad was busy packing shells with explosives. Don't bother Daddy, kids, he's working.

Beyond the office and playground stood a tall barn-like structure that Simon knew was used for constructing ground displays. It looked like the renovations that had started with the painting of Lugosi's pee-wall had continued there. The barn had been stripped of the white paint Simon remembered from his last visit, the bare barnwood prepped for painting. The three long, narrow process buildings that radiated out from the barn like spokes on a wheel were likely next on the "To Do" list.

The Firenzes ran a good operation. Everything clean and up to code. With explosives, neatness counted, and so did a lot of other things.

Knowing that he was coming to the factory, Simon had dressed in cotton fabrics: jeans and a cotton golf shirt. Static electricity, the kind that gives you a little shock when you walk across a carpet and then touch metal, can kill you in a fireworks factory.

Simon pulled open the office's wooden screen door and ducked in. No one was at the reception desk, but Tudy stuck his head around the corner when the door slapped shut behind Simon. "Simon, come in. You want a cup of coffee? A doughnut?"

The old man looked bad. His face was gray, like *he* needed to prop himself up against a wall like Lugosi. Yet Tudy was offering refreshments. And, like the aging dog, wouldn't appreciate pity.

"No, thanks." Like the night before, the man wouldn't quite meet Simon's eyes. As the potential bearer of bad news, Simon had experienced that reaction from people before. It was like they thought if they didn't look at him... "Are you sure you should be here, Tudy?"

Now Pat came out. "That's what I asked him, but the old fart wouldn't listen. Made me pick him up on the way out here."

Tudy led the way to the coffee room and sat down heavily--as heavily as a bantamweight could sit--on one of the mismatched chrome chairs set around the green linoleum-topped table.

He spread his hands. "Where'm I going to go, huh, Pat? Home to cry? No. My place is here with you, like it was with your dad. Besides, we got work to do. We got shows coming up for the Fourth. We got shells to finish."

Pat squeezed the old man's shoulder before sitting down next to him. "I know, Tudy. I'm glad you're here." He looked a question across at Simon, who had pulled up a chair.

Simon understood and shook his head to indicate there was still no sign of Ray. "You have a full staff on today?"

Pat shrugged. "Not on purpose, but everyone came in. Almost like it's a tribute to Ray and my dad to be here."

"Angela?" Simon asked.

"She's with Ma. They're seeing the priest. My ma, she has a cold, so she didn't come to the show last night. She saw it on TV instead." Pat looked down at the table.

"I'm sorry, Pat." Simon hoped Sadie Firenze hadn't watched the close-up. That would be too much for anyone, but especially for a sixty-year-old woman who had devoted her life to the man on the screen. "I'm hoping, though, that some of the film can help us figure out what happened."

Pat lifted his head. "Any theories yet? I mean from what you have seen?"

"I think the lift charge failed for some reason." What that reason was, Simon couldn't say yet. He hoped he would know more when the results came back from the few samples he was able to gather on the barge.

Tudy was nodding, seeming to buck up a bit. "That's what I told you, Pat, you see? Your father, he went back, thinking he had to relight it."

"That's the way it looks," Simon agreed, pulling out a notebook. "I need to know about the shells. Can you give me the actual date the blue one was made?"

Pat got up to pull a calendar off the bulletin board next to the coffee machine and bring it to the table. "Let's see."

He was squinting at the calendar, trying to make out the scribbling. "Jesus, Dad's handwriting is getting..." Pat didn't glance up at his accidental use of the present tense, but Simon saw his face flush, "...*was* getting bad. I think it says Channel 8 was here to tape on May 28. That would be it."

"But the stars," Tudy interjected, "we made the stars in March or April maybe." He turned to Simon for the first time. "They have to be made when it's cool. We make them in the spring and store them, then we just put everything together when the TV was here."

The stars were the color, the guts of the fireworks shell. Their size was determined by the diameter of the shell they were going into. "How big were the stars for the sixteen-inchers?" Simon asked.

Tudy closed one eye as he thought, looking like an Italian Popeye without the "musckles." "Oh, I think an inch, maybe? The stars were okay, though, we used them in the twelve-inchers, too."

"Even the blue?"

Pat leaned forward on his elbows. "No, you're right. Not the blue. We saved the blue stars for that one shell."

Simon looked back and forth between them. "What was in them?"

Pat answered with a casual shrug, but the irritation in his voice contradicted it. "Potassium chlorate. Dad didn't think anything else, anything new, would do. Color wasn't blue enough for him, or bright enough."

Simon who'd half-expected Pat's answer, shook his head. "But potassium chlorate? Jesus."

Pat just shrugged again. "You couldn't tell the old man anything, Simon. He lived in the past."

That was the truth. On both counts. "Your dad made the blue stars?"

"Like I said last night, he didn't trust anybody else with them from start to finish." The phone rang and Pat got up to answer it. "This better not be Mrs. Fetcher from the Waverly again, or I'll go over personally and take her dog out," he muttered.

"Between me and you, Simon," Tudy said, picking up the conversation where they'd left it, "I don't think Pasquale wanted his kids messing around with the chlorate. Nasty stuff."

Tudy fixed his eyes on Simon's. "But it wouldn't have caused the explosion we saw. You know that, and I know that."

Tudy was probably right, though when potassium chlorate was mixed with the other ingredients in a shell, it formed copper chlorate--an unstable chemical, especially when it got wet.

And Pasquale had taken it out on a barge on Lake Michigan. Humid day, to boot. Humidity could wreak all kinds of havoc with explosives. "Do you have any more of the blue stars around, Tudy?"

Tudy pushed away from the table. "You want I should go get some for you?"

Simon shook his head. "We'll put one in the day box before I leave and an Explosions Enforcement Officer will be out to pick it up." Simon had no intention of carrying a star around with him in the Explorer.

Bam. Pat hung up the receiver hard, nearly knocking the smudged plastic base right off the wall. One of his guys walked by the door, looked in to see what the noise was, then kept right on walking. A wise decision.

"Great," Pat said, "now we've got OSHA in our hair, too."

"You got to expect that, boy," Tudy said, standing up.

OSHA--the Occupational Safety and Health Administration--was the federal entity responsible for worker safety and would be doing a full investigation.

Pat turned on Tudy. "I know, dammit, but we've finally recovered from the accident with Uncle Frankie and now it's going to start all over again. The bastards are already going after our shows."

Since everyone else was standing, Simon got up, too. "Which bastards?"

"Which? Our competitors. Gustafsen for one. He's been on the phone to our customers this morning, already, full of sympathy, offering his help in case--quote--'Firenze can't fulfill your contract under the sad circumstances.' Unquote."

Pat picked up the calendar on the table and shook it at them. "My father's not even cold. Hell, Ray's body hasn't even been found and these bastards are already picking over their bones."

Tudy flinched at the word "body."

"Let's all go for a walk." Simon said quietly.

"Been swimming, huh?"

Jake looked up as Luis flopped down in the chair next to her. She'd arrived at the station shortly after eight a.m. to dupe the tapes Aamot wanted, and try to do some research for Martha. "Try" being the operative word. She'd already had five telephone calls--two from Martha, one from Neal, one from Cara, the morning producer, and one heavy breather--all nearly three hours before she was scheduled to begin work at eleven.

Her own fault, of course. She regularly came in early and left late, meaning everyone at the station was used to her being in the production suite and at their beck and call at all hours. She'd have to retrain them when she had time.

But first, Luis. "How do you know I was swimming?" she asked, feeling her hair to see if it was still damp.

"Easy--you swim every day. But besides that," Luis reached out and touched her on the cheekbone below the right eye. "Goggle eyes. Big time."

Jake backed away and felt the indentations around her eyes for herself. She'd been experimenting with different brands of swim goggles for nearly two years now and all of them left rings that lasted varying lengths of time after her swim.

"Apparently the Gecko Goggles are no better than the SuperSwimmers," she muttered.

Luis laughed. "Aww, I don't know. I think *these* rings are particularly cute on you." He leaned back casually in the chair, hands clasped behind his head. "I used to dive back in high school--was really good at it, if I do say so myself. You dive, Jake?"

My, my, weren't *we* dripping in charm and self-confidence all of a sudden. "Only feet first," she said dryly. "Okay, spill it, Luis. "Why so chipper?" she asked.

"I was on-air with Neal this morning, and I just got a call from CNN wanting to use my footage of the explosion."

"You'll have to get Gwen's permission," Jake cautioned. "I'm not sure what the network will say about an affiliate sharing tape with another network."

"Right, I know." Luis leaned forward in his chair, his head nodding up and down like a bobble-head doll. "But this is so cool, Jake. Suddenly it's like I'm a star or something."

A shooting star, Jake thought. But let the kid enjoy his five minutes of fame, even if it did come at the cost of at least one and probably two lives.

"Once Gwen says okay," Luis continued, "I'm going to need the close-up I shot of the old man. They used the fire in the box thing this morning, but Neal said Cara couldn't find the stuff I shot of Firenze getting blown up."

Hence Neal's call this morning. And Cara's. Jake apparently was alone in thinking the tape of Pasquale at the mortar was too graphic to be shown on the air. Everyone may have looking for it, but Jake had stashed the master in a file drawer under "F" where she could find it, but nobody else could.

"Cara must have just missed it on the dupe," she lied, thinking about her chances of persuading Gwen that the footage shouldn't be used. Or shared. Probably slim to none, given the ratcheted-up level of television violence these days. "I'll find it."

And she *would*. What she did with the thing, though, she couldn't promise.

"It's really important, Jake." Luis was bouncing his right leg up and down now. "That tape could make my career."

Jake put her hand on Luis's knee to stop the bouncing before it sprang up spasmodically and blackened his eye. "Relax Luis, I--"

Just then the phone rang and she picked it up, grateful for the interruption. The relief lasted until she heard Martha Malone's voice on the other end. "Jake, I need that info on the earlier Firenze explosion now. Now!"

Yikes. The whole place should be on Ritalin. "Yes, Martha," she said, as she turned to her computer. "I have it in front of me."

Jake scanned the computer screen. "This is interesting. This Simon Aamot guy was the investigator on that accident, too."

As she spoke she saw Luis sneak out the door, on tiptoe, like Martha was going to climb right through the handset. Some days Jake wouldn't put it past her.

With Luis safely gone, Jake pulled a videotape out of a file drawer and pushed it into a slot on the console. "That's Aamot, pronounced..."

Simon, Pat and Tudy walked out to the process building in silence. One of three spokes radiating out from the barn, the building was really a metal shell with a concrete floor. No chemicals were kept there, and the place had to be completely cleaned out after each use. If heat was needed in the winter, it was steam or hot water--nothing with an automatic pilot light to spark an explosion.

Inside, the space looked like any workshop, and smelled of fresh wood, paper and glue. Long wooden tables ran down the center of the room and a sink occupied one corner. In another corner near the door, stood a set of what looked like window screens.

"You mix in here?" Simon asked. Mixing was sifting the dry chemicals of the stars together. Pasquale had called the formulas he used for his stars "recipes," and the process did resemble baking in a way.

First, the ingredients were sifted together using a series of increasingly fine screens. Though the individual "recipes" were kept under lock and key, all stars contained the basics: oxidizers, fuels, binders, special effects, color and the propellants, of course. The black powder and the flash powder.

Once properly sifted, water would be added and the whole mess kneaded into what looked like black bread dough and pressed into trays or loaf pans to dry. Once dry, the dough could be cut into cubes or formed into balls. The cubes were used in cylindrical shells, the balls in round. Both shapes were called stars for some reason Simon never quite understood.

Tudy answered Simon's question as Pat wandered over to a woman slicing stars in the opposite corner. "Nah. Mixing's too messy, so we do that outside. We just keep the screens in here. We mostly load and wrap here." He pointed toward a workbench where the man who had come by the coffee room earlier was wrapping brown paper around a cardboard cylinder. "You remember how we do this, Simon?"

Since Simon's job consisted of a whole lot more bombs and structure fires than fireworks, he figured a refresher course couldn't hurt. Besides he wanted to observe the Firenzes' methods, given it had been two years since his earlier investigation. "Show me."

Tudy called out to the man building the shell. "Maxie, bring that here."

Maxie carried the shell over. He was wearing an apron now, not only to protect his clothes from the chemicals, but to cover any belt buckles and zippers that might accidentally strike something and cause a spark. "Yeah, Tudy?"

Tudy gestured toward Simon. "This is Simon Aamot." Tudy always pronounced it A-met, long "a," but Simon never bothered to correct him. He was used to mispronunciations and, besides, probably only relatives he'd never met in Norway were really sure how the name should be pronounced. "Show him what you're doing."

Maxie held up the large cardboard tube. "This is an eight-incher. I've already got the stars in here and a salute."

Salutes were the noise. Without a salute, a breaking shell would pop instead of boom. Salutes were what rattled windows and caused babies to cry. Pasquale had loved them.

Simon looked into the cylinder. "Are the stars already primed?" Priming was rolling the stars in black powder--a high explosive--like cookies in coal-colored powdered sugar.

"Oh, yeah," Tudy said, "the stars are primed before they're dried, remember?" He took the shell from Maxie. "This here is a weeping willow, right Maxie?"

Maxie stepped back and nodded.

A metal tube ran down the center of the larger cardboard tube and the stars were packed around it. "Black powder in the tube, Tudy?" Simon asked.

The old man sucked on his tongue as he scooped the black powder into the tube. "That's right. You remember, huh? Black powder for the bursting charge, and we let a little spill over into the stars. Just a little more priming."

Finished with the powder, Maxie pulled out the metal tube, leaving a ring of stars with a black powder center. Then he topped the cylinder with a cardboard disk attached to a fuse. The fuse, this one an internal time fuse, delayed the break of the shell until it had climbed high enough to be safe. Or at least that was the idea.

"You said there were ten-second internal time fuses on the sixteen-inchers, right?" Simon asked.

Tudy nodded as he folded the brown paper down around the shell and added another cardboard disk to hold the time fuse in place. He seemed happier now with fireworks in his hands, like working with them would lessen the horror of having his best friend and probably his own son killed by them. "The sixteen-inchers, they had a four-inch time fuse: two-and-a-half seconds an inch. This little girl has a four-second delay cuz she doesn't have to go so high."

"Do you spike the shells then?" Spiking was wrapping the shell tightly in string soaked in wheat paste. The wheat paste made the string shrink as it dried, creating a tighter shell and a better break when the black powder exploded.

Tudy nodded. "And then three wraps."

"Three?" Simon asked.

Pat came up behind them. "First a band, then a cover, then a final wrap."

Tudy explained. "They're all brown paper covered in paste. The band just goes around the shell. We let that dry, then the cover goes around the whole thing--even the time fuse. Then the final wrap." He picked up a sheet of craft paper and crumpled it. "We wrinkle it all up. That breaks the grain of the paper and makes it dry nice and tight."

"And you did all that to the sixteen-inchers?" Simon asked.

"Sure," Tudy said, "and Pasquale added a fourth wrap for the TV. Colored paper--red, for one, silver for another and blue for..." He let it trail off.

Simon turned to Pat. "I assume the wraps were intact when the shells were loaded on the barge?"

"Of course they were."

"Who transported them from here to the lakefront?"

"We had two semis full. Ray drove the one with the finale and the twelve and sixteen-inchers. I drove the one with the body of the show." He met Simon's eyes and then looked away. "And yes, the wraps were intact. I carted each of the sixteen-inchers onto the barge myself."

Simon thought about that. "Where were the shells dried? Here?"

Pat eyed him. "In a magazine, of course."

Finished aerial shells were considered low explosives and could be stored in Type Four magazines, masonry buildings with metal doors and double locks. The black powder and flash powder, though, were high explosives and had to be kept in more secure Type One or Type Two magazines. Simon knew that, of course, and Pat knew that Simon knew.

"A Type Four?"

"No." Pat pointed out the open door. "Our north magazine. It's a Two."

That was the way Pasquale had operated: If a Type Four was required, Pasquale went a step further and used a Two. In addition to the requirement for Type Fours, Ones and Twos also had to have quarter-inch thick steel doors lined with two inches of hardwood and be bullet-resistant. The mandatory double locks on the doors also had to use two different keys. Type Three magazines, called day boxes, were used for temporary storage of high explosives.

If the shells had been kept in a Type Two magazine, they were pretty damn secure. Depending, of course. "Who had keys?"

Pat's jaw tightened. "My father, myself, Angela, Ray and Tudy. Why?"

It might be a moot point. "But the shells didn't have lift charges yet?"

"No, they were brought back out for fusing," Pat said. He turned to Tudy, who'd been uncharacteristically quiet. "Do you remember when Dad fused them?"

"I know he wasn't feeling too good, so he put it off." Tudy shrugged. "Last week maybe?"

"Would he have done that here?"

"Probably," Pat said, "this building is the closest."

"Can you show me how the lift charge was added?" Simon asked.

Still carrying the 8-inch shell, Pat led him over to another table, which held a small bin of black powder and lengths of quickmatch. "First, we attach the quickmatch to the bottom of the shell and then we cover it with brown paper, letting the paper overlap the end of the shell."

More brown paper. "The excess paper makes the pocket for the lift charge, right?"

"Right." Pat turned the shell over, dipped a little black powder out of the dish and poured it into the pocket he'd just made. "The higher the shell has to go, the more black powder you need."

"So let's think about yesterday," Simon said. "The quickmatch would have ignited the lift charge on the first shell sending it up. At the same time, it would have lighted the internal time fuse. Meanwhile, the flame continues on down another timing fuse to the second shell. That shell's lift charge and internal time fuse ignites, sending it up, and the flame continues on to shell number three."

Pat lifted the shell up by the quickmatch. "Right."

Simon looked the shell over. Eight inches in diameter-- peanuts compared to the one that had killed Pasquale, but lethal nonetheless. "So what are we saying? That the time fuse between the second and third shells failed?" he asked.

Pat set the shell down harder than Simon would have liked. "Then why did it explode at all?"

"Something your dad did when he went back?" Simon offered.

Pat and Tudy didn't answer. They didn't look at each other either. Simon wouldn't press for now. He gestured to a group of shells wrapped and ready for the drying racks. "You have a lot of shows scheduled for the Fourth?"

Pat nodded. "Seven, including the big County show back in Liberty. God knows what's going to happen to that. Or the other ones if people start thinking we screwed up somehow." He stopped. "Shit, my father's dead, God knows what's happened to Ray and I'm worried about the business that caused it all." He looked at Simon. "Does that make any sense?"

Tudy touched his arm. "You've said it yourself, boy. We've got people depending on us. Our families. Our workers. The people who're coming to see our shows."

"If anybody comes." Pat sighed. "I'm sorry, Simon. What else can we show you?"

Simon thought people would come--out of morbid curiosity, if for no other reason. He looked around. "Nothing else here. I need to send some guys out to get samples, though. Try to match the residue on the barge." They started toward the office.

"I suppose it's possible the chlorate was set off, but not by the fuse," Simon said as they rounded the building. "A spark, maybe--"

The roar of an engine drowned him out, and all three of them turned to see a cloud of dust moving up the gravel drive. A red Miata was bouncing through the ruts. If Simon owned that car, he'd be a hell of a lot more careful with it.

The Miata crunched to a stop next to the Explorer. The woman in the driver's seat whipped off her sunglasses as a TV8 van pulled up behind her.

Martha Malone had arrived. Or made her entrance, more precisely.

Martha slid out of the car and strode toward the three men, leaving her camera man behind to unload his equipment.

She'd already met Pat Firenze and Tudy Guida. But even if she hadn't, she would have been able to pick out the ATF agent, and not just from the glimpse she'd had of him when she interviewed the sheriff.

She stuck out her hand to the ATF agent when she reached the three men. "Martha Malone, TV8 News. I'm sorry I missed you yesterday, but I'd like to talk with you later."

Without waiting for a reply, she turned to Pat. "I'm terribly sorry about your father, Pat."

Stepping neatly between Pat and Tudy, she walked them away from Simon and down the drive to the office, one hand resting lightly on each of their backs. "I feel awful bothering you at a time like this, but I think it's important that we get your side of things as soon as possible."

She turned her best sympathetic smile back toward Aamot, who was trailing. "Don't you agree, Mr. Aamot?" She pronounced the name as Jake had told her, but waited for a correction in case her producer got it wrong.

None was forthcoming, at least of the name. "Me?" Aamot said, with a twang she suspected was a put-on, "I like to have all the facts first. Just funny that way."

Martha turned to face him as her camera man caught up with them. "But you're the lead investigator on the case, you already know more than the rest of us."

Dave brought the camera up and trained it on Aamot as she continued. "One person is dead and one is missing. Do you truly have nothing to tell us?"

Aamot waited half a beat before answering, making her wait for it. He'd undoubtedly had television experience and from the way he was reacting, it hadn't been pleasant. That could work to Martha's advantage. People often say more than they intend when they're angry.

"I'm afraid that until I have something conclusive to report, Ms. Malone," the agent said evenly, twang gone, "it would be a disservice to the public and to the people personally involved in this tragedy to speculate. Don't you agree?"

Damn. The quote was unusable unless Martha wanted to make herself look like a jackass.

But as good as Aamot might be, she was better. "People are already speculating," she pointed out. "Especially in light of the accident on Pat Firenze's barge last night and the fact that there was an earlier fatality here at the factory, one that was ruled an accident."

She waited that same half beat and then added, "By *you*, coincidentally."

Direct hit. Aamot's eyes narrowed. "We're looking at everything, Ms. Malone, and now I'm afraid you'll have to excuse us." He had Pat and Tudy precede him into the squat red fireworks office as he held the door. And his position.

You had to give the ATF agent points for a quick recovery. Martha signaled her camera man to lower the camera. "Listen," she said, purposely getting closer to Aamot than most people found comfortable. "I don't want to play games with you. We've reported that a shell landed in a box filled with unexploded fireworks last night. We even have tape of it. We also have information on the earlier explosion. People are saying there may have been carelessness involved in all the...accidents." She put the emphasis on the last word.

"People are saying? Or TV8?" Aamot asked, not giving ground.

Martha wasn't going to back down either. "Both. And if it's *not* true, then someone had better say so. Otherwise, we have no choice but to go with what we have."

She widened her eyes and Aamot held her gaze for one more second, then lifted his eyebrows. "Really? Well, then I think you'd best just...go."

He stepped inside and let the screen door bang closed behind him. At its sound, two German shepherds bounded out from behind the barn and Martha retreated to her car. As the animals circled the Miata, Aamot opened the door and whistled for the dogs.

Big of him.

Leaving Dave to stash the equipment in this van, Martha started the Miata, slammed it into reverse and stepped on the gas. She'd intended to make a big exit, but the parking brake foiled her. Having learned to drive on the hilly streets of San Francisco, she still set the hand brake out of habit when she parked. Even if it was in a fucking farmer's field.

As Martha reached down to release the brake, she caught sight of her new red Sergio Rossi pumps covered with fine gray dust from the driveway. Which, come to think of it, meant they went perfectly with her formerly red car.

Damn dusty gravel. Damn smug ATF agent. Damn rutted road.

And did one of those dogs have just two legs?

FIVE

It was nearly noon when Simon arrived at Lake Days. The festival grounds proper were just north of the area where the fireworks crowd sat the night before. Now empty of the quarter of a million spectators, that part of Shore Park was being used for parking at ten bucks a pop.

The TV8 truck was still where it had been last night--on the bluff to the south, overlooking the grounds. The barges were gone, though, towed back to the commercial docks for inspection.

In their place, sailboats dotted the lake. In fact, if it weren't for the Coast Guard boats still searching inside the breakwater, it would be easy to pretend that nothing unusual had happened yesterday. That Pasquale and Ray were back at the Firenze factory, happily concocting more missiles.

Simon pulled down the street past a giant inflatable beaver billowing in the wind, and parked next to the TV8 truck. As he got out of the car, he could hear music from the main stage and could smell the mingled salty/sweet scent of corn dogs and cotton candy. It reminded him of church festivals when he was a kid, and summer weekends spent hanging around the carnie games, eating trash and trying to win giant teddy bears to impress the girls.

Also reminded him he was hungry.

Jake had a videotape on the screen when Simon Aamot tapped on the door of the production truck. It was one she'd seen before. In fact, she'd produced it. Watching it this time, though, she had a whole lot more respect for, if not understanding of, the content.

Pasquale Firenze was talking. "We roll the dough in the black powder, so it don't stick, just like you use flour when you bake. Then you cut 'em." As he spoke he sliced through the black dough like he was making slice & bake cookies.

41

Aamot stuck his head in the door. "That the tape from the factory?"

Jake nodded, pausing it. "It's amazing how they handle this stuff. I mean, how can they just cut explosives?"

Aamot folded himself into the tech director's chair next to her. "Special non-sparking knives--and they're not considered explosives until they're dry. At this point," he pointed at the screen, "the stars are 'in process.'"

"Yeah," Jake muttered, pushing stop and then rewind, "in the process of killing you." She realized what she had said, and how it must have sounded. "I'm sorry, that was a lousy way to put it."

Aamot shrugged. "It's a dangerous business. No one expects to get hurt, but all the same, they know it can happen. You have to respect the powder, Pasquale used to say."

"So you knew him." Jake turned awkwardly to stack the tapes she'd copied earlier in a box.

She was hitting a wall, fatigue-wise, probably because after the late night, early swim, and tense morning at the station, she finally had *time* for a let-down. Or maybe a breakdown. "We'd have these meetings, production meetings, you know? And everyone would be arguing--Bryan Williams, the mayor, Martha, Pasquale--and I'd just sit there, waiting for them to make up their minds so I could do my job."

She swiveled back to Aamot with the box of tapes. "And after every meeting, Pasquale would come up to me and say real low, 'Don't you worry, Wendy.' He called me Wendy, nobody's called me that for years. Anyway he'd say, 'Don't you worry, Wendy, I'll give you a show like nothing you've ever seen. I'll do it for you. You'll see.' Like I was his daughter or something."

Her eyes were starting to tear up, and she swiped at them. What a stooge she was being. "Sorry, I guess I could use some sleep. Here are the tapes you wanted." She handed him the box.

"What about--"

"Oh." Anticipating his question, she hastily searched through the papers on the console and pulled out an envelope. "You wanted the crew list, too. I put in their assignments and a diagram showing exactly where they were."

He took the envelope and looked her up and down. "Have you eaten lunch?"

"No," she said, surprised. "Why? Am I acting like I need food?"

He grinned and unexpected laugh lines appeared in his face. "You're acting the way I feel. Let's go grab us a hot dog."

Aamot stepped down out of the truck, keeping his head low so he wouldn't crack it on the door. He turned to help Jake, but she'd already hopped out.

"Just how tall are you?" she asked.

"Six-four. You have to tell anybody you're going?"

"Nah. Everybody has already taken off," she said as they set off across the parking lot. "There's no Noon News today, because it's Saturday, so I'm just handling the News Breaks with Neal. The next one is scheduled for 3:30, during the baseball game."

Aamot put his arm out like a crossing guard to stop her as a car rolled by. "Why are you working on a Saturday?"

Jake looked sideways at him. "Someone said he needed tapes this morning. He was pretty pushy about it."

Aamot dropped his arm, and they continued down the road that led from the bluff to the festival grounds. "Pushy is what I do best. So how long were you on the air last night?"

She shrugged. "We wrapped it up about two."

"That's almost two hours after the Coast Guard found Pasquale's body. What did you find to talk about after the search was called off for the night?"

"Recap, recap, recap. Chicago-style dogs or gyros?" she asked, pointing in opposite directions.

Aamot, having baited her with hot dogs, switched to gyros. They veered left.

"It would have been a whole lot easier if we'd been able to interview you," Jake said, as they got in line behind a gaggle of teenage girls in tank tops.

Aamot shrugged and backed up to let one of the kids cut through the line with her food. "Like I said: I don't talk when I have nothing to say."

Jake rolled her eyes. "Then you're the only one."

"Sometimes I think that's true."

"Believe me, you don't know the half of it." She stepped up to the counter and ordered a gyro deluxe--double the meat--and a Diet Coke. Aamot had the same, but with a Mountain Dew. Jake was impressed. She liked a man who could handle his caffeine.

He passed her both gyros and took the soft drinks himself. Jake remembered to grab napkins and straws as they left the window. The day was pleasant--a change in wind direction had pushed all the heat and humidity further inland and left only a gentle lake breeze.

"Anyone who wants to say or do something outrageous," Jake continued as they sat down at a picnic table, "anyone who wants to take a stand about anything, can get on TV these days."

She took a bite of her gyro--a real gyro with spit-roasted lamb, not that compressed garbage you got some places. Meat and grease and yogurt sauce spilled out the end. Heaven. Assuming you had a napkin. Preferably a pile of them.

"That's pretty cynical for someone who makes her living in television." He said it more like a lazy aside than an accusation. Sitting there coiled up, he reminded her of a big cat--a big sleepy cat with watchful green/gold eyes.

She shrugged. "I've been around this business for nearly ten years, first as an intern, then as a reporter, then as a director/producer. That's long enough to see a lot of change. I've gotten used to local news time being used to promote network shows, and 'News that can save your life!' that's so vitally important to people that we can tease it for two weeks."

"Meanwhile, people are dropping dead all over the place, huh?" Aamot asked with a grin.

"You got it," she said, smiling back. She shifted on the picnic bench. "But what really bothers me is the warped view of the world you can get by only watching TV news."

She set down the gyro and leaned forward on her elbows. "We do a story about someone who is protesting something--chunks in their peanut butter, say. If you didn't know better, you'd think there was this huge anti-chunk movement out there instead of one old lady with dentures."

Aamot laughed and handed her a napkin. "Do you think the public is that gullible?"

She took the hint and wiped her chin. "Gullible? No, I don't think the public is gullible necessarily, it just wants to be entertained, instead of informed. People don't read the newspaper or news magazines or watch real news programs, unless something catastrophic happens. Then they're insatiable--they just can't get enough of the story. The rest of the time, though, they're happy to catch our 'eleven minutes of non-stop news' and be done with it."

"So, don't stations like yours," he nodded at her, "have tremendous power to shape people's perceptions?"

"Yesss." She said it warily. Aamot wasn't looking like such a pussycat anymore. Jake thought about the research she'd done on the Firenzes: The fire in the box she'd told Martha about, the earlier explosion at the factory, and the fact that Aamot was the investigator then, too. How would those facts--kneaded, shaped, and fed to the public in easily digestible tidbits--be perceived?

"Then don't you also have a responsibility?" Aamot followed up. "To present both sides of a story, to have balanced coverage?"

"In eleven minutes? Don't be silly." Realizing sarcasm probably wouldn't cut it here, Jake took a pull on her soda. "I take it you're not thrilled with our coverage of the accident."

Aamot sawed off a chunk of pita bread with his plastic knife and speared it, then a chunk of lamb and some onions with his plastic fork. Geez, the man ate gyros with a knife and fork. It almost offset the attractiveness of the Mountain Dew addiction. "No."

Jake waited, but no more seemed forthcoming. It was Jake's nature to feel responsible for everything that happened around her, but, honestly, the one-sided coverage wasn't all the station's fault. Aamot wasn't helping his cause.

"If the coverage of the explosion isn't balanced, isn't that partly your fault? Why don't you agree to an interview?"

"I told you, I don't have any concrete information for you yet. It's not my responsibility to keep you in sound bites in the meantime."

Jake wiped off her hands and set the napkin carefully down on the table, ready to do battle. "So what are we supposed to report?"

"The news. Just don't invent it."

"We--"

"Mind if I join you?"

The voice came from behind Jake. She twisted and saw Bryan Williams. Bryan was the owner of Festivities, the event marketing firm that was managing Lake Days. He was also Jake's former boss. And former lover. Emphasis on "former."

Bryan had a junior-size orange drink in hand. Wimp.

Aamot stood up to introduce himself. The two men shook hands. Bryan was about five-foot-nine and slender. His silver hair made him look distinguished and ten years older than his forty years. Even dressed casually today in jeans and a shirt with the Refresh Yourself Lake Days logo, he looked smooth and immaculate. Jake just knew his jeans had been pressed.

Aamot was wearing jeans, too, but looked entirely comfortable in them. And in himself.

But it was Bryan who was speaking. "I blame myself. I should have known this show was too much for the Firenzes."

Here we go again, Jake thought. Bryan appearing to blame himself, but only so nobody else would. *Don't be silly, Bryan, it's not your fault the Firenzes blew themselves up.*

Aamot had swiveled on the bench to face Bryan squarely. His eyes had that watchful look back. "You think so?" he asked, his voice slowing.

Jake tucked one leg up under her on the bench across from the two men and settled in. This could be good: Bryan's comma-bracketed, qualifying parentheticals against Aamot's shoot-straight-from-the-hip way of speaking.

"Oh, definitely." Bryan tapped his fingernails on the table. "I told Clementine--Mayor Cox," he explained for Aamot, "that we were taking a risk. Not with safety, of course, or we never would have gone with the Firenzes. She felt--and rightly so, I thought at the time--that, obviously, given they were the hometown company, we had to give them a chance."

Jake wanted to scream at the sentence construction, but Aamot just raised his eyebrows. "The Firenzes may be local, but they're one of the best in the business."

"Oh, of course. But you, as a regulator, would be interested in safety, reliability. As an event manager, I'm interested in those things, too, but also in the creative aspects. Showmanship, technology, visual effects." He shook his head. "Do you know what Pasquale Firenze said when I suggested adding lasers to the show?"

Jake knew the answer to that, because she'd been there. It had been at one of the production meetings she had mentioned to Aamot.

Ideas had been bouncing around the table, everybody--Mayor Cox and Bryan, mostly--talking excitedly over everybody else. A Venetian Night parade, or maybe a symphony concert, and then lasers had been brought up.

Pasquale rubbed at one bushy white eyebrow. "No," he said quietly.

Bryan had turned to him. "What?" The surprise on Bryan's face almost made Jake laugh.

"I said no. No lasers. Lasers and my fireworks don't mix. You want lasers, you do them after my show."

Mayor Cox's turn, and she looked angry or maybe embarrassed. "Pasquale, we're paying you for this show and you will--"

Pasquale leaned forward to shake his finger at the mayor, sitting across the table from him. "That's right, Clementine, you're paying me. You want to go with Gustafsen Fireworks or somebody else, you just go ahead. If you want to shoot the whole goddamn show yourself, I'll hand you the flare. You work with Pasquale Firenze, though, you get the benefit of his experience. Thirty years of shooting fireworks and maybe I know something you don't. You understand?"

The mayor glanced sideways at Bryan, who hesitated before finally tilting his head.

Pasquale continued. "Lasers are light. You put light with fireworks, you wash them out. You lose the color. Like doing fireworks when it's not dark. You put fireworks with lasers, you wash the lasers out, too. You understand?"

Back in real-time, Jake was aware that Aamot was answering Bryan, and she was surprised to hear him echoing her thoughts. "He probably said lasers and fireworks don't mix."

Jake jumped in, if only for the pleasure of crossing Bryan. "We'd have lost both of them on the coverage."

"Well, that's something we didn't realize at the time, of course," Bryan said, looking hard across the table at her. "Still, as I think we can all agree, the Firenzes were in over their heads with the sixteen-inch shells. I wish to God, in hindsight, they'd simply admitted as much. We would have formulated alternative, less ambitious, plans. But, well, if you knew Pasquale..." His open expression invited them to agree with him.

Bryan was into Act Two of his usual performance when something went wrong. Not coincidentally, it dovetailed nicely with news coverage of a disaster. Act One: Horror, Regret. Act Two: Recriminations, Outrage. Reluctant recriminations on Bryan's part. "I'm sorry to say," he'd preface it with, then he'd flay the Firenzes.

"I *did* know Pasquale," Jake said pointedly, "and I would have trusted him with my life."

"You certainly trusted him with a microwave truck," Bryan retorted, "and see where it got you."

Jake must have struck a nerve. It wasn't like Bryan to lose his temper in public. It made absorbing the counter jab from him about the truck almost a pleasure. "Yeah, and you can look for that little item on your production bill. You were the one--"

Aamot held up his hands. "Why don't we cool it? The fact is we still don't know what happened. Until we do, blaming anyone, including the Firenzes," he looked at Bryan, unconsciously--or not--mimicking the other man's speech rhythms, "is a mistake. It would be a shame to say something we'd have to retract later."

"But, as I understand--" Bryan was interrupted by the siren song of his own name being called by a female. A young female. He waved over his little blonde assistant, Lillian, who nodded hello to Jake, and then leaned down to whisper in Bryan's ear.

Aamot was observing closely, but Jake didn't know if he was trying to listen or looking at Lillian's breasts bouncing in the tight Lake Days T-shirt.

Bryan stood up. "Simon, have you met Lillian White?"

Aamot stood up, too. "No," he said, holding out his hand. "Nice to meet you."

Aamot and Lillian shook on it, and Bryan picked up his orange soda and drained it. "I'm afraid, according to Lillian, we have a fire to put out." He smiled at the irony of his words, then turned to Aamot. "It's been a pleasure meeting you, Mr. Aamot, although I'm sorry it had to be under these circumstances."

He and Aamot shook hands, too. There was a whole lot of shaking going on, Jake thought. She didn't partake, settling for a cheery little goodbye.

As the two Festivities people walked away, Bryan doing all the talking, Aamot said: "Please don't tell me the Whites named their little girl 'Lily.'"

Jake laughed. "At least she has sense enough to use Lillian." She picked up the empty cup Bryan had left behind and tossed it across the table and into the trash. Basket! The crowd roars. "I'm still cleaning up after him," she muttered.

"Still?"

"I used to be Lilly White," Jake said.

Aamot cocked his head, not understanding.

"I was Bryan's first assistant when he started Festivities," Jake explained, pausing to give that fact some thought.

Criminy, she'd been buxom and blond back then, just like Lillian. Funny, it had never occurred to Jake that Lillian White was an awful lot like yesterday's--or more accurately, last decade's--Wendy Jacobus.

47

"I thought you'd been at the station for ten years," Aamot said. "You work for Williams when you were twelve?"

"I'm older than I look." But not than she felt. "I worked for Bryan for two years when he was just starting out. He sold sponsorships and I managed the events. In other words, I did all the work, and he got all the money and glory."

"He's done very well," Aamot said mildly.

Jake shrugged. "Bryan's smart. And he's a very good salesman. Take Lake Days. He sold my station on the idea of a live broadcast of the fireworks and then turned around and encouraged our competitors to line up along the street to shoot the finale for their news. Not *his* fault, he says. It's a public street, how could he stop them?"

"Slick," admitted Aamot.

One man's slick is another man's oily, Jake thought.

The ATF agent was nodding. "It's like giving NBC the rights to broadcast a baseball game and then letting CBS, ABC, Fox and ESPN show the bottom of the ninth live."

"Exactly," Jake said with a smile. "Bryan secured a live broadcast of his event, with the ad revenues associated with it, and still didn't have to sacrifice coverage on the other stations.

"And you're right, he is slick," she continued. "His only problem is he considers himself a 'big picture' kind of guy, and sometimes a detail or two falls through the cracks." She pointed at the Refresh Yourself Lake Days banner flying above them. "See this? Refresh Yourself, the sports drink, is the title sponsor of Lake Days. They paid big bucks to buy the sponsorship, only to have CoolSplash ambush them."

Aamot didn't seem to follow. "Ambush them how?"

"CoolSplash is Refresh Yourself's biggest competitor. That's their beaver." Jake gestured across the street with her now tepid gyro. An even bigger banner there proclaimed "Make a SPLASH at Lake Days."

"So, let me get this straight, the beaver is ambushing someone?" Aamot seemed to be having trouble keeping a straight face.

"Uh-huh." Jake knew what he was thinking, but she wasn't going to give him the chance to be beaver clever. Okay, so she could be sophomoric, too. "Ambush marketing is fairly common in events. It used to happen a lot with the Olympics. A company pays a huge amount of money--millions, in the case of the Olympics--to have official sponsor status. They are the 'Official Whatever' of the Olympics. That's fine, but it doesn't buy them anything but the right to call themselves 'The Official Whatever of the Olympics.' They have to buy their own ads to promote the sponsorship.

"So," Jake continued, "a competitor theoretically could come in and buy up a whole bunch of ad time on other stations or rent all the billboards in town, congratulating the athletes. Now, even though Company A is the

Official Whatever, Company B is all over the air and all over the city. If it's done well enough, the public perception is that Company B is the sponsor."

"Sounds like a big problem for the event itself." Aamot rubbed his chin. "Why would someone buy a sponsorship if you can ambush it for nothing?"

"Exactly." Jake gathered up the rest of their trash and stuck it in the barrel as she stood up. "That's why you have to prevent it."

"How?"

"Well, for one thing," she said, "you make darn sure you reserve the park across the street, so they can't fill it with giant beavers." She saluted the CoolSplash Beaver with one finger and giggled.

This time Aamot beamed his approval. "You're what? Thirty?"

"Thirty-five. Told you I was older than I look."

"Still. So young to be so cynical."

She laughed. "It's been a long thirty-five years, believe me."

"What about this microwave truck? Who really pays for it?"

"Sore subject," Jake warned. "Tread there and, rest assured, cynicism will follow."

He didn't say anything.

She sighed. "Okay, okay. I'm hoping that the station's insurance will cover it."

"Why wouldn't it?"

They were approaching the production truck now. Jake picked her hair up off her neck. The air was getting sticky again. "They could argue that losing a microwave van off a barge during a fireworks show was beyond what they consider a 'normal business risk,' even in our abnormal business. If that happens, either we go after Firenze's insurance company or the station takes it out of my hide."

"You're the one who decided to put it out there?"

Jake shrugged. "I'm the one who let Bryan talk me into putting it out there. Just like Pasquale let Bryan talk him into making those big shells, no matter what spin Bryan is trying to put on it now. And see where it's gotten us?"

SIX

Simon followed Jake back into the production van. "You think they'll fire you?"

Jake settled into her chair at the console and slid the box of videotapes he'd left there toward him. Interesting woman, he thought, looking down at her. Strawberry blonde hair, but eyes so dark brown they looked black.

She shrugged now. "I don't know. You can't lose something that big, that expensive..." She broke off with a laugh. "But life goes on--or not--one way or another. You know that verse, 'The Indispensable Man?' by the prolific poet, Anonymous?"

He smiled, but shook his head.

"It's used by a lot of inspirational speakers. I may be paraphrasing, but here goes." She clasped her hands theatrically.

"Sometime when you're feeling important
sometime when your ego's in bloom.
Sometime when you take it for granted,
you're the best qualified in the room.

Sometime when you think that your going
would leave an unfillable hole,
just follow these simple directions
and see how they'll humble your soul.

"Take a bucket and fill it with water,
put your hand in it up to the wrist.
Pull it out, and the hole that's remaining
is the measure of how you'll be missed."

She grinned at him as she continued.

"You can splash all you want as you enter.
You can stir up the water galore,
But stop, and you'll find that in no time
it looks quite the same as before.

"Now the moral of this quaint example
is do just the best that you can.
Be proud of yourself, but remember
There is no indispensable man."

"And you find this inspirational?" To Simon, it sounded downright depressing.

"I find it...reassuring," Jake countered. "No one's as important as they think they are--not me, not you, nor even Martha Malone, Bryan Williams or the honorable Clementine Cox."

She smiled now, and it lighted up her face. She just missed "beautiful" when she smiled.

"Would you--" Simon started and then stopped.

"Would I what?"

Damned if Simon knew, but he feared he had been about to ask her out. Not a good idea in the middle of an investigation, as past experience had proven.

Yet he lifted up the uppermost tape in the box and asked, "Would you go over these with me?"

"Me?" She looked surprised. "Why?"

Simon was fumbling for a reason, and now one--lame, though it might be--came to mind. "Because I assume you have something more efficient than a regular VCR to view them on. Besides, I'm hoping you can provide context. Who's shooting and such."

"I can, but right now I have to get ready for a three-thirty News Break, and then get back to the station for the Six O'clock News. If you can wait until after that, we could use the editing suite there and go through the footage frame by frame. But...," the "lameness" of Simon's request seemed to be sinking in, "aren't you worried I'll leak something to our news guys?"

"I don't think you'd do that," Simon said, honestly. "Do you?"

From Jake's expression, she apparently wasn't as sure.

Kathy McCutcheon looked up from her desk when the electronic access pad on the ATF office door beeped. Three seconds later, Simon Aamot entered.

"Howdy, cowboy."

Simon sat down on the corner of her desk and straightened the "Investigative Assistant" name plate. "Howdy, ma'am. Anything from the lab yet?"

"Please." She gave him a look over the top of the reading glasses she'd recently adopted. She didn't need them, but she liked the way they made her look. "It's Saturday, and you dropped the samples off maybe ten hours ago. You're lucky I'm here."

"You won't get an argument from me on that," Simon said wearily.

"I do have the *preliminary* cause of death on Pasquale Firenze," she offered hesitantly. Kathy knew Pasquale was a friend, and Simon didn't have many friends. Not because he wasn't good, or funny, or clever. Simon was all of those things. It was because he didn't attach himself to people easily or lightly. But once he did--once you were his friend--it was for life. Kathy liked that about him, and she hated to see him hurting. Though no one but Kathy would probably notice.

"It looks like heart failure from the concussion of the explosion," she said. "There was no water in the lungs."

Meaning Pasquale hadn't drowned, but had died instantly.

"Good," Simon said softly, then changed the subject. "So how's by you, Kath. All well with the doc?"

She followed his lead to the lighter side. "You are absolutely transparent, Simon. You want me to be a nun or what?"

Simon gave her a slack-jawed leer. "What."

She smacked him lightly. "Get off my desk, you cretin."

Simon and Kathy had started with ATF the same year, Simon, twenty-eight, and Kathy, just eighteen. Unbeknownst to Kathy at the time, he'd warned off all the other guys in the office, not because he was interested in her himself, but because he felt protective of the young woman barely out of high school. After two dateless years, Kathy finally realized what was going on and told her protector to mind his own damn business.

Now--at twenty-eight herself--she was officially engaged to a doctor. A pediatric cardiologist. But it didn't stop her from loving Simon.

The ATF agent rubbed the shoulder she'd hit and stood up, smiling. "Just watching out for you, Kath."

She shook her head. "When are you going to find yourself a nice gal, Tex, and settle down?"

"I did that once," Simon said, heading into his office. "Remember?"

"I said a nice gal," Kathy muttered under her breath.

Neal: *"...has taken its toll on the Firenze family. Francesco Firenze was killed two years ago in an explosion, and just last night we saw, live on TV8, his brother Pasquale suffer a similar fate.*

In addition, Pasquale Firenze's son-in-law is still missing in last night's blast and is presumed dead, leaving only the patriarch's son, Pasquale Jr., and daughter, Angela. A sad ending, some say, for the Firenze Fireworks dynasty."

Brett: *"Neal, I understand the Firenzes are scheduled to fire next week's Fourth of July fireworks in Liberty. Any word--"*

Jake swiveled away from the monitor in her control room and took a hit of the latte she'd picked up en route from the lakefront.

Even on a Saturday, the energy at the station was palpable. Talk about luck, the general consensus seemed to be. TV8, the exclusive Lake Days Fireworks station, as catastrophe struck. Oh, sure, the other stations had one, maybe two cameras down there to film the finale. But nobody else had anybody on the barges or the seawall.

News programs from all over the country were clamoring for tape and even to interview Luis Burns. Luis, for his part, was clamoring for footage, too--the close-up Jake had buried under "F" in the file cabinet.

Speaking of tapes... Jake sipped her latte, eyeing a different tape, this one containing the footage Luis shot *after* the microwave van went down.

The tape had been in his camera, though Jake didn't quite understand why Luis was recording to that when he was already hard-wired to the microwave van. A backup, in case something happened to the truck or to the signal? That should have been Jake's call, and not a bad one in retrospect. But for Luis to have done it--for Luis even to have *thought* of it--would mean he was a belt-and-suspenders kind of guy. And Luis was anything but.

Besides, with Luis on the barge, Jake wouldn't have access to the footage in his camera for the live show anyway. It was worthless unless later coverage was required for some reason, and Luis would have no way of knowing, when he'd put that tape in the camera, that--

The phone rang, breaking her train of thought. Jake picked up the receiver. "News."

Silence. Probably just another yahoo thinking the newsroom number would ring in the studio and, therefore, on air. "Get a life," Jake said into the phone, before replacing the receiver.

She stared into her now empty coffee cup. Running on latte vapors and still with nearly five hours to go.

The producer watched the monitor as Neal diagrammed the accident on a chalkboard. Even Neal--a genuinely nice guy--was eating this stuff up. Now if only there were criminal negligence on Firenze's part, this story could go on for months. The gift that just keeps on giving.

Vultures. Feeding off Pasquale's body. And probably Ray's. And worst of all, Jake was right down there with them, elbowing her way to the dinner table.

Finding TV8's front entrance locked, Simon Aamot pushed the after-hours buzzer to the right of it. A voice over the intercom answered a moment later.

Simon identified himself. "I have an appointment with Wendy Jacobus."

"Who?"

"Jake," Simon tried.

"Just a second. I'll get her."

Five minutes later Wendy "Jake" Jacobus was leading him through a labyrinth of laminate half walls to a real one with a real door in it. Inside was a windowless room that looked like an enlarged version of the production van, but with even more monitors.

The editing suite, as Jake called it, included a small studio, now dark. The whole suite--walls, floor and ceiling--looked to be encased in some sort of sound-deadening insulation. Most of the monitors were black, but one showed a studio somewhere else in the building--the news set, with Neal Cravens was sitting at the desk talking. The sound was off.

"Sorry I'm a little early," Simon said.

She smiled. "They're done. Neal's just jabbering to the guys. Come on in and sit down."

"Is Cravens your weekend anchor?"

Jake went to the console and pushed a button, then looked over her shoulder at him. "Don't tell me you don't watch our news."

"Nah, I'm too busy reading the newspaper and Newsweek."

"Slum and watch us instead. I need my job."

Simon looked around. The light in the room was subdued and, like any sound they made, seemed to be sucked in by the walls and ceiling. The space felt dead, like an isolation chamber.

In the midst of all that isolation, Jake was plainly alive and in her element. She looked tired, though, with small dark thumbprints under her eyes.

"How long have you been working?" he asked. "You were on until two last night, then here to make the tapes for me this morning. Lake Days at noon, then back here again. Did you sleep at all?"

She flopped into the chair in front of the editing console and tucked her feet up under her as the chair swiveled. "Time to sleep when I'm dead."

When Simon didn't respond, she sighed. "Okay, about three hours, maybe. I finally gave up and went to swim laps, thinking it would relax me."

"Did it?" Simon asked. He was a runner when he had the time, but the thought of paddling up and back the same narrow strip of pool over and over again sounded like nothing short of torture to him. Water torture.

"No." Jake folded her arms across her chest. "And what about you? Did you sleep?"

He nodded, feeling a little guilty about it. "I've gotten to the point where I can just turn it off. I have to."

"Yeah, I suppose you do. How long have you been with the ATF?" She gestured for him to sit in the chair next to hers.

He did, setting the box of videotapes he'd brought along on the console. "About as long as you've been here, ten years."

"You like it? Or is that a silly question?"

He shrugged. "No more than my asking if you like your job. There are good days, and there are bad days."

She thought about that. "I suppose. But I've experienced just a part of one of your days, and it has kicked the living daylights out of me."

"It's...you get used to it. And when it gets too bad, you move over to the Secret Service for a while."

"The Secret Service?" She was laughing.

"Seriously. Both ATF and the Secret Service are under the Treasury Department. At ATF, we deal with motorcycle gangs, illegal arms dealers, bombers--not exactly the upper rungs of society's ladder. After a while, it drags you down, too."

"Must be hell on a home life."

"It's hard to leave your work at the office. Or your mood."

"Are you married?" Jake asked.

Simon shifted in his chair. "Not anymore. She's an attorney, a partner in a good firm. The marriage didn't last long."

"Your job? Her job?" Jake's hair was back-lighted by the glow coming off the monitor behind her. It looked like a tangled halo around her white face and dark, dark eyes. She looked very fragile all of a sudden.

He cleared his throat, reminding himself that during lunch she had been about as fragile as a fox terrier. Little in stature, but wiry and, he was willing to bet, tenacious. "Both. Days spent in my world and nights in hers. Dinner parties. Benefits. I'd come home feeling like I should check my shoes to make sure I didn't drag the crap from my life into hers."

They were both quiet, the dimness of the room almost intimate. On the monitor, Neal Cravens got up from the news desk and walked out of the picture. A moment later, the studio lights went off and the screen went black.

Jake reached over and flicked off the monitor. "We'll look at my masters instead of the ones I made for you. We'll get better resolution with them."

"This one has the breaking news coverage from last night," she continued, lifting the top tape in her stack of three. "The next is the actual fireworks program up to the explosion, and this one," she indicated the third cassette, "is all the B-roll, the stuff we didn't use. What do you want to see?"

"The close-up view you showed right after the explosion. I assume Burns shot it from the next barge."

Jake flushed. "Actually, I *will* need your tape then. That footage isn't on any of these."

She set down the tape she had picked up, and Simon cocked his head at her. "I thought you had the masters. How can there be something on mine that isn't on yours?"

Jake was squirming. She looked at him, then away, then back again. "There's a gap on the masters. Like the Watergate tapes."

"A gap? You mean they've been erased? By who?"

"Taped over, actually. And by me." She was back to not looking at him.

He didn't get it. Why would Jake destroy the footage unless there was something on it she wanted to hide? But if that were so, why did she give it to him in the first place?

He asked her, swiveling her chair around to so she faced him.

"I didn't want to chance anyone airing it again." She cleared her throat. "The night of the explosion, it felt like the worst kind of voyeurism. Pasquale deserved better. We all deserve better."

Simon nodded. You could question the woman's methods, but not her motives. "But isn't that destroying station property?"

"Heck, yeah." Jake cracked a grin. "But you're talking to the woman who lost an entire truck. What's one little section of tape?"

Simon didn't think she was quite as unconcerned as she pretended. He held out the box to her. "Let's see it."

Jake selected a tape and stuck it into a slot on the console. She turned a knob clockwise, and the image on the screen raced ahead. When she reached the place she was looking for, she turned the knob the other way, and the tape rewound and then slowed to normal speed. Sure beat the clunkiness of a regular VCR. Sometimes Simon felt like he could go out for pizza in the time it took for his machine to move from rewind to play. Yet another reason why DVDs deserved to send videotapes into extinction.

"Here it is," Jake said.

Simon leaned forward. You could see Pasquale clearly in the reflected light of the flare he held. As they watched, he came forward and leaned down to light the quickmatch. A flash of light and the fire ran up the fuse to the first shell as the old man stepped back and turned his face skyward.

A small flash and a whoosh as the first shell went up. Simon checked the clock on the editing console. Three seconds later, another flash, another whoosh. And three seconds later...nothing.

"Stop it here," Simon said, "and run it back for me. If you slow it down, will the clock still show elapsed time?"

"It will slow down to match the tape," Jake confirmed. "Why? What do you see?"

"Nothing, that's the thing." Simon pointed at the screen as the tape started to run in slow motion. "Look here. Pat said there was a three-second time fuse between the first and second shell and the second and third." He counted as the clock on the console ticked off the seconds, also in slow motion. "One...two ...three... There goes the second shell, see it?" He traced the path of the shell with his finger. "Three more seconds, the third one should go up."

"But we know it didn't. It exploded on the barge," Jake stopped the tape.

"That's right, and Pasquale realized it hadn't gone up." Simon touched the figure of Pasquale on the screen. "Start it again, and watch. One, two, three, four... See? Here's where he realizes the shell didn't go up, so he heads back to the mortar to re-light it."

"And it explodes when he touches the torch to it?"

Simon shook his head. "I don't think so. Here rewind again." They went back to the beginning of the sequence. "After the lift charge blasts the shell out of the mortar and into the air, there should be a ten-second delay before the pyro, the color, actually bursts. That ten seconds gives the shell time to climb high enough in the sky.

"That means," he continued, "since they were timed three seconds apart, the red shell would burst at ten seconds, the white at thirteen, and the blue at sixteen."

Jake zeroed out the clock, and Simon counted as the red shell went up. "Eight...nine... This is when Pasquale starts back to the mortar. He already knows something is wrong. There goes the red burst. Eleven...twelve...the white...fourteen..."

Pasquale reached the mortar.

"Fifteen...sixteen..."

The screen went yellow, then white, then black.

"Geez," Jake muttered.

Simon sat back and thought. So the blue shell's internal time fuse--the ten-second fuse in the shell itself--*did* light. That accounted for the ten-second delay before the shell burst.

"Can you go back again?" Simon asked. "Just to the blast."

She rewound it again and started through it slowly.

"Stop there," Simon said. "Did you see that?"

"See what?" Jake asked, getting closer and freezing the image.

"There." Simon pointed. "That arc of light going off to the side--"

"And being extinguished," Jake finished for him. "Pasquale's flare hitting the water." Jake didn't turn to look at him when she spoke, just stared straight ahead at the still image.

Simon's head was very close to hers now, and he could see the tears pooling in her eyes. "Probably," he said softly.

Jake stabbed at a button, and the tape started up again, only to go black. As Jake reached to stop the tape, there seemed to be a hiccup, the image got lighter, then bucked and got black again. Simon reached out to prevent her from pressing stop. "What was that?"

They watched for a few seconds, but nothing else happened.

"Luis must have been trying to adjust the camera and get the image back," Jake said. Then the swell hit and there went the microwave link. You've already seen the other tape--the backup he had in his camera." She popped out the cassette and cleared her throat. "Anything else?"

Simon leaned back in his chair and stretched. He'd seen what he needed to, even if it only confirmed what he already had suspected. "No, I guess that'll do it for tonight. Can I get a copy of anything shot at the fireworks factory, too?"

Jake got up and crossed the room to a large metal shelving unit filled with neatly labeled videotapes. She came back with the tape and held it out to him.

Simon stood up to take it, and the movement put him closer to her than he'd intended. "For what it's worth, I think you were right to erase the tape. I'm glad you made a copy for me first, though."

Jake didn't step back, but she didn't look at him either. "You needed to see it, but no one else does."

Simon took the tape from her and set it down on the console. She was looking down at the floor, any place but at him. He sucked in a deep breath and reminded himself how complicated things could get when...

A tear rolled down her cheek.

Aww, damn. He reached out and brushed it away.

Her eyes closed, and a hint of a tremor ran through her body. Unable to resist, he rubbed his thumb across her bottom lip.

Jake's head came up and her eyes snapped open. They were even darker than usual now, if that were possible, but soft and unfocussed. Her lips parted as she started to say something and he slid his thumb ever so slightly in between them. Another shudder, this time unmistakable. She reached up and pulled his head down to hers, and he kissed her.

She kissed him, sex-starved tart that she was.

Right there on the editing console.

Jake was a good ten inches shorter than Simon, so their parts didn't quite match up. She was tottering on her tiptoes, arms twined around his neck, and he hopped her up onto the edge of the console.

The room was quiet and dim. It felt surreal--like they were about to make love in the womb. A bizarre thought, one that would likely put her into therapy for the rest of her life.

Jake was all raw nerve endings, every part of her screaming "yes, yes, yes!" like some shampoo commercial. Under Simon's right arm she could feel what she presumed was a gun in a holster. She could also feel his lips starting to move down from her mouth, and his hands gravitate upward from her waist...

He must have felt her freeze up and lifted his lips from the notch at her throat. "What?" he whispered hoarsely. "Did you hear something?"

That was as good an excuse as any. She nodded, struggling for breath, and for an irrational second she thought that maybe all the air had been sucked out of the sealed room.

"Are you okay?" Simon asked. He took a step back, and she slid off the console and turned away from him, feeling like an idiot.

Much as she wanted it, much as she wanted him, it was way too complicated. A bad idea on a lot of fronts. She almost giggled at her own joke. Then he'd *really* think she was nuts. "I'm sorry. I'm okay. But we can't do this."

"No, *I'm* sorry. This was inappropriate. Here in your office. Us working together." He seemed to be fishing, trying to pin down exactly what had caused her reaction.

Jake knew she should explain, but then he'd just be embarrassed or even repelled. Whichever, better to end this now and save them both the trouble.

She wet her lips and, as Simon took a step toward her, put up a hand. "Listen, it's fine. I kissed you, or if not--" she held up the hand again, as he started to interrupt, "it was certainly mutual. This...it's just not such a good idea."

Simon raised his hands in surrender. "Okay, message received and understood." He picked up the tapes she'd given him. "I hope you'll still give me a hand with these if I need it." He studied her face. "During the day. With the door open."

Jake smiled, wondering which of the mixed messages she was sending he understood. "Deal."

Simon started out the door with the tapes, and then turned. "I lied before."

"Lied?"

"I'm not sorry. I enjoyed every second of it, appropriate or not."

Same here, was what she thought.

"Goodnight, Simon," was what she said.

SEVEN

The next day was Sunday and for Simon that meant church, or more precisely, church choir. The choir was singing in the ten o'clock service and Simon got there at quarter to, just in time for warm-up. The choir director at St. Joseph's was a short balding man, with the biggest, whitest teeth Simon had ever seen. His name was Ryan Orwell, and Simon considered him a friend. He also considered him gay, though he wasn't absolutely sure.

"Simon," Orwell greeted him, "I'm glad you're here. We're short baritones today."

Simon pulled on his choir robe and looked around. He didn't see any baritones at all, with the exception of himself. "Don't tell me I'm the whole section again."

Orwell smiled at him from behind the piano. "Simon, old man, you're all I want."

It was Orwell's stock line, invariably delivered with a quirk of one eyebrow.

Simon was capable of carrying the baritone part himself and didn't half mind doing it, even if he pretended he did. In fact, one of the reasons he liked St. Joseph's choir was that it was small--twenty people at full strength, and they were never at full strength. In Ryan's choir you had to be able to sing, had to be able to read music, and had to be able to carry your part alone if need be. In that way, it was very much like life.

In fact, the only negative Simon really saw was that the church choir was, well, a church choir. Meaning you had to go to church to sing in it. So far he'd managed to use his job as an excuse for leaving before the sermon. Three years it had been now.

At first, St. Joseph's pastor had gotten after Ryan, positing that it looked bad for choir members to up and leave at the start of each sermon. Ryan had prevailed on Simon's behalf, arguing that Simon was the best baritone he'd ever had and, besides, fifteen minutes in church singing God's praises was better than nothing. Especially considering what Simon did the rest of the week.

So it came to pass that after a rousing rendition of "God is Great," Simon rose from church and descended into the Hardee's next door. Over four cinnamon raisin biscuits, extra frosting, and a large black coffee, he tried to read the op-ed section of the Sunday paper. Instead, he thought about Wendy Jacobus.

Capable, responsive--professionally and personally, judging from last night. Nice little body.

There was something wrong, though, and Simon had realized last night--in his bed, alone--that although she had asked him if he was married, he had never asked her the reciprocal question.

His ex-wife, Dianne, used to say that Simon needed to be the center of his own universe. Simon didn't quite see what was wrong with that. Everyone should be the center of his own universe, shouldn't he? Or she?

Still, he should have asked Jake about herself--specifically, if she was married. She didn't wear a wedding ring, but that didn't necessarily mean anything. If she *was* married, that would explain what had happened last night in the control room. And the explanation was more to his liking than that she just wasn't interested.

Whatever the reason, it was for the best. Since his divorce, Simon had made it a habit not to make women a habit, or to become a habit for one of them. His job gave him enough to deal with, and he had his big screen TV to keep him warm and his house to keep him busy at the odd times his job didn't.

The house, an old Victorian-style fixer-upper right on Lake Michigan, had been the one thing both he and Dianne fought for in the divorce settlement. It was set picturesquely on a bluff that probably wouldn't erode in his lifetime. The "probably" was the reason they had been able to afford it in the first place.

Simon had worked on the house most every Sunday for the two years he and Dianne had been married and every Sunday since. First the exterior, then the interior--stripping off layers of paint and wallpaper, sanding hardwood floors, and exterminating colonies of rats, ants and yellow jackets. He was on the last room now.

The study was on the first floor at the back of the house. Before Simon had removed the wainscoting, three of the walls had looked pretty much like you would expect them to look in an old-style den: dark, masculine, lots of bookshelves.

The fourth wall, though, was as spectacular as it was unexpected. The previous owner had knocked out the entire east side of the room and put in floor-to-ceiling glass, exposing the room to the lake. Although Simon was enough of an architectural purist to cringe at the thought of 1979 "improvements" to an 1890s house, he had to admit the view was magnificent.

And it was his.

Throughout the divorce proceedings he had pursued possession of the house single-mindedly and against all reason. And, the advice of his attorney.

He knew Dianne had been surprised at his tenacity. Until then, Simon had been extremely easy-going about the divorce and the property settlement. "Things" didn't mean much to him, probably the result of seeing so many "things" burnt to a crisp. Still, he had to have the house--not so much for what it was, as for what it represented.

And what it represented was Simon, of course. You didn't need a shrink to tell you that. By coming out of the marriage with the house, he was affirming that he was still intact. That he had recovered his investment and then some. The fact that he'd given up everything else in order to get it didn't matter. Dianne was, after all, an attorney. And Simon, for all his stubbornness, was a realist.

He drained his coffee cup and folded up the still unread newspaper. He had to stop for a gallon of paint on the way home.

After days of scraping and steaming, Simon had finally gotten all the wallpaper and glue off the study walls and primed them. He was ready to paint. Problem was he couldn't decide what color.

It was almost a ritual. Every Sunday morning, Simon stopped to pick up a can of paint on his way home from Hardee's. Every Sunday noon he painted a swath next to the door and stood back to look at it. Every Sunday just after twelve, he stowed the can of paint in the basement.

This week it was "Creme de la Creme." He had just set the can down in the front foyer when the phone rang.

The caller was Pat Firenze. "I'm sorry to bother you on a Sunday, but Angela is going out of her mind. Is there any word on Ray?"

Simon, who had checked on both the search and the lab results before church, could believe that. "Sorry, but no. And...well, it's been thirty-six hours, Pat. If Ray was picked up by a boat, or floating on debris or something, we should have heard by now."

"Unless he drowned, you're saying. Jesus. How in the hell did this happen to us?"

Pat sounded dazed, and who could blame him? His whole world had literally exploded in a second.

Simon chose to answer Pat's question in practical rather than rhetorical terms. "The lift charge didn't detonate, just as we suspected. The timing fuse to the shell lighted, though, so your guess is as good as mine as to the cause.

There just wasn't much left on the barge to go on: Some chemical traces we're having analyzed, canvas, silica, sand, string, brown paper..." he trailed off.

Pat didn't say anything.

"Pat?"

"Sorry," Pat said. "I was just thinking how twisted it is that paper and string survived the blast and my father didn't."

Explosions were like that, Simon thought. The bombing of the Murrah Federal Building in Oklahoma City had killed 168 people, 19 of them under the age of six. Yet toys were found in the building's day care center still ...

"Why don't you come for dinner, Simon?" Pat said out of the blue.

"Come where?"

"My parent's house. We can talk," Pat said. "And besides, my mother cooks to forget. You'll be doing us a favor by giving her another mouth to feed."

Right. Pat apparently had something to say, but he couldn't--or wouldn't-- say it over the phone. Simon agreed to six-thirty and hung up.

He was still puzzling over Pat's sudden invitation as he painted a stripe of "Creme de la Creme" on the study wall just to the right of "Ivory Tower" and below "Ecru To You." The ecru he'd bought more for the name, than the color. Or the absence of color. He stepped back to look.

Nope. Still not right.

Simon tapped the lid back on the can and carried the paint and brush down to the basement, where he stacked "Creme de la Creme" on top of a gallon of "Suddenly Sudan." The brush he stuck in a can of thinner to soak.

He checked his watch. Just after twelve. Simon needed to track down any footage the other stations had shot of the finale, just in case they'd captured something TV8 had missed. Normally, it would be tough to get hold of station officials on a Sunday, but he figured they might jump at a chance to be part of the investigation. And say so on the air.

All in all, he shouldn't have any trouble getting that done, paying a courtesy call to the mayor, and *still* getting to the Firenze's for dinner by six-thirty.

Stroke/kersplat...stroke/kersplat...stroke/kersplat...

The sound followed Jake up-and-back, up-and-back, like the tick...tick...tick of the alarm clock inside the crocodile in Peter Pan.

Nuts. Swimming was supposed to be therapeutic, a place where you let your mind wander, thinking the great thoughts you only think as you swim up-and-back thirty-six times. And have nothing to write them down on.

Stroke/kersplat...stroke/kersplat...stroke/kersplat...

Today, the man--or the Croc, as she'd taken to thinking of him--was in the lane next to her. Each time she kicked off from the shallow end, he'd do likewise and swim like they were racing. Each time he finished ahead of her.

Each time he stood and waited in his lane for her to finish. And, each time, he'd start the whole thing all over again for the next lap.

Although people like Doug often swam alongside her, this guy was different. It was like he was taking pleasure in beating her over and over and over again for thirty-six laps. It gave Jake the willies.

She grabbed the end of the pool and turned, avoiding eye contact with the Croc, who again was waiting in the next lane.

Stroke/kersplat...stroke/kersplat...stroke/kersplat...

He was behind her at the half-length. At her heels at the turn. Passing her at the three-quarters mark.

Stroke/kersplat...

Another non-eye-contact turn. Jake started her last lap.

So if this guy was the Croc, that would make Jake Captain Hook wouldn't it? Funny, she'd always fancied herself more the Tinkerbell type, everybody clapping hard as they could, to save the flighty little Tink.

Stroke/kersplat...stroke/kersplat...stroke/kersplat...

Or Tiger Lily, an assertive female if there ever was one.

Stroke/kersplat...stroke/kersplat...stroke/kersplat...

Jake had never identified with Wendy Darling. In addition to having a stupid name, she was a fool for giving up Peter Pan in order to grow old and die.

What was the point of *that*?

Stroke/kersplat...

Thirty-six.

Finished.

Jake pulled herself up and out of the pool, waving over Doug, who had just walked in, to take her lane.

She felt badly sticking him next to the Croc, but it was time to fly.

The other local TVs had been a washout for Simon. None of the three had more than one camera on the scene and they were all too far away to catch anything significant. No matter, you had to check these things out, even if it did waste the better part of the afternoon.

It was nearly five when Simon arrived at Shore Park. Mayor Clementine Cox had left word that she could be found at the Lake Days headquarters tent there. Simon liked talking to politicians almost as much as reporters, but he'd found keeping local officials informed was the best way to keep them out of his hair. Mostly.

The TV8 production van was still in place, as was the smell of corn dogs and cotton candy. As Lake Days drew to a close on its final day, the park was jam-packed with people and the Coast Guard continued its search for Ray Guida's body.

Lake Michigan was beautiful--blue and tranquil. Like Jake's "bucket of water," the lake's surface was "quite the same as before."

Simon watched as a young couple picked up beers and nachos at a concession stand and boosted themselves up on the seawall to monitor the Coast Guard search. A real life Reality Show, except the couch was made of rocks.

The ATF agent steered toward the red-and-white-striped headquarters tent and stuck his head in. A woman of about thirty-five sat behind a table. She had dark hair cut short around a freckled face and was wearing khaki shorts and a royal blue Lake Days T-shirt. On the telephone as he ducked in, she looked up and waved him over.

The place was bare bones, just a tent set over now parched grass crisscrossed by heavy duty extension cords. Four tables were arranged along the walls of the tent, two held telephones, another was piled high with T-shirts and Lake Days souvenirs, and the fourth held just a single box of Dunkin' Donuts and a 30-cup percolator. The coffee smelled like pencil lead.

Behind the table was a wall of cardboard boxes labeled "Beer Cups" and "Toilet Paper." There was something cosmic about the combination. The circle of life.

The mayor was still talking. "That's fine, Bryan, but we only have three days until the Fourth. We need to make a decision here." She eyed Simon as she spoke. "I know, I know. Okay. Get back to me, then."

She hung up the phone and turned to Simon, who had settled himself in a chair across the table from her. She stuck out her hand. "Clementine Cox."

"Simon Aamot. I'm with ATF, investigating the explosion Friday night. I wanted to introduce myself."

"A terrible thing." She gestured toward the phone. "I was just talking to Bryan Williams, our event manager, about it and what it means to us."

"Means?" Simon said politely.

"Yes, the explosion has been a horrible set-back for everyone involved with Lake Days."

"Some more than others," Simon pointed out.

"Of course." Cox picked up a pencil and tapped it twice, then set it back down. "Do we know what happened yet? The Firenzes are supposed to fire our County Fourth of July fireworks on Wednesday. I have to say, I'm seriously thinking of trying to break the contract."

"The Fourth of July show is here, too?" Simon asked.

"That's right, and we expect a very large crowd. We'll be using the park across the street, as well."

Home of the beaver. "You're in charge of that celebration, too?"

Cox nodded. "It's a county event."

"And you're thinking of replacing Firenze?"

She leaned forward across the desk, like she was taking him into her confidence. "If Firenze Fireworks was negligent in the Lake Days show, we certainly have grounds."

"I've seen no evidence of negligence on their part, at least up to this point in the investigation."

"But if there was no negligence, why did the shell explode? And what about the other thing? The fireworks in a box?"

"Fire in the box. From what I can tell, that was a freak accident." Simon leaned forward, trying to explain something that seemed harder and harder for people to understand these days. "Despite human beings' best efforts, things go wrong sometimes--it's inevitable in life. And when you're dealing with fireworks and high explosives, the potential for those incidents to have major consequences is going to be greater."

The mayor opened her mouth, but Simon kept going. "It's something fireworks people understand. People who hire them to put on displays need to understand it, too."

The mayor held up her hands, fingers spread, as if waving off responsibility. "So you're saying, essentially, that if you play with fire, you should be expect to be burned?"

Simon wasn't going to let her off that easily. "Or if you *hire* someone to play with fire."

"We are having a fireworks display on the Fourth of July," Cox said, unequivocally. "The question is, do we use the Firenzes?" She eyed him. "It's not as if this were their first deadly accident. I understand you investigated an explosion at the factory a couple of years ago."

"I did," Simon said simply, determined not to get defensive like he had with Martha Malone.

"So you're familiar with the Firenzes?" The mayor pursed her lips.

"Familiar enough," was all Simon said, suddenly wary of where Cox was going with all this.

She surprised him and backed off. "So bottom line: Is it safe to use Firenze Fireworks for this show?"

Simon relaxed. "Safe as anyone. Safer than most."

She seemed to mull that over.

"According to Bryan William," Simon continued, "you were the one who suggested the Firenzes in the first place."

The mayor flushed now, all but obliterating the spattering of freckles across the bridge of her nose. "Public sentiment demanded we give them a chance because they're local. In truth, I want to make this a regional show, something that people will come from a hundred miles in any direction to see. I don't think Firenze has that kind of appeal, and I never did.

"But all in all," she continued, picking up her pencil again, "it will probably be best to go with Firenze for Wednesday's show. As Bryan points out, our contract with TV8 stipulates it, and it would be a difficult point to renegotiate."

So why all this discussion about the Firenzes if Cox was contractually bound to use them one way or the other, Simon wondered. Was the mayor trying to elicit Simon's endorsement, so if something *did* happen she wouldn't be.... Then he realized what she had just said: "TV8 is broadcasting the Fourth of July Fireworks, too?"

"Yes. They hadn't planned to, but--" The phone rang and Mayor Cox picked up immediately. She seemed glad for the interruption. After listening a moment, she put her hand over the mouthpiece and said, "I'm so sorry. I'm going to have to take this. Was there anything else?"

It was a dismissal and Simon complied, figuring he'd walk up the bluff to TV8 and see what he could find out about Wednesday's show. He was about halfway there when someone called his name and he turned.

Bryan Williams, wearing khakis and a blue golf shirt, was at the wheel of a "Lake Days Staff" golf cart. "Can I give you a lift?"

Simon stepped into the cart. "Sure, I was just going to the TV8 stage."

"And I, as well." Williams stepped on the gas. "I need to discuss details of our Fourth of July broadcast with Martha Malone."

Simon nodded. "The mayor was just telling me about that. I don't remember the celebration ever being televised before."

Williams nodded, keeping his eyes on the crowd slowly parting to let them through. "It's quite the coup. The Lake Day ratings were so high, TV8 negotiated for the Fourth of July, as well. Ad time is selling briskly, I understand."

This is what *Cops* and *America's Worst Whatever* hath wrought, Simon thought. Ratings would be sky-high, fueled by people hoping for another live, on-camera bloodbath. "I bet," was all he said.

When they arrived on the bluff, Martha Malone was standing on a corner of the set, the lake behind her as she spoke to the camera. Williams stopped the cart, and Simon got out with a nod of thanks and moved toward the monitor that faced the crowd.

Malone: *"So as the search for Ray Guida's body goes on, so do the questions.*

"TV8 research has found that Simon Aamot, the ATF special agent who is leading the investigation, also headed the inquiry two years ago when Francesco Firenze was killed by a blast at the Firenze Fireworks Factory. That explosion was caused by, quote, "lightning in the atmosphere." That despite the fact that according to our meteorologist, no lightning strikes were reported in the area.

"Now Simon Aamot is refusing comment to the media, while at the same time our own Luis Burns reports seeing Aamot and Pat Firenze on a friendly, first-name basis.

"Can Aamot be objective, people are asking? That may be a fair question.

"And, finally, should Firenze Fireworks--given the history of "accidents"--be allowed to produce the Fourth of July show scheduled to be aired live right here on TV8 Wednesday night?"

[Aamot headshot] "Again, Simon Aamot has refused comment."

Well, look at that, thought Simon--a photo suitable for framing. Plus, they had spelled his name right.

Damn it to hell. First, TV8 decides to broadcast the Fourth Fireworks show because of the great ratings they got for Friday's disaster, and now they were using Simon to goose the drama quotient. And what about Malone with her "should the Firenzes be allowed to produce the show"? According to the mayor, TV8's contract virtually *demanded* Firenze Fireworks do just that. Of all the hypocritical...

But Malone had returned to the anchor desk and was in an on-camera exchange with George Eagleton, so Simon couldn't very well vent on her. That left the one person he *could* vent on.

When he reached the TV8 production truck, he yanked open the door, purposely letting it slap back hard against the metal shell of the truck.

Jake, inside at the console, jumped. "Hey! We're on the air."

He pointed at her tech director. "Let him take over. I need to talk to you. Now."

Jake shook her head. "I don't care what you need. *I* need to finish this broadcast."

Simon's eyes narrowed. "Now."

She started to refuse again, but in truth the anchors were signing off and she was pretty much done for the day. "Fine." Jake shoved past Aamot to hop out of the truck and then turned on him. "Now, just what in the heck was *that* all about?"

The ATF agent took a step toward Jake, making it necessary for her to look up--way up--at him. "That's what I want to know. Is this supposed to be TV8 news or some kind of docudrama? Where do you people get your facts?"

What a difference a day makes. Last night he was all lips and hands, and today he was all mouth. "Which facts are you talking about? The fact that the shell exploded when it wasn't supposed to? The fact that one person is dead and another is presumably dead? We're making that up?"

"You're exploiting, dramatizing." Simon paced away and then back. "For what? Ratings?"

Gosh, Jake thought. He says it like it's a dirty word. Despite the fact she'd been known to voice similar sentiments at times, the producer automatically sprang to the defense of her employer and industry. "Without ratings, we can't--"

But Aamot interrupted, moving in even closer and bracing one hand against the truck, effectively trapping her between himself and the production van. "I understand you're broadcasting the Fourth of July Fireworks. Your coverage of 'Blast at Lake Days' pulled in quite an audi--"

"'Disaster at Lake Days'" Jake automatically corrected.

Aamot stopped mid-word. "What?"

"A festival in Kansas has the word 'Blast' trademarked," Jake mumbled. "We're using 'Disaster'.

"Wait a second," Aamot started, "you're telling me someone can trademark a word that's in common usage? That's...," he caught himself, "...beside the point. Whatever you call it, the Firenze explosion has been great for business, hasn't it? What's your commercial time for the Fourth going for?"

Jake flushed. She knew that despite sky-high rates, the ad time already was sold out. She didn't like what that said about the station or humanity in general, any more than Aamot did.

But the ATF agent wasn't coming up for air. "Cravens thinks he's a war correspondent. The same for your camera man. And Martha Malone is doing a made-for-TV movie, with herself in the central role. And implying that I'm in collusion with the Firenzes. Not to mention disputing the results of my earlier investigation, when she doesn't know a damn thing about it."

Almost in spite of herself, Jake was fascinated by Aamot's sudden temper tantrum. He'd been so laid-back yesterday, that seeing him get mad was like watching a heretofore tranquil mountain erupt into a volcano. One minute there were deer grazing on his slopes, and the next minute his head blew off.

"I'm not sure what you mean," Jake said. "I read the reports myself and there were no lightning strikes--"

"No lightning *strikes*, but lightning in the atmosphere." The vein above his right eye was throbbing. "Static electricity."

Jake thought about it. A little information could be a dangerous thing, especially when it was patched together with a lot of other partial information to fit a foregone conclusion. "Then you need to clarify. On the air."

Simon was quiet. But still simmering underneath, Jake was willing to bet.

"Listen," she said. "You can blame me. You can blame Martha. You can blame Neal, and you can blame Luis. But you sure have to include yourself if you don't show us where we're wrong."

He looked at her like she was a fly who'd had the audacity to buzz him. Then something flickered in his eyes, like a sudden thought had struck.

"What are you doing for dinner?"

EIGHT

The drive out to the Firenzes was long and very quiet. Simon was driving the Explorer, and Jake was in the passenger seat. Instead of reacting to his tantrum by being angry right back at him, the producer seemed to be enjoying the outing. Which, of course, made Simon feel downright sheepish.

Government agencies were used to being criticized in the media. Hell, *he* was used to being criticized in the media, though usually not by name and accompanied by a full-color photo. Yet he'd overreacted again, making him look like he *had* been treating this explosion differently than other investigations.

All was not lost, though. He could still get back on track tonight and set a professional tone with the Firenzes. And Jake would be there to witness it, even better. He looked over at her, and she caught his eye and gave him a big smile.

Jesus, what in the hell was he doing bringing Jake along? As a witness? A buffer?

Simon turned the truck into the Firenze driveway, and they bounced past the factory parking lot and up to a cream-colored brick farmhouse. Pasquale and his wife, Sadie, lived on the northern-most portion of the old farm in the original farmhouse.

Pat was in the front yard with the two dogs and called to the shepherds as the truck pulled up. Only Lugosi obeyed, flopping over onto the ground while Bela chased the truck's back tires, trying to snap at them as he ran.

"Sorry," Pat said as Simon and Jake got out of the truck. "Bela's a little high strung today."

"As usual," Simon said, stepping around the dog as it practically stood on its head trying to fit its mouth around the steel-belted radial. "Lugosi's looking mellow, though." The two-legged shepherd was lying on the grass chewing on his rear leg.

Pat shook Simon's hand. "He's been off his feed lately." He turned to Jake. "I'm glad you could join us."

He didn't sound glad. Simon had called on his cell phone to make sure it was all right to bring a guest, but now it occurred to him that the Firenzes might well have seen Martha Malone's report, too.

Jake, who had been studying Lugosi, turned innocently to greet Pat. That's why I brought her, Simon thought, she's the TV8 sacrificial lamb.

Just then, Sadie Firenze flew out the screen door and down the wooden porch steps to throw her arms around Simon. "Oh, Simon, Simon, what will we do without our Pasquale?"

Sadie Firenze was all of five feet tall. She had her arms wrapped around Simon's waist now and was sobbing and murmuring something he couldn't understand into his shirt. So much for appearing professional.

Coming from a family of Norwegians, Simon felt awkward around public displays of emotion. Grief in his childhood home was something to be contained until it could be spilled out safely into a pillow or behind a closed door. To do otherwise was considered self-indulgent and stagy--like rending your clothes or sitting in ashes.

But before Simon could do more than start to put his arms awkwardly around Sadie, she was backing up, wiping at her eyes with the corner of the dish towel she held. "I'm sorry, Simon. I know you're here to do your job."

She looked up at the ATF agent, and he could see that grief had taken all the horizontal lines of her face--the crinkles at the corners of her eyes, the laugh lines around her mouth--and turned them into harsh verticals. Sadie's face seemed to sag, and her mouth trembled as she struggled to control herself.

The older woman took his arm. "You come in and you eat. Then we talk about what happened to my Pasquale." Sadie looked toward the kitchen window, where a figure could be seen moving behind the sheer curtains. "And to my daughter's husband."

She turned toward Jake as they entered the big living room. "And this? Is this someone else from the ATF?"

"I'm sorry, I thought you already knew each other. Sadie Firenze, this is Wendy Jacobus, she's with TV8."

Sadie's brown eyes got small and shiny. "Yes, I remember you," she said to Jake, then turned on Simon. "You bring this person to my house, Simon? After what they say about my family? And about you?"

Oh, boy. Simon started to answer, but Jake leapt into the breach. "I'm sorry, Mrs. Firenze. When there's an accident like this, we try to explain what happened, given the best information we have at the time. Sometimes we..."

"Speculate," Simon finished for her, feeling even guiltier for putting the producer in the situation. "But the fact is, it's my responsibility to find out what really happened so Jake's station can report it."

Sadie eyed the TV8 producer speculatively and then dropped Simon's arm to take hers. The Firenze media relations department. "My husband Pasquale, he was so careful making those shells. No way he make a mistake." She made a violent negative gesture with her free hand to shush Pat, who had opened his mouth. "No way. You understand?"

Jake was nodding as Sadie led her off into the dining room. Trailing alongside Pat, Simon saw dinner was already laid out.

"Everybody makes mistakes." Pat glanced over at Simon and then quickly away. "And sometimes accidents just happen, like with Uncle Frankie."

Sadie etched a sign of the cross at the mention of her late brother-in-law and took the chair on the end of the table closest to the kitchen door. She motioned for Jake to sit on her left.

Simon, waiting to be told where to go, wondered if that was what Pat was hiding: A mistake. One his father had made. Or did Pat think Simon was the one who had made a mistake?

Pat sat on the opposite end of the table from Sadie in Pasquale's chair at the head of the table. He motioned for Simon to take the chair next to Jake.

As he did, Angela's voice floated out from the kitchen. "But Uncle Frankie should not have been working in the factory at all. He should have been in the Pathways Center in Ohio, like Aunt Nicolene wanted."

Angela came out of the kitchen with a dish of stuffed shells. Simon stood up to greet her, having experienced Firenze dinner conversations--which bounced from table to kitchen and back again without a break--before.

"Your Aunt Nicolene was full of prunes," Sadie snorted. "You have to be a Shriner to go there, and one thing your father said his family had no truck with, was those Shriners."

"I think he meant Teamsters, Mamma," Angela said gently, as she hugged Simon in greeting. Her slightly woodsy perfume wafted over him. "But the important thing is that Uncle Frankie died doing what he loved. We should all be so lucky when our time comes, my father would say." Her huge eyes filled with tears, and she took Simon's hand and led him around the table to sit next to her.

Simon, feeling awkward, sat down diagonally across the table from Jake. He didn't want to react to Angela's tears in front of the TV8 producer, and certainly not the way he'd reacted to Jake's the night before. Instead, he turned his attention to the food. On most American dinner tables, the pasta would have been the main dish. Here the shells were just a side dish, like potatoes--which they were also having, along with roast chicken. And green beans. And an antipasto.

"Your father, he wasn't old and crippled, Angela," Sadie was saying. "Ten years younger than his brother, my Pasquale was, and very healthy. Even if I tell him sometimes he's a hippo...what's that word, Little Pat?" She looked to her son.

"Hypochondriac, Ma," Pat supplied.

"Hypochondriac, what with those pills and vitamins he took. And a real romantic, your father."

Pat laughed. "That's not what you said last month when he gave you new pots and pans for your birthday."

Sadie waved him off and turned to Simon. "My children, they don't like to hear this. But I'll tell you, Simon, that man was lusty and virile-like, until the day he died. Liked to have worn me out the night before."

Simon could hazard a guess what *one* of the pills Pasquale had taken was.

"Soup?" Sadie asked, oblivious to the horrified expressions on her children's faces.

"Italian Wedding Soup, we call it." Sadie took the lid off a large tureen. "Chicken, you know, with escarole. My sister Marie made this one. When I make it, Angela she makes me beautiful itsy-bitsy meatballs to add and then makes sauce, too, so she can use up the rest of the meat. Waste not, want not, my Angela says. Even puts in the heel of the pepperoni, if we have it.

"But, Marie, she's lazy. Just pinches off little bits of chopped meat and drops them in. But it's okay." She wrinkled her nose, and started passing bowls of the inferior soup down the table. "But God-bless my sister for thinking of us, and God-bless that we are here to eat it." She paused just long enough to make the sign of the cross, and then kept right on ladling. "Now you have some wine. The white used to be my Pasquale's favorite, but the red, she's good, too."

Simon glanced over at Jake. She was already working on her soup as Pat poured the Firenzes' trademark homemade wine, sort of the Wild Turkey of wines. God knew what proof the stuff was.

"Red or white?" Pat asked. "Tudy made the red, Angela made the white." He held up an old Coke bottle in one hand and what looked like a recycled champagne bottle in the other.

Simon opted for red--the Coke bottle--as Angela passed him a bowl of soup. "There is still no sign of Ray?" Her color was high--a spot of red on each cheek, like the emotion had pushed to the surface only there.

"I checked with the Coast Guard on the way over," he answered. "Still nothing. I'm sorry."

She nodded and looked down at the table.

Sadie turned to Jake, who was wolfing down her soup. "My husband, when he started this business, it was only him and Tudy and my son. It was too much, too much, especially with all the paperwork. Pasquale's heart wasn't in those things. He was an artist, my husband.

73

"When Ray, Tudy's son, was old enough, he started helping with the books."

"Where is Tudy?" Simon asked. The old man was family, in heart if not by blood. Simon was surprised he wasn't there.

"He's home, taking care of Mary Ann, his wife. She's not Italian," she said to Jake, as if that explained why the woman needed taking care of.

"After that," Sadie continued, "Ray and Angela, they married, and now Ray is a partner just like my son. When my Pasquale is gone, Ray and Pat will take over."

Sadie beamed at her daughter, as if forgetting her own husband was dead and that Ray Guida had been missing in Lake Michigan for nearly forty-eight hours. Next to Simon, Angela looked down at her hands. The rest of the table was silent.

"Antipasto?" Sadie asked.

Sadie had a talent for segues, Jake thought.

Conversation about Pasquale's funeral arrangements:

"Cremated. My Pasquale wanted no dirt or worms or such. Stuffed shells?"

Discussion of Ray's fate:

"That water, she's so dirty, so cold. More chicken?"

The phone rang just as they were finishing a dessert of sublime home-made chocolate éclairs, filled with what Angela called yellow cream.

Pat went to answer the phone, suggesting Simon take his coffee out to the porch. That left Jake alone with Sadie, Angela, and the dishes.

Jake would have given anything to be out on the porch with the men. Even if Simon had scarcely been able to take his eyes off Angela during dinner. But then who could blame him? Angela was gorgeous, *and* she was a lady in distress. Besides, what business was it of Jake's? She'd turned Simon down flat just last night.

Pat slammed down the phone and stomped out the door. Maybe being a lady in the kitchen *did* trump being a man on the porch.

Sadie shook her head sadly. "Another show, she's down the drain," she said, as she set aside a cast iron pasta pot and then proceeded to fill the sink with hot soapy water.

"We've had calls all afternoon," Angela explained to Jake as the two of them cleared the table. "Our clients canceling their displays."

"I'm so sorry," Jake said, and she was. First, she had aired the close-up of Pasquale's death, and now she'd aided and abetted Martha's reports which were painting the Firenzes as reckless. And that didn't even include the secret sin of being jealous of Angela. Yup, Jake was really racking up the points with the Big Guy.

Angela carried a stack of plates to the counter, Jake trailing behind with two wine glasses in one hand and the empty white wine bottle in the other.

"My father is dead, and all is in shambles," Angela said, as she set down the plates. "Everything is ruined." Her long hair had swung forward to cover her face, but Jake could hear the tears in her voice.

"No," Sadie said, as she pushed her daughter's hair back behind her ears. "It's not ruined, but we need to be strong. We had your father for a long time, and we must pray God and thank Him for that. Ray, for not as long. But if he is gone, we need to be thankful for the time we had with him, too."

Angela nodded, still looking down at the plates in front of her. Jake set the glasses and bottle quietly on the counter next to her, feeling like an intruder. Over Angela's shoulder, she could see Simon through the window, lounging on the porch.

Sadie took the corner of her apron and wiped away Angela's tears. "Now," she said, "pulling off the thick green rubber band that circled her wrist like a bracelet, "get that hair off your face before you get it in the dish water."

Angela laughed, and Jake realized that there was a method to Sadie's segue madness. "My mother has been saying that to me since I was four years old." Angela held up the rubber band Sadie had handed her. "Do you see what it says?"

Jake looked closer. "Broccoli?"

Angela pulled back her hair and wrapped the band around it. "At school the girls would laugh at me because one day I would wear 'Asparagus,' the next day 'Broccoli.'"

"But they know you ate good," Sadie said, shaking her finger and laughing.

"Yes, Mamma, they did." Angela kissed her mother on the forehead.

"That *was* a wonderful meal," Jake said, wanting to contribute something.

Sadie looked her up and down. "You're a good eater, for somebody so skinny. I remember when you were on the TV. You called yourself 'Wendy Jacobs,' and you were so sick. Thank the Lord," she crossed herself again, "you're here to eat. Isn't that right, Angela, didn't I say 'that newsgirl, she's not long for this world.'?"

"Mamma, please." Angela gave Jake a sympathetic smile. Her eyes flicked down, but she seemed to catch herself and looked Jake square in the eye. "You are very lucky, you know."

Jake started to come back with a canned response, but Angela continued. "I must be very careful about what I eat."

Jake, grateful for the artful steering of the subject, smiled back. "I swim every day, which seems to help."

"See?" said Sadie, waving a soapy dishrag at her daughter. "You should start that running again. Now, Simon," she said, turning the cloth in Jake's direction, "I bet he likes a girl with a little muscle, isn't that right?"

Jake felt a blush rise. "I, we..."

75

Angela saved her again. "Please, Mamma, you're embarrassing her. Would you mind drying?" she asked Jake, handing her a dish towel. "Then I will put away, since I know the kitchen."

Jake took the towel from her.

"My daughter plays softball, and she ran tracks in school," said Sadie proudly. "My husband, he would say 'my Angela, she runs like an angel with wings on her feet.'"

Sadie rinsed the first plate, set it in the dish drainer, and picked up another. "'Pasquale,' I told him, 'that's the FTD flower man who has wings on his feet. Angels, they have wings on their backs.'"

And with that, Sadie Firenze finally broke into tears, then near hysteria.

After Pat hung up the phone, he picked up his coffee cup and stood for a second.

Jesus, what were they going to do? They already had lost three shows for the Fourth, and now a fourth was threatening to pull out. Small community park shows, for sure, but each of them worth fifteen to twenty thousand bucks. He walked out onto the deck with his coffee and sank onto the timbered porch glider.

Simon was straddling the hammock. "I assume that wasn't good news."

Pat studied his coffee cup. "Prairie Pleasant wants to cancel their show on the Fourth."

"Don't they have a contract?"

Pat shrugged. "Sure, and I'm in my rights to demand payment whether we do the show or not. Problem is, then I can kiss the display goodbye for next year, and the one after that, and the one after that. I'm hoping when this all blows over..."

He stopped and looked up from his coffee cup. "But maybe that's stupid. Maybe it'll never blow over."

Sadie's laughter floated out to them from the kitchen. "Your mother seems to be holding together pretty well," Simon observed. "That's good, at least."

"My mother is manic," Pat said. "One moment she's cooking for a hundred, the next she's sobbing so hard she can barely stand."

"Has she seen a doctor?"

Pat shrugged. "She has a GP, who's nearly 80. My dad never believed in doctors..." He let it trail off.

Simon slid his coffee cup out from under the hammock and took a drink. An owl hooted in the woods beyond the house. "What aren't you telling me, Pat?"

Pat wondered what he'd done to give himself away. "What do you mean?"

"There was something when we talked on the phone this morning. Something that bothered you. What was it?"

The owl hooted again. The sound reminded Pat of the old "Give a hoot, don't pollute" commercials. He and his dad would watch Saturday morning cartoons in their pajamas, big bowls of Cheerios on TV trays in front of them. Now his father was gone, but Pat still felt like the little kid who watched THE JETSONS and dreamed of taking over his father's company some day. Now that he had his wish, would there be anything left to take over?

Pat hadn't answered Simon, and the ATF agent turned and followed his gaze. The owl was silhouetted in the very top of one of the trees. Beyond it, they could see the bare wood of the barn glistening in the moonlight.

Simon, who had been about to set down the coffee cup, stopped mid-air. "Are you sandblasting the old paint off the outbuildings?"

Pat nodded. He knew that Simon, who had done his share of remodeling, would know that silica sand--one of the substances Simon had mentioned on the phone earlier that day--was used in sand-blasting.

"Of course," Simon confirmed. "I noticed the silica sand shining on the floor of your father's barge that night, but I assumed it was mixed with the sand in the sandbags used to stabilize the shells."

Pat was still looking toward the woods. "We use coarse sand in the sandbags, the same stuff we use on the roads and driveways here in the winter. We bought the silica sand for the sandblasting. There are a couple of bags in the storeroom."

The big bird took off, wings pounding the air, and struggled to gain altitude. Woodsy Owl, that was the name of the "Give a Hoot" owl.

"Can you tell what's missing?" Simon asked, finally setting the cup down.

"Nah. You'd only need two pounds out of a fifty-pound bag. Who would notice?"

"How can you be certain someone didn't make a mistake and use it in the sandbags?"

Pat turned to him as the owl hovered on the air currents overhead. "I made up those sandbags myself, Simon. They did *not* have silica sand in them."

"So if the silica wasn't on the barge before you set up, and it wasn't in the sandbags," Simon said slowly, "there's only one place it could have been."

Pat had seen Simon work before--the way he laid out all the facts in his head before he was ready to lay them out in words, so he said it for him: "The lift charge.".

"But why use silica?" Simon asked. "Why not just use regular sand? That way there would have been no trace at all."

"Silica is fine, like the black powder."

"But would anyone have noticed once it was wrapped?"

"You know how it is, Simon. You develop a feel for it. Any of us might have noticed something was wrong. My father, or Angela, or Tudy, or me."

"Or Ray?" Simon asked.

Pat shrugged and in the silence that followed, Woodsy Owl glided down to make his kill.

Simon was alone on the porch when Jake stepped out. She and Angela had finally gotten Sadie calmed down, though Jake suspected it was finding the coffeemaker empty that had jolted the woman from her tears. God forbid the men should be without their coffee. Taking care of others was what Sadie Firenze had done for the sixty-odd years of her life, and though it wouldn't have been Jake's choice, that routine seemed to be sustaining her now.

Just as Jake sat down on the glider, Pat came back out carrying a couple of thick, black 3-ring binders. "The last two years of financials, Simon. Is that enough?"

Simon, who had been lying on the hammock lost in thought when Jake came out, set down the coffee cup he'd balanced on his stomach and sat up to take the binders. "For now. I'll get them over to our auditors in the morning and let you know if they need anything more."

Angela had followed Pat out the door. "More coffee, Simon? Jake, would you like some?"

Simon stood up abruptly. "No thanks, Angela. We should get going."

Jake guessed she didn't want any coffee. Sadie, who apparently was equipped with radar, came out of the kitchen with plates covered in plastic wrap. "You take these with you," she said. "It's stuffed shells and chicken. I have a little antipast left in the kitchen. You want to take that, too?"

"Not me," said Simon. "Maybe Jake?"

Jake regretfully declined the antipasto, too, not wanting to be a pig. Or a bigger pig than she'd already been. She took both plates, one in each hand, and nearly dropped them as each bent under the weight of the chicken and the pasta.

Angela helped her stack one on top of the other. "There's one éclair left. Why don't I get that, too? It will just go to waste here."

"Won't someone eat--" Simon started to ask. Jake wanted to clap a hand over his mouth. No one in their right mind would turn down one of Angela's chocolate éclairs.

Angela, to Jake's relief, was having none of it. "No, no, you must take it. My mother doesn't eat sweets, and I--"

She broke off, startled, as rustling sounded in the woods nearby.

"Probably just that owl we saw earlier," Pat said, putting an arm around his skittish sister. "Or the dogs."

"We should bring them in tonight," Angela said. She turned to Simon and Jake. "We have coyotes nearby and I worry about Bela and Lugosi."

"The coyotes are probably more frightened of the dogs than the dogs are of them," Pat assured her.

"I know, but they seem very hungry. The paper said there have been attacks on small pets." She disengaged Pat's arm and held up two hands in surrender. "I know, I know. You will say the dogs are not small, but I worry about Lugosi, since he's a cripple."

"Lugosi is fine," Sadie said. "Now you go get that éclair from the ice box."

Angela went to do her mother's bidding. Sadie watched the screen door close behind her. "My daughter, she worries Lugosi suffers." She shrugged. "I say to her, 'So what's better, that he's dead?'"

Sadie certainly did know how to cut through the clutter.

Angela came out with the wrapped éclair in one hand and her handbag-- the Coach Hamptons Leather Carryall, if Jake were any judge of handbags--in the other. She gave the éclair to Jake, who balanced it on top of the plates.

"Mamma, I need to run home for some night things, then I'm going to come back and stay with you."

Jake thought that sounded like a good idea given Sadie's state of mind. It would at the very least give her somebody to feed in the morning.

As they all started down the porch steps, the "crippled" dog Angela had been talking about came bounding up the steps, made an astonishing u-turn and bounded back down. Then he stopped, tail-wagging, and fell over sideways.

"My God, is he dead?" Jake asked.

"No," Angela said, dropping her Coach bag on the ground with a thud in order to fish a cigarette butt out of the dog's mouth. "That's how he lies down."

Jake, amazed to see the chic Angela now giving the two-legged dog a tummy-rub, just managed a "Wow."

Angela straightened up, tucking her bag up under her arm. "Poor puppy."

"He does really well, though. It's incredible." Jake reached down to give the dog a scratch, too. Lugosi's back leg moved rhythmically in time with the scratching and his tongue lolled out one side of his mouth.

"Not as well as he once did," Angela said, watching him with a sad smile. "He's getting old. I hate to see him in pain, not able to do the things he loves."

"Like chasing cars?" Pat had followed them down the steps and was en route to his car. "That's what got him into trouble in the first place."

NINE

Jake nodded off on the drive back. The result, Simon assumed, of the home-made wine and all the food she had shoveled in. He'd never seen a woman, especially a woman who probably went all of a hundred and ten pounds, eat that much.

Simon welcomed the quiet. A chance to think. Assuming he and Pat were right, the lift charge had been replaced with silica sand, which according to Pat would have been similar enough in weight and texture that it couldn't have been detected without opening the wrap on the shell.

That meant not only wasn't the explosion an accident, but it was sabotage perpetrated by someone who had access to the shell.

Pasquale had built the shell.

Pasquale had finished the shell with the lift charge.

Pasquale, Pat, Ray, Angela, Tudy, Sadie, and presumably anyone who worked at Firenze, had access to keys to the north magazine, where the shell was stored.

Ray had driven the shells to the lakefront.

Pat had placed them on the barge.

Pasquale had fired them. And been killed by them.

Ray was missing. And did the Firenze's accounting.

If there was something hinky in the Firenze financial records, that would provide motive, meaning Ray might very well be gone, but not in the dearly departed sense. More in the skipped-with-company-funds sense. With the explosion that killed Pasquale little more than a diversion.

And if that was true, Simon would make Ray pay.

About halfway to Liberty, Jake woke up with a start. "Uh-oh."

Simon glanced over at her. "What?"

She made a face. "My car. It's not in Liberty--it's at home."

"Where's home?"

"Shorewood. One of the camera guys is a neighbor and we carpooled in. They'll all be gone now, though."

Shorewood was on the north shore--as far north of Milwaukee as Simon's house was south. He checked the clock on the dashboard. "It's after eleven. I'll take you home, but we'll have to stop on the way and let my dog out. By the time I take you up there and get back to my place, she'll have all four legs crossed."

"At least she has four legs to cross," Jake pointed out.

File that, Simon thought, under "Count Your Blessings."

Jake was impressed as they pulled up the long driveway. Simon's house was right on the lake. When he pulled up in front, she hesitated for just a second before hopping out of the car. She had to see the house.

"Why don't you wait here," Simon said, not budging from the driver's seat. "It's a real mess."

He'd have to get out of the car sometime if he was going to take the dog out. Jake started up the walk. "Whose isn't? Besides, I'm not interested in your dirty dishes, I want to see the house." She stopped and turned, realizing she was being wine-pushy. "Please?"

He shook his head, but got out of the truck. Jake waited as he retrieved his briefcase and the videotapes out of the back, and then remembered the leftovers. She took Simon's plate, leaving hers--and the éclair--for the second leg of the trip to her house.

Speaking of houses, Simon's was gorgeous, but of a style she couldn't quite place. Sort of Raul Julia's THE ADDAMS FAMILY meets Steve Martin's FATHER OF THE BRIDE. Victorian, Gothic, Traditional...who knew? Not her, but it was both beautiful and lovingly maintained, with pink roses blooming under every window. And it was as much an individual as its owner.

Simon unlocked the door, and they stepped in. "I'm still working on it, so 'a mess' is more understatement than euphemism in this case." He let the dog, an Irish Setter, out the side door as Jake tucked the leftovers into the refrigerator.

"Go on Irish, but make it quick."

Jake watched the dog bound out the door barking. "Irish, the setter? And you're making fun of Lily White?"

"Could have been worse. Could have been just 'Dog.'" He peered off into the darkness. "She's after something, so she'll be a couple minutes. I'll show you around."

He took her through the house, talking easily now and pointing out what he'd done in each room. Apparently he had started rehabbing it when he and his wife were still together. Only the room Simon called the study seemed incomplete. Just inside the door, the wall was striped with nine or ten different shades of yellow, cream, and white paint.

"Having trouble deciding?" Jake asked.

Simon shrugged. "I don't know. They look good in the paint store. Then I bring them back here, and they just don't work. It's the last room, though." He moved aside so she could see the rest of the room. "I'm finished after this."

Jake gasped when she stepped past him. The moonlight reflecting on the lake outside shone through the glass wall and filled the room. "It's absolutely gorgeous."

"It is, isn't it?" He'd brought the tapes in and set them on the entertainment center. Now he was standing just behind her, looking over her head at the lake.

"No wonder you can't decide what to do in here," she said softly. "The view is so magnificent, it will put everything else to shame."

"That's part of it." He laid his hand tentatively on her shoulder. She could feel his breath on the top of her head. It would be the nape of my neck, she thought, if I wasn't so short. Still, an involuntary tremor ran through her, and she backed right up into him. Betrayed by her own butt.

Evidently taking it as a good sign, Simon lifted her hair and kissed her neck. That's when her knees turned to Jell-O. It had been an awfully long time... She whimpered involuntarily and he turned her around to face him.

His eyes were half closed, but asking a question. *The* question. Oh, heck. Blame it on the moonlight. And the homemade wine. She snaked her arms up around his neck as he ran his hands down her sides to her waist. Another tremor.

"I want to make love to you." Then he kissed her. Not like in the editing suite, when they'd both been going at it tooth and nail. Gently. Exploratory kissing. First he kissed her top lip, then the bottom. Then both of them. Then he slipped his tongue into her mouth. Meanwhile, his hands were on her butt, holding her up against him.

She kissed him back, sucking on his tongue, then on his bottom lip. His hands moved up under her T-shirt, and she abruptly let go of his neck and staggered back. He reached out for her.

"Wait," Jake croaked. "Wait."

He reeled her back in. "Not again. I've waited long enough. So have you, from the way you're reacting."

She put her hands flat on his chest and held him off. "There's something I have to tell you."

His eyes looked wary now. He was probably thinking she was married, or gay. Or maybe both.

She led him to the couch. "What?" he asked again. More than a trifle impatient now.

She'd never had to explain before, having avoided it by avoiding any complications like this. Any relationships, any love affairs. She took a deep breath. "Two and a half years ago, I was diagnosed with breast cancer."

He started to say something.

"No, wait," she said. "Let me finish. Then you get your turn. I'm okay now. So far, at least. I mean, I'm not dying or anything--at least no more than most people. I had treatment and a double mastectomy."

There. That was all she had to say. Jake took a deep breath and waited.

Simon's eyes looked almost entirely gold now, and she couldn't quite read the expression in them. He sat for a moment, then said softly, "Show me."

"What?"

"Show me." He took her hands and put them on the bottom of her T-shirt. His eyes didn't leave hers. "Take off your shirt. Please."

"Wait," Jake said. "There's something else."

He waited.

"I didn't have reconstructive surgery. I'm just...flat. No nipples, no nothing."

"Show me," he said again.

So she did. She did it because he asked her with those eyes, and he asked her nicely. Then again, maybe six months of treatment had just conditioned her to expose her chest upon request.

Jake slipped off the shirt, and Simon took it away from her. Then he got onto his knees in front of her on the couch and ran his fingers lightly over the horizontal scars that marked where each breast had been. "They've healed well."

"I...," she started to say, but as she said it, he leaned in and ran his tongue lightly over the left scar.

Geez. She normally didn't have any sensation around the scars, but... Her back arched as he did the same with the right.

"Equal enjoyment opportunity," he murmured against her.

"Funny." She pulled his head up to eye level. "But you don't mind? You don't think it's--"

"What? Disgusting?" His eyes were soft, the pupils dilated.

"I'll tell you a secret," he said, touching her lower lip. "sometimes breasts just get in the way. Distract you..." He let his fingers lightly trail down her throat, past her chest, along her stomach... "from the important things." He pulled her close.

"One thing," Jake murmured.

"What?"

"Is that a pistol in your pocket," she asked, "or are you just happy to see me?"

"Both, in fact."

Now that they were both disarmed, they made love--first on the study rug and then again in the shower. No small accomplishment, Simon thought, given their difference in height. Good thing she was light--not to mention, athletic.

Afterwards, they slipped into Simon's bed and he pulled the blanket up over both of them, before tucking himself around Jake, spoon-style.

"Are you warm enough?" He ran his hand over her shoulder, feeling the muscle definition, presumably from swimming.

"I'm fine, thanks. Perfect, in fact." She wriggled her butt and he had an urge to go for the hat trick. Before he could pursue it, though, she continued. "I should probably go home soon. It's almost two, and I have to work tomorrow and so do you, I suppose." She twisted around so he could see her face. "I'm just sorry you have to drive so far to take me home."

Was that a "talk me out of going home" statement, Simon wondered, or an expression of genuine regret for putting him to any trouble? It was always so hard to tell with women.

Opting for a regretful-yet-chivalrous reply, he kissed her and followed it with, "I'm sorry you have to go, but I certainly don't mind taking you. After all, I practically kidnapped you to take you to the Firenzes' in the first place."

She pulled back, studied his face for a second, and then laughed. "You did, didn't you? And for the record, I wasn't fishing for an invitation to stay." The woman didn't miss a thing. "Let me get dressed and we'll leave."

But all of a sudden, Simon wasn't quite ready to let go of her.

He'd fallen asleep after the third time they made love that night.

Jake knew she should either wake him up, so he could take her home, or go to sleep herself, so she wouldn't be completely exhausted the next day. She didn't want to do either.

What she wanted to do was to enjoy the moment. The feeling of exhilaration...contentment...relief, even. She'd survived something she'd imagined and dreaded a thousand times. The boob confrontation.

Disengaging Simon's right arm, which was draped over her, she slid sideways and away from him and then flipped over on her back to study the ceiling.

There was a time when she had believed she would never be with a man again and hadn't cared a whit. Times when she would lie awake all night, staring at the ceiling like this, and bargaining with God:

"Please God, let the biopsy comes back "benign," and I'll never skip another mammogram.

"Please God, let me keep my breasts, and I'll never complain about their size again.

"Please God, let me stop throwing up, and I'll eat right and exercise every day.

"Please God, let me live, and I'll never use your name in vain again. I swear.

And, some nights, just, "Please God, let me die."

No, sex hadn't even entered into it.

But, boy-oh-boy, had she missed it.

And with Simon it had been magical, she had to admit. He was a sensitive, considerate lover who said the breasts--or lack thereof--didn't matter.

And she believed him, that was the miracle of it.

The other miracle was that Simon didn't appear to be looking for anything serious in a relationship. Look at the way he'd promptly fallen asleep after sex. And that was just fine with Jake.

Rent over buy, individual-serving over economy-size, short-term floating over long-term fixed, six-pack over keg, goldfish over dog. No commitments. No one depending on her.

No one to get hurt.

Just in case.

Simon felt sick.

In his dream, the smoke was thick and the stench overwhelming. Though Simon would never admit it to anyone, the smell of smoke literally turned his stomach. Some fire investigator. The first thing he always did when he returned from a fire scene was to shower and change.

But now in his dream, he was wading through smoke as he imagined Jake would wade through water.

He was thinking of Jake because she was in his dream, too, her hand feeling cold in his hand, despite the flames. He was trying to lead her out of the fire, but she didn't seem to care that she might die--that *they* might die, and his house...his house was...

Simon awoke with a start, but the smoke didn't evaporate along with the dream. Neither did Jake. She was on her back next to him, breathing shallowly.

He reached over and shook her shoulder and she sat bolt upright, like she wasn't used to being touched. "What?!" The blanket fell to her waist as she looked around, probably trying to figure out where she was.

"Fire!" Simon said urgently, sliding off the bed and pulling her down onto the floor with him. "Stay low and follow me."

Now completely awake, Jake nodded. Simon noticed she didn't bother with questions, other than the important one: "Which way?" she asked.

"The window." He crawled toward it and she followed.

"I'll open it," he said when they reached the window. The smoke was hanging about a foot above the floor, filling up the room now. "You stay low."

It was only when Simon turned back after unlocking and raising the sash, that he noticed Jake had dragged the blanket from his bed along with her. Good thinking, since they were both butt naked.

"Throw it out ahead of us," she hissed, as she passed it up to him. "There are rose bushes under your windows."

Okay, so it was *doubly* good thinking.

Simon folded the blanket double and tossed it over the sill and onto the prickly shrub roses. Jake followed, with a tiny "ouch," as she crossed over. Simon was next, and he tugged the quilt off the bushes and threw it over his shoulder, before taking her hand.

Jake's hand was cold, like in the dream, but she seemed as intent as he to get away. Together they ran from the heat and smoke of the house until finally, a football field away, they turned and looked back, coughing.

The window they'd just escaped through was on the north side of the house, and smoke was billowing out that window, along with the one next to it, though there were no visible flames. Simon angled around to the lake side.

It was quite a sight. The lake was still bright with reflected light like it had been earlier, but now that light wasn't from the moon, but from the flames dancing behind the glass study wall.

Simon stood there staring until Jake finally tugged at him. He looked down at her, standing naked next to him, and thought to tuck the quilt around her. "Are you warm enough?"

In the glow of the fire, he could see a scratch on her cheek where the rose bush must have nicked her as she climbed out the window. "I'm fine," she said, like she had to the same question after they'd made love, but sadly this time. In the distance, a siren screamed. "I'm sorry, Simon--your house..."

There was a long, low *craaack* then, and Simon turned away from Jake, and back toward what had been the love of his life.

He was just in time to see the window wall of the house shatter and fall, releasing the flames into the night.

TEN

By the time the firefighters arrived, the back of the house was gone. If Jake was the fanciful type, she would have said she heard Simon's heart break at the exact moment the windows of his house had.

Now he would never find just the right color for that room. Never feel the satisfaction--or the emptiness--that comes from finally being done with something that has consumed you.

Simon had scared her a little, standing there staring endlessly, and Jake had pulled him away from the house and eventually back to his Explorer. Simon's brain seemed to switch into gear then, and he'd used a key he'd hidden somewhere under the truck to move it out of the way of both the fire and the trucks converging on them to fight it.

In the back of the SUV, under the binders Simon had brought from the Firenzes, he'd dug up sweatpants and a T-shirt. His running clothes, he said, and she realized how little she knew about the man she had just had sex with and nearly died alongside.

At her insistence, Simon pulled on the pants and, at <u>his</u> insistence, she had taken the shirt. He kept asking her if she was cold, seeming to forget that it was early July, and the temperature, a balmy seventy-five degrees.

Hoses were laid out. Firefighters were everywhere.

Simon was enough of a professional, even at his own personal fire, to stay out of the way. He identified himself to the Fire Captain, confirmed that there was no one else inside, and then he and Jake settled on the hood of the Explorer to watch.

Simon was worried about Jake. He thought maybe he should take her home or someplace warm, but she kept saying she was okay, and not to worry.

87

He was also worried about Irish. He had let her out when he and Jake had arrived at the house and had forgotten to let her back in. A good thing in this case. The Irish Setter finally bounded up at about 3 a.m., apparently having had a fine time prowling the neighborhood.

Paramedics checked them out. Firefighters passed by. Someone asked what was in the basement. Paint, Simon said, lots of paint. And thinner. The guy gave him a "You stupid fuck" look and moved on. Simon just shrugged.

At about 4 a.m., Irish got hungry. Simon found the pasta and chicken in the back of the Explorer and, after offering it first to Jake, took the chicken off the bones and fed it to Irish. Jake volunteered to eat the chocolate off the éclair when Simon explained that chocolate could kill a dog and Irish already had gotten into the Oreos that week. Then Jake tossed the remainder of that to Irish, too.

By 5 a.m., the fire was controlled, though controlled was probably the wrong word. All that paint, all that thinner. The firefighter was right: he *was* a stupid fuck. He'd burned down his own house. Must be against the law. Housal abuse. Simon almost laughed at the thought, but figured Jake would think he was nuts. And she'd probably be right.

The sun was up when the firefighters picked up their hoses and went home. The game, for now, was over.

Jake's neighborhood was quiet as they pulled up behind her car in the narrow driveway. Simon was so out of it that he didn't even comment on her Jaguar. The classy black convertible with its tan roof never failed to elicit male comment; but, for now, Simon seemed oblivious.

And Jake was exhausted. After she let the three of them--Simon, Irish, and herself--into the house, she turned and wrapped her arms around Simon. He held her, resting his head heavily on the top of hers.

Jake was glad Simon was alive. And Irish, too, even if the dog had gotten most of the éclair. But beyond that, Jake didn't know quite what to say. Platitudes--like the only thing that mattered was that everyone was okay, and that houses could be replaced--seemed lame, even if they might be true.

So they hung there like that, not talking, until Jake thought Simon's weight was going to compress her spine. Finally, as she rubbed his back and started to wish someone was rubbing hers, he straightened up.

"You're okay?" he asked, for what had to be the tenth time that night. He tipped her chin up to trace the scratch on her cheek. "You're not hurt except for this?"

"I'm fine, thanks to you. And you? Are you okay?"

She meant beyond just the physical, and he seemed to know it. He rubbed at the stubble on his face and closed his eyes. When he opened them a fraction of a second later, there was more "Simon" there, and he smiled. "We're both alive, and houses can be replaced."

Jake smiled back. "I was going to say that, but I thought you'd smack me one."

"You're the one who should smack me for treating you to dinner, sex and a smoke."

That made her laugh. "I'm just thankful it was 'le petit mort,' and not just 'mort.'"

Simon's mouth dropped open, and then he laughed, too. "That is very, very clever. I just wish I was a little less tired, so I could show you how much I like it."

"I'm tired, too, or I'd take you up on that." She stood on tiptoe and kissed him. "What do you say we go to bed? To sleep this time."

"To sleep, perchance to--"

Jake covered his mouth. "Ay, but there's no rub tonight, Hamlet." Simon put up a token objection, and Jake led him to her bedroom, which was the only one of the three in the house that actually contained furniture.

"Maybe we should shower before we smoke up your sheets-- literally, if not, sadly, figuratively," he said, surveying her neatly made-up bed and sparse furniture.

"I truly don't care about the bedclothes, but if it will make you feel better..."

"Sounds good." Simon sat down on the edge of the bed, the weariness seeming to overtake him after his show of Shakespearean bravado in the face of modern disaster. "Why don't you go first?"

Jake went into the bathroom and stripped off the stinky T-shirt, then showered and washed her hair as quickly as she could, before sticking her head out the door. "Your turn."

No answer. Coming out of the bathroom, she saw Simon fast asleep on her bed. Still smudged with ash from the fire, he looked like an extremely grubby eight-year-old, albeit a very tall one.

Jake pulled a spare blanket out of the closet, thinking that maybe Simon's concern over Jake being cold was because he, himself, was chilled. She covered him with the blanket and then slipped into bed, spooning around him like he'd spooned around her earlier. Simon roused momentarily and took her hand, pulling her in even closer. Within seconds, though, he was asleep again.

Irish, having taking stock of her new surroundings, padded in and dropped to the floor next to the bed with a thud. Soon her breathing slowed and became regular, too.

Jake lay awake. Worrying.

About Simon, certainly, but also about herself.

Angela was staring at the young JFK.

Though her own bedroom had been turned into an office when she'd left her parent's house to marry Ray, Pat's room had been kept virtually intact after he moved out.

Mamma pretended it was "the guest room," but the only concessions to guests were the white chenille bedspread and frilly pink throw pillow that covered the DUKES OF HAZZARD sheets Angela slept on tonight. The crucifix still hung at the head of the bed, facing President Kennedy on the opposite wall.

Funny, how some things had changed not at all. And others, they had changed completely in the blink of an eye.

Her father was dead, and the company he had built was in terrible trouble. Customers that Angela thought would forever be loyal to her father and to her family were running like frightened rabbits. She was glad her father wasn't here to see it. That he, at least, was beyond the heartache and confusion. She worried, though, for Pat. And for herself.

Angela studied the portrait of JFK. It was actually an election poster her mother had glued to a piece of corrugated cardboard salvaged from an old appliance box. Long ago, the glossy paper of the poster had buckled and pulled away from the backing to reveal the word "Kenmore" above JFK's right ear.

Angela had begged her mother repeatedly to let her replace it. "Mamma," Angela would ask, "why do you keep that old thing?"

"Oh, Angela," her mother would say. "he was *so* good-looking. So much better than that Tricky Dick. What a man, my Johnny was." Then she'd blow a kiss to the late president.

Angela's father sometimes would pull out the yellow thumbtacks that held the poster and hide it, just to tease his wife.

"Pasquale," Mamma would scold as she scurried around in her housecoat and slippers looking for the poster, "did you steal 'My Love' again?"

And Angela's father would say, every time, "No, Sadie. Don't you remember? You gave me your love of your own free will." And then he would give her the ratty old picture, and they would kiss.

Angela smiled at the memory. Pat would snort and say it was corny and walk away, but Angela thought it was romantic. Her father and mother had been a true love match, and she had imagined they would be together forever.

Because that was the way it was in the Firenze family. Marriage and love were forever. Angela had expected that for herself, too, had even planned for it.

But sometimes, she told herself, sometimes we don't get what we expect. Through the open kitchen window tonight, she had overheard Pat telling Simon that Ray put sand in the lift charge of the shell that killed her father. That her husband might have stolen money, too.

Angela shivered and made the sign of the cross. God help them all, she wouldn't be surprised if Simon found evidence that Ray had done just that. And now Pat would take over Firenze Fireworks, but Angela didn't think that would be what he expected, either.

Angela turned over, pulled up the chenille bedspread and buried her face in her brother's pillow.

The sound of punk rock propelled Jake out from under Simon's right arm and halfway across the room before her eyes were fully open. That posed a problem, since she'd forgotten Irish was sleeping on the floor.

Nearly tripping over the dog, she managed to catch herself on the edge of the dresser and turn off the radio alarm in one fell swoop.

Jake kept the alarm clock on the dresser instead of the bedside nightstand, so she wouldn't be tempted to lean over and hit "Snooze." She also kept it tuned to a punk-rock station, so she wouldn't be tempted to lie there and listen. Odd thing was, she was starting to like the stuff.

She looked at the time: 9:30. She'd slept for maybe two hours. She and Simon simply did not fit on her queen-size bed. Actually, that wasn't quite true. Simon fit just fine, he just didn't leave any room for her.

Jake yawned and wandered into the bathroom. It had been quite a night, but she needed to be in early this morning for an eleven a.m. planning meeting. That meant getting to the Y by nine-thirty in order to swim, something she wanted desperately to do in order to clear her head.

She quickly and quietly washed her face, brushed her teeth and pulled on some sweats. Then she grabbed her gym bag and work clothes from the chair next to the door, and started out of the bedroom. She was in the hallway before she realized she should leave a note for Simon.

She looked back at him. If he'd awakened at all when she'd launched herself out of bed, he'd recovered. He was fast asleep and snoring--the blanket scrunched up under his head on one end of the bed, his bare feet hanging off the other, and Irish snuggled up next to him in the spot Jake had just vacated.

When Simon woke, Jake had already gone, leaving a scribbled note saying she had an early meeting, and he could reach her on her cell phone. She'd signed it simply, "Jake." No "Love." No "Cordially." Not even a "Sincerely."

To be honest, Simon was relieved he hadn't needed to face her this morning. The morning after was always awkward, but especially when you've moved in--lock, stock and Setter--a mere four-and-a-half hours after making love for the very first time. Oh, and your house had burned down with the two of you nearly in it.

What did one say under the circumstances? Thanks for letting me stay? Sorry you were almost incinerated? And by the way, you are one *hell* of a lover?

Simon rolled over on his back, dislodging Irish who grunted sleepily at him, then settled her head on his stomach. He scratched her behind one ear and stared at the ceiling.

Funny, if someone had asked him, he would have said he didn't give a shit about physical possessions. Easy to say when you have them.

Now Simon didn't have so much as a toothbrush, much less all those "sentimental" things one thinks about losing in a fire: Photos. His favorite T-shirt. His old chair. His '70s soft porn literature. They didn't write classics like *Hot Pants Karen* and *Tongues of Lust* anymore. Those things were damn near irreplaceable.

Simon had an uncontrollable desire to get to work all of a sudden. At least he had "stuff" there--things that were familiar, untouched by what had happened.

He sat up, and Irish hopped off the bed and turned to look at him, tail thumping. "Gotta go out?" Simon asked. The setter turned around gleefully and headed for the door. The closet door, from what Simon could tell. "Wrong door, genius," he told her, and then realized he wasn't sure himself where the outside door was either. Luckily, Jake had a small house and they managed to find their way out in time.

He left Irish happily investigating the fenced-in backyard and went back in the house to shower. The bathroom was original to the house, spare and functional like the rest of the house, with those funky pinky-beige fixtures from a few light-years back. He ran the water hot into the tub, then hit the trigger to divert the water to the shower head. Also original, thank God, not of those wussy water-saver things.

As he ducked his head under the torrent, Simon sucked in the stench of ash and fire that the shower raised from his hair and almost gagged. He put his hand on the wall and waited for the feeling to pass. Then he lathered up over and over again until all he could smell was the scent of Jake. Or Jake's shampoo to be exact. He stood a while longer and let it wash over him until the water grew cold.

Out of the shower and feeling substantially better, he rummaged around the medicine cabinet until he came up with a new blue Bic razor, plastic cover still intact. At least it looked new, though he couldn't be absolutely certain it hadn't been used on female legs. He'd be able to judge by how many pints of blood he lost when he shaved.

He rinsed around the grit in his mouth and spat into the sink. God, do people who smoke and purposely inhale this stuff have *any* idea what they were putting in their lungs? He considered using his finger with toothpaste on it, but found a toothbrush--the cheapo kind you get from the dentist--in a drawer filled with miniature bottles of hotel-labeled shampoo, mouthwash, lotion and shower caps. Jake apparently cleaned out the bathroom freebies in every hotel she visited. Bless her.

Too bad she didn't collect men's clothing. He pulled on the smoky sweatpants he'd slept in, and borrowed back the T-shirt he'd given Jake. They would have do until he got to the office, where he kept a change of clothes.

Let's see, what was on the schedule today? Luckily his personal vehicle was safely parked in the structure at the office, or it would be under the pile of rubble formerly known as his garage.

So he just had to buy clothes and call his house insurance agent. Oh, and find a place to live. He wished that in the hurried note Jake had left, she'd said something akin to, "Hey, stay as long as you want."

Simon let the dog in and watched her nose around the kitchen floor. He couldn't just leave her roaming Jake's house, but he couldn't very well take her into the office with him either.

He sighed and picked up the phone to call Jake. He wanted to make sure she was okay, then he'd apologize, thank her, and ask yet another favor--or two. This didn't seem to be the best way to start out a relationship: Temporary cohabitation and joint custody of a seventy-pound dog who shed.

ELEVEN

By the time Jake hit the parking lot of the Y it was nine-forty-five. She'd only have time for a half-mile swim today--not even that, if she didn't get moving.

She ran for the door, gym bag thunkking her in the side, and then stepped back to let a woman with a pink baby in a carrier and a blue toddler on foot, enter ahead of her.

"C'mon, Billy," Mom said to the toddler. "Push the big silver button, and the door will open for Sarah and me!"

The big silver button was the automatic door opener, intended for people with disabilities. Kids love them. Parents love that their kids love them. For her part, Jack wondered whether tickets should be issued to people who pushed them and weren't disabled. Like when you park in a "Handicapped" space, and aren't.

Still, she waited patiently for the door to slowly open and then helped the mother wedge the baby carrier, diaper bag and toddler through. As Jake started in after them, she almost collided with a man who was playing the same waiting game on the other side of the door. He stepped back to let her through.

Jake smiled a thank you and barreled around the corner, nearly mowing down her fireman friend, Doug.

"Hey, Doug," she said, pulling out her membership card for the man at the front desk. "Don't tell me you're done already?"

"I only did three miles today," he said, "I have a doctor's appointment."

"Your ears?" Jake asked, worried.

He banged his right ear with the heel of his hand. "Yeah, we're trying a hearing aid for this one. See if that helps."

"It's not getting worse, is it?"

"Nah, it's okay."

Not that he would tell her if it wasn't, she thought as she changed into her suit in the locker room. Doug's off-hand way of dealing with his own physical problems was one of the reasons Jake felt so comfortable around him.

Jake had started swimming soon after her mastectomy, both because it was the perfect exercise for her chest and back muscles, and great therapy for her head. It had taken every ounce of courage for her to put on a suit--no fake foam boobs, they create drag when you swim--and walk into the pool area that first time, but it was one of the best decisions she'd ever made.

Doug had been there then, and a lot of the other people she still swam with. Even though they'd likely followed her treatment on TV along with the rest of the viewing area, no one at the pool had ever made her feel the least bit uncomfortable.

Until now.

Jake had finished her eighteenth lap and was walking to the showers when she heard it behind her.

Stroke/kersplat...stroke/kersplat...stroke/kersplat...

The Croc. Then it stopped.

She didn't have to turn to know he was watching her.

Simon had reached Jake by cell phone, and she agreed both to Simon staying another night and to his leaving Irish in her fenced-in back yard, since he wasn't sure how civilized the dog would be in a strange house. Jake even told him where to find old margarine containers as makeshift water and food dishes and a box of Cheerios that would substitute for kibbles until Simon was able to go shopping.

An unusual woman, Simon thought. Even more so, because she hadn't even mentioned nearly being burned to death, until he'd asked her how she was. Like the whole thing had slipped her mind somehow.

Not a bad model to follow, Simon thought. After getting the dog fed and watered, he walked down the driveway to his truck on the street. He'd left it in the driveway, but Jake apparently had moved it to get her Jag out.

The XK8 was quite a car: seventy-five grand, new. And this one was new. He had clearly smelled "showroom" when he walked by it last night in his post-disaster haze, though it had seemed inappropriate to comment on it at the time.

Simon wondered how well television stations paid. Maybe Jake had inherited money. It occurred to him that despite what had happened to them, and despite the fact he had slept in her bed and showered in her bathroom, he knew very little about Jake.

Simon had barely settled in the driver's seat of the Explorer when his cell phone rang. He had left it in the cup holder overnight and when he picked it up to answer, he saw he had missed six calls.

"Aamot."

"Where the hell have you been?" The question was probably Collins', but the voice was Kathy's.

"My house burned down last night."

"No shit, Sherlock, the fire department has been calling all morning, looking for you. Something about accelerants in the basement. Are you okay?" The last was Kathy's own question and sounded a little frantic.

Simon felt ashamed he hadn't called her immediately to reassure her. He also felt more than a little stupid. Accelerants. Like paint, paint thinner, rags. "Fine, Kath, and it was my own damn fault. You know I've been working on the house. I had all sorts of shit down there." Simon started the engine, shifted into gear and pulled away from the curb.

"Piled next to the water heater, no doubt?" Kathy asked. "Simon, you know better."

"I know, Mom. And now I'm suffering the 'consequences of my actions,' as my parents used say. Is Collins looking for me?"

"Of course. Where are you? Are you coming in?"

"Twenty minutes away. Be right there."

Jake was already in her second planning meeting of the day--this one about the Fourth of July broadcast. Today was Monday, July 2, and on Wednesday she would be back at Shore Park, back in the production van, back producing a fireworks show.

Jake hoped the Fourth of July broadcast would prove to be one big snooze in comparison with Lake Days, but she felt alone in that hope. Everyone else at the station seemed to be banking on the fact that viewers would tune in *because* something could happen. That maybe lightning would strike twice in the same place and they would be watching to catch it.

"'...safe from the comfort of your own homes?'" she read from the promo script. "Why don't we just bill it as 'Fireworks Island: Let's See Who Survives!'"

Bryan Williams, sitting across the table from her, laughed. "Actually, the shells are going to be fired from land this time, so the island theme won't work." He leaned across the table and put his hand on hers. "Not that I didn't think of it."

Jake pulled her hand back and Neal, sitting next to her, gave her a friendly nudge. "C'mon, lighten up, Jake."

Weren't we all feeling good about ourselves this morning, Jake thought.

Gwen, a tiny brunette who nevertheless knew how to throw her weight around when she needed to, cleared her throat to get their attention. Neal, Jake, and Martha sat on one side of the table; George, Bryan and Luis across from them. The news director's gaze landed on Bill Laverenz, the station manager, seated on the end opposite Gwen.

Laverenz stood up. "I need to get to another meeting, but I wanted to announce our team for this broadcast. We're going to mix things up a bit."

"We've arranged to have a camera on the "Lake Mist," an excursion boat on Lake Michigan." He nodded toward Martha, but managed not to look at her. "Since Martha showed us how well she thinks on her feet after Friday's explosion, she'll handle the coverage from there. In another change, Luis Burns will be in front of the camera for the first time, at least officially."

Laverenz smiled over at Luis, but Jake was busy watching Martha who sat next to her. The anchorwoman's face was a calm, cool mask. Oooh, she's ticked, Jake thought. She leaned ever so slightly away from Martha and waited.

Laverenz turned and nodded toward Neal. "Neal is going to be anchoring this time around, with George." He held up his hands. "I know, I know. It's unusual for us to pair two men, but I think this puts the strength where we need it. Neal, I understand that Angela Guida has agreed to be a guest, so I'm counting on you to get her to open up about her husband's disappearance. As for the rest, I'll leave the details to all of you. Have a good show!"

With that, the station manager picked up his yellow pad and left the room, not once having looked at Martha.

There was an apprehensive silence, the calm before the storm. In fact, Jake could have sworn the room took on that same eerie green cast that signals the approach of a Midwest thunderstorm.

Martha stood up. "What the hell is going on here, Gwen? I'm an anchor for God's sake, not someone you stick on a boat in the middle of the lake, while you let a scrub reporter take over. Laverenz, the spineless fucker, didn't have the courtesy to look me in the face when he stabbed me in the back."

Sitting across from Martha, Luis was torn between wondering how you could stab someone in the back while looking them in the face, and if he was the "scrub reporter" Martha was talking about.

"You're calling me a 'scrub reporter?'" Neal Cravens yelled, answering one question. "I have as much as experience as you do, just not the legs. Maybe it will do you some good to put them to the use God intended, and do some actual reporting for once. You call *George* a talking head? You're nothing but a talking ass with tits."

Whoa. Low blow.

Jake started coughing, and Luis slid his bottle of water across to her, a cartoon of a "talking head, ass and tits" playing in his mind. Might make a great animated short or maybe even a series. You know, sort of a SOUTH PARK meets SPORTS NIGHT thing.

"Experience?" Martha screamed at Cravens, interrupting Luis's creative flow. "At those podunk stations you worked at?"

Gwen jumped up. "We're all professionals here..."

97

The guy across from Jake laughed for some reason, and Martha gave him a dirty look. Then she turned back to Gwen. "Yeah? Well, you can take your 'professionals' and stick them up your ass."

Then she walked out.

Now Martha always wore these really high heels, so it was worth taking the time to watch her leave. By the time Luis swiveled back to the table, Gwen was already sitting down and waving Cravens and Eagleton to do likewise.

"Should we get down to work?"

God, Luis loved this business.

"I think I've had enough asses, talking or otherwise, for a while," Jake muttered to Bryan as they left the room an hour later.

"Francis," he said.

She hesitated, then got it. "The talking mule?"

He just grinned, but Jake shook her head. "Sometimes, Bryan, you surprise me. You seem almost human."

"Almost," said Williams, as he opened the door into the production office for her, "is the operative word."

Amen to that, Jake thought, though the exchange did serve to remind her of what she had seen in him so many years back. She nodded toward Neal's back disappearing down the hall. "Neal really went off back there. I was prepared for Martha to throw a fit, since she was demoted, but Neal..."

"Neal is like a snake that's been caught under Martha's stiletto heel--or hoof, if you want to extend the ass metaphor--for years. He's figured out, at long last, how to turn and strike back."

Jake stopped at her doorway and raised one eyebrow. "So Neal's a snake and Martha's an ass?"

Bryan shrugged. "Strange bedfellows, no?"

He winked at her and hurried after Neal. Jake continued into her office. There was something lizard-like about Bryan winking. Like the eyelid stretched, but couldn't quite close. Yuck.

Jake sat down at her desk and stared at her still-blank computer screen, ignoring the question of whether lizards actually *had* eyelids for the far larger one: was Bryan insinuating that Neal and Martha were lovers? Neal, the family man? Martha the...well, never mind. But then, Jake reminded herself, Bryan thought everyone was "doing" everyone, because *he* always was. In fact, the one he'd been doing fairly recently, according to station gossip, was Martha.

The snake, the ass and the lizard. They made quite the interesting menagerie *a trois*.

TWELVE

Kathy looked up and sniffed when Simon came in. "Lordy, you smell like a smoked salmon." She got up and hugged him.

"Thanks," Simon said, flopping down in the chair next to her desk. "And is that 'Eau d' Pediatrician' I smell emanating from you?"

"I think you had best mind your own business, Tex," she said, eyebrows raised. "Which reminds me, where did *you* spend last night?"

Simon turned red. "A friend's house."

Simon? Blushing? "Must be a good friend," she said, but didn't inquire further for now. She'd nail him on it later, when he was feeling better. It would be more sporting and just as much fun.

"Do you need somewhere to stay tonight?" she asked. "I'm sure Ned wouldn't mind." She knew Ned *would* mind, but that was just too bad.

"No, I'm fine," Simon said, not sounding fine at all. And why should he? He'd just lost the only thing he loved. Well, almost the only thing.

"Is Irish okay?"

Kathy had helped Simon pick out the setter puppy as a gift for What's-her-name, as she liked to call his ex. Simon had kept Irish after the divorce, since the woman couldn't be bothered with a dog anymore than she could with a husband.

"Everybody's fine," Simon said. "The dog was outside when the fire started, fortunately for her."

"The luck of the Irish," Kathy offered automatically, but she was wondering who "everybody" was.

But Simon didn't explain, or even smile. He stood up. "You said the fire department called?"

She handed him the message. "Call this guy back, and Collins wants to see you."

"I figured." He tapped the binders he had carried in. "Can you get the auditors to go over these?"

Kathy nodded. "Looking for something in particular?"

"Anything irregular, funds diverted--you know the drill. And tell Collins I'll be right in after I get out of these clothes."

Simon went into his office and closed the door behind him.

Kathy turned to her computer, typed in "depression +male" and clicked "Search."

Simon took another shower and changed into his spare jeans and shirt. Stuffing his smoky sweats into a plastic grocery bag, he tied it shut and stashed it deep in the corner of the closet in his office. Even in the plastic bag, even with the door shut, he still could smell it. The smoke from the fire had seeped into his pores and permeated his nostrils, like a nauseating cologne you accidentally got on the tip of your nose. Simon knew from experience it would take hours, maybe days, for him to shake it, no matter how many showers he took.

Clean, if not exactly feeling fresh, Simon sat down to gather his thoughts before he went in to see Collins. As always, his desk was neat, probably because he spent very little time there. He was on the road nearly half the year. He kept a pad of yellow paper in the center of the desk and his in-and-out box in the upper right-hand corner. That was it.

He pulled the pad toward him. Then he sat and stared. Whether his mind was over-cluttered or absolutely empty, Simon couldn't seem to snag a coherent thought and put it down on paper.

A knock at the door interrupted his reverie, or lack thereof, and Collins stuck his head in. "Glad you're okay. Got a minute?"

"Sure." Simon stood up and followed his boss back to his office. Ed Collins was tall, broad-shouldered and good-looking, with dark hair and blue eyes. The day he had been introduced as the new RAC, Kathy had practically swooned. Since then Collins had grown progressively more rumpled. Simon suspected he regretted taking the promotion from field work to paperwork.

Unlike Simon's desk, Collins' desk was covered with stacks of files. He settled into his chair. "I was sorry to hear about your house. How much did you lose?"

Simon shrugged. "Pretty much everything."

"Have they come up with a cause yet?"

"I have to call the department this morning. I've been doing a lot of remodeling, so there are all sorts of possibilities." Simon left it at that.

Collins pushed back in his chair and put his feet up on the desk. "Speaking of possibilities, any chance someone with a grudge might have seen you on TV yesterday?"

So Collins had seen Malone's report, too. "I suppose it's possible, but why now? I haven't been undercover for years."

Collins shrugged. "Maybe it's been long enough that someone you took down is out on the streets again."

Could be, Simon thought, perking up. Having a murderous freak trying to exact revenge was so much more palatable than being a stupid fuck.

"Think about it," Collins said, "and if the locals turn up arson, we'll take over the investigation."

Simon nodded.

"In the meantime, let me know if there's anything I can do."

Collins pulled his feet off the desk and leaned forward to pick up the phone. "Anything on the Lake Days explosion?" he asked as Simon got up to leave.

Simon hesitated. The sand, the lift charge, Ray, the still-to-be analyzed financial records--all of it seemed too nebulous to explain right now. Besides, Simon had learned not to share theories with his RAC until all the facts were in. That way Collins couldn't latch onto a favorite. It was tough to run an investigation when your boss has already decided what the outcome should be.

"Nothing definitive," Simon hedged. "I'll keep you up to speed, though." The "up to speed" was Collin's favorite line, and Simon threw it in as a bone.

But Collins was already dialing. "Great. Keep me up to speed," he said absently as Simon left.

Simon shook his head and went back to his office. It would take a while for the auditors to analyze the Firenze's financial records. In the meantime, he might as well check out some other possibilities.

Pat had said that rival fireworks companies were cherry-picking their accounts. Simon wondered if the fireworks business was lucrative enough to make putting a competitor out of business worth the risk. He reached for the phone.

"Calling the fire department?" Kathy was at his office door.

Simon felt a twinge of irritation at her and set down the phone. "I will, but I have some other things to do first."

"Are you going out there? See what you can salvage?"

The thought of pawing through what was left of his life made him sick.

Kathy read his expression and gave him a sympathetic smile. "I understand, Tex, but plug your nose and do it. Let me know if I can help." She turned to leave.

Damn, the woman knew him better than he knew himself. "Kath?"

She turned back.

"I love you, you know."

She gave him a dirty grin and a Mae West voice. "Keep the pistol in your pocket, Tex. I'm spoken for."

The remark reminded him of Jake. He cracked a small smile and picked up the phone again.

"Jake!"

Only Luis's head was visible in the doorway of Jake's office, the rest of his body apparently idling like an Indy car on the other side of the wall. "You got the master of the tape I shot on the barge? We still can't find the close-up on the dupe."

"It's here somewhere," Jake said, playing for time or postponing the inevitable, depending on how you looked at it. "Congratulations on your reporting assignment. Was that a surprise?" She gestured for him to come in and sit down.

He came in, but didn't sit. He could barely stand still, in fact. "Not really. I had talked to Gwen and Bill about it. I mean with all the interest from the networks and stuff, I figured this was my chance to move up. You gotta strike while the fire's hot, you know?"

Yeah, and the early bird catches the germ. Jake hoped Luis would be scripted on the air, though she had always suspected the kid was shrewder than he let on. Witness the fact that he had been smart enough to run tape so he could keep shooting when the truck went down.

"The networks are interested in what? The footage or you?" As she spoke, she pulled the master tape from the hundreds on the metal shelves next to her desk.

"The tape first," he said, grabbing it out of her hand. "Then CNN wanted an interview and MSNBC and, well, I guess I came off pretty good. All of a sudden, I'm a reporter." He smiled delightedly, and Jake found herself smiling back. Sucker.

The cameraman-cum-reporter held up the tape. "Gwen's letting me put together a package about the explosion--what it was like to be out in the middle of it."

Jake knew about the two-minute package from the morning meeting. "Not quite in the middle of it, thankfully, or you could have ended up like Pasquale or Ray Guida."

Luis was already backing out of the room. "Yeah, but the camera really did put me right there with Firenze when he got it."

He stopped at the door and held up the tape. "You know, I was kind of pissed you didn't show that close-up footage more, but now I'm glad. I mean, I can do it as part of my package and it will have more..." He hesitated, searching for the word he wanted. "Dramatic impact. Yeah, that's it."

He grinned again and was gone.

Jake wondered what the "dramatic impact" would be of Luis's finding that the close-up of Pasquale had been replaced with ninety seconds of a two-year-old Tornado Safety Special. If he had been "pissed" when she hadn't run the footage, just wait until he found out it no longer existed.

Jake leaned back in her chair, imagining how Richard Nixon must have felt after he erased his tapes. And knew he was about to be found out.

When Simon pulled up to his house, there was a red Chevy with official plates in the drive. Evidently someone else already was pawing through the ashes of his life.

He walked down the driveway and around to the lake side, bypassing the door in the front facade of the house. And facade it was: why go through the front door when the entire back of the house was gone?

Stepping over the shattered glass of what had been the window wall into the den, he heard sounds from below. The floor boards of the study were burned right through in places, so all he had to do was look down to see the fire investigator picking through the rubble in the basement.

Not that there was much to investigate. The source of the fire was evident even from where Simon stood above. The burned and burst paint cans, the scorch marks, the glass of the basement window shattered next to the furnace, the--

Wait. Even in his current funk, Simon knew that was wrong. The glass should have exploded *out* from the heat like the glass wall had, not in toward the furnace. That meant... "Someone lobbed something through the window."

Simon said it out loud, and the man in the basement jumped at the sound of his voice. Simon recognized him from the local fire department--Jensen, Jansen, something like that.

"I'd say so." Jensen/Jansen stuck his hand up. "Don't know if you remember me. Walt Johannsen."

Yeah, that was it. Simon got down on what was left of the floor to reach through and shake Johannsen's hand. "Sure, thanks for coming out." He stuck his head down between the joists to get a better look.

Johannsen obliged by shining his light around. "Looks to me like someone broke the window from the outside, like you said, and tossed in an incendiary device."

"Can you tell what it was?"

Johannsen shrugged. "I found an old Zippo lighter outside and there's thick green bottle glass in here. I'm thinking somebody lobbed a Molotov cocktail in your window. Hard to tell about the accelerant, though, with everything else down here."

Simon sniffed. Was he getting a whiff of gasoline? Johannsen was right, it was hard to tell. The basement was filled with paint and thinner cans warped from the heat, soggy cardboard file boxes, scorched skeletons of overstuffed furniture, and sagging duct work. It reeked of all of those things, torched and then wet down and left to ferment.

"For what it's worth," Simon said, pulling back a little to get away from the stink, "there wasn't any gasoline stored down here. Just regular thinner and oil paint." Latex just never covered as well.

There was that "stupid fuck" look again, this time from Johannsen. Simon passed his card down. "My RAC is going to want to be kept informed, since this appears to be arson."

Johannsen was looking surly, all of a sudden. "ATF taking over?"

Simon shrugged. "Maybe. But I've found the best way to keep my RAC out of something is to keep him up to speed." Handy little phrase.

The fire investigator grunted and went back to sifting through garbage. You'd think he'd jump at the chance to dump this all on ATF, Simon thought, standing up.

He looked around the study and wanted to laugh. Jesus, what a mess. The only damn wall that had survived was the one next to the doorway. The one he'd covered with swath after swath of paint.

Blue. That was it. He should have picked blue.

Simon walked the perimeter of the room, looking for anything that could be recovered. The couch was reduced to metal springs and ashes, the rug that he and Jake had made love on, melted into the floor boards. His TV--his beautiful big-screen TV--was melted, too, into a big-screen hunk of tortured black plastic. Next to it was a metal shelving unit holding two rectangular hunks of melted plastic. The DVD player and the VCR--the DVD player topped with a small hill of melted clear plastic DVD jewel-cases, and the VCR, a dollop of destroyed videotapes.

The tapes Jake had given him. Damn it all to hell and back.

Jake tried to occupy herself with the rundown of the show, expecting Luis to reappear any minute. It took twenty-three minutes.

"Jake."

Jake jumped. See Jake jump, she thought. See Jake jump and run.

The fact that she was taking mental cues from her kindergarten reading primer probably wasn't a good sign. She was going to have to do better if she was going to brazen her way through this.

"Yes?" Jake raised her eyebrows at him.

Luis's eyebrows, in contrast, were hanging low and ominous. He held up the tape. "Where's my close-up footage?"

"Close-up footage?"

He came in and slapped the tape down on her desk. "You know damn well what I mean. Firenze going up to relight the fuse. There's a tornado on here."

"Tornado? Are you sure?"

"Am I sure? Hell yes, I'm sure. Now, you better have another copy." He was standing very close, and he was very angry.

Feeling threatened, Jake got angry, too. "Why? So you can get a raise? A better job?" Jake was on her feet now, toe-to-toe with Luis who only had about six inches on her.

She'd taken on bigger and better. She poked him in the chest with her finger. "Does it bother you at all that you're using a man's death to further your career?"

Luis backed up. "You really did it, didn't you? You ruined my tape."

"So what if I did?" Ahh, kindergarten rears its ugly head again.

"So, so..." He was red in the face. "So, I'm going to tell Gwen!"

Jake watched him race down the hall, intent on telling teacher. What a weenie.

It didn't take twenty-three minutes for the other shoe to drop, that shoe being Gwen, and Gwen's office being just a few doors down.

Since the tape was still sitting on Jake's desk, Gwen didn't come in and slam it down for effect. She did the power equivalent. She had her secretary call Jake to her office.

Jake answered the summons.

It took Simon less than an hour to walk through the rest of the house. He was having this weird push-pull, yin-yang reaction: the nearly uncontrollable need to get away, versus the admittedly macabre attraction of picking through the debris, looking for something familiar that remained. That tooth amongst the ashes in the cremation urn.

The house was a total loss, including the bedroom from which he and Jake had escaped. What wasn't burned by the fire or ruined by the water, was so smelly Simon couldn't have stood to have it in his truck, much less his home. If he had one.

His bed was a sodden shadow of its former self. The dresser, a pile of burnt plywood and genuine "solid oak" laminate, the contents charred beyond recognition, except for a bottle of Versace cologne he'd been given--ironically by a woman who suggested it would counteract the smell of smoke that seemed to follow him everywhere. It figured that the cologne would be the one thing that survived, when what he really needed was a clean pair of undershorts.

When Simon finally left the house, carrying only the VCR with the tapes welded to the top, he exited by the front door, shutting it carefully behind him. He had his keys in his hand and came *that* close to locking the door out of habit. Stuffing the keys back in his pocket and feeling stupid, he walked down the sidewalk and put the VCR in the Explorer before turning to look back.

Eerie. From this angle, assuming you ignored the black scorching under the windows, you could scarcely tell there had been a fire. Freshly painted door, gleaming brass house numbers, pink shrub roses still blooming hopefully out front.

Just a facade, thought Simon again. Normal on the surface, but empty, burned out, within.

Like him.

THIRTEEN

Jake was sitting in one of the two visitors chairs in front of Gwen's desk, and the news director had come around to sit in the other. Gwen believed that sitting behind her desk was too hierarchical, too chain of command. She thought this felt friendlier. Jake thought it felt condescending.

Gwen Sonntag had been around TV news for a lot of years, first as a reporter in Cincinnati, then as an anchor. She'd come to TV8 as news director about the same time Jake had started at the station.

Everyone, Gwen included, had assumed she would move into the station manager's job when it opened up last year. Instead, the owners had pulled Bill Laverenz in from a sister station. Gwen had been furious, though she covered it well.

Since then, though, Jake had noticed a subtle shift on Gwen's part toward the company line--which was, of course, the bottom line. Gwen wasn't going to be bypassed again.

And that didn't bode well for Jake's future, given her boss's current state of mind toward her.

Gwen was talking now, knee-to-knee with Jake and looking her directly in the eye. Firm, yet sympathetic.

"Jake, I'm not going to kid you. We've both been around long enough to know you can't pull this kind of thing. That tape was the station's property. You had no right to alter it."

Jake knew she should just take her whacks, apologize and move on. Or better yet, lie and say it was an accident. But noooo: "I'm a producer, an editor. That's what I do. Edit tapes. I made an editorial decision that the footage was too graphic."

"It wasn't your decision to make, Jake. It was mine."

Jake got up and crossed to the file cabinet by the door before turning back to the news director. "Fine, Gwen, I'll grant you that. So tell me what you would have done--and whether it's different from what you would have done five years ago."

Gwen sat back in her chair and sighed. "I know you think I've sold out, Jake, but local news is different today. The threshold for acceptable violence has gone way up, I don't have to tell you that. Viewers want to see things as they happen, not be told about them later. And whether we like it or not, if we don't attract and retain viewers, we won't be here tomorrow to tell any of our stories. As for the close-up footage of the blast, I don't know. Maybe I would have canned it, too. But I sure as hell wouldn't have destroyed it."

Jake thought about telling Gwen there still was one copy intact, the copy she had given Simon. Then again, Simon had taken the videotapes into the house last night, so maybe it wasn't so "intact."

But the news director was asking a question and it was a good one. "...you're the one who showed the tape the night of the explosion. Why?"

"Sometimes I..." Jake hesitated, searching for a way to explain the push-pull she felt. "...sometimes I revert to reporter-mode. I still want that rush you get when you're the first one to put something on the air."

Gwen was nodding and Jake realized all of a sudden what she doing. Dancing. Giving Gwen the answer the program director could understand, respect even. Thing was, it wasn't true. Not this time.

Jake took a deep breath. "But this wasn't one of those times, Gwen."

Gwen stopped nodding.

"Truth is, I screwed up. I didn't preview the entire segment, and I didn't realize it was as graphic as it turned out to be." Jake leaned forward, wanting to make the point. "But what is 'acceptable violence'? Is any amount of violence acceptable, if it involves your husband or your father or your child? I hate the way we're turning news into one big reality show. Live car chases and gun battles. What's next? Public executions? Feeding Christians to the lions?"

Gwen started to speak, but Jake held up her hand. To her dismay, it was shaking. "Wait. Let me say this, then if you want to fire me, do it.

"We crawl into people's lives, Gwen. We climb all over them, like so many bugs. The famous. The tragic. The tragically famous, it doesn't matter. We consume them, and then we're on to something else. More 'news.'"

Jake tried to laugh deridingly, but it came out just this side of maniacal to her ears. "We leave them with nothing. We've taken it all--their images, their words, their dignity--and used them as sound bites. We're modern versions of carny workers and they're our side-show." This last was barely audible.

"You're talking about yourself, Jake. Nobody else." Gwen got up and came over to her at the file cabinet. "*You* felt on display, *you* felt like we had taken something from you."

Jake met the news director's eyes and saw pity. She hated pity.

"You didn't take it from me, I volunteered it. And *that*, Gwen, is the true hell of it."

Simon still sat in the Explorer, and the Explorer still sat in the driveway. Somebody had torched his house.

But why?

Was Collins right? Did it have something to do with an old case? Someone Simon might have put away while undercover? Someone who had seen him on TV yesterday and now, thanks to Martha Malone, had a name to go with the face?

Fifteen years ago, Simon's next question would have been, "How would they know where I lived?" With the Internet, that information was no more than a couple of clicks away for anyone with half a brain.

Or was the arson tied to something more immediate, like Simon's investigation of the Firenze explosion?

Simon looked at the pile of melted plastic on the seat next to him, wishing he had a plastic bag big enough to seal it in until he turned the mess over to the experts. Maybe someone had wanted to destroy the tapes. If so, they'd done a good job of it. Still, maybe something could be salvaged.

So who knew Simon had the tapes?

More importantly, who knew he'd left them at his house?

More importantly even, who knew there was a small part of one tape--the close-up of Pasquale--that couldn't be replaced?

Jake.

But she'd given him the tapes in the first place.

Irrationally, the thought of Jake--even as an unlikely suspect in a fire that could have killed her, as well as Simon--cheered him. At least enough to enable him to start the car and back the Explorer down the driveway and away from what was left of his house.

He tried again to focus on what he had to do next. Report to Collins. Drop off the tapes. Call his insurance guy. Pick up some clothes. That should get him back to the house by dinner.

He wondered if Jake liked Chinese.

Jake, for her part, was wondering if Simon had lost his mind. Chinese?

"I won't be home for dinner tonight, Simon," she said patiently. "Actually, I'm never home for dinner. I work until eleven. Now, if you and Irish want Chinese..."

Hanging up the phone after assuring Simon she'd be home by eleven-thirty, she put her head in her hands. Be careful what you wish for, she thought. And the truth was that Simon was pretty much everything Jake had wished for since she was...oh, say, five. But even so, things were moving unnaturally fast. Last night Simon seemed undecided about even inviting her to stay over, and tonight he was ordering in Chinese for the two of them. At "their" house.

Nice of him, of course, and he *had* likely saved her life last night. But Jake had this weird feeling he was imprinting on her after the disaster, like a bird emerging from its shell and forming an attachment to the first thing it sees.

Poor Simon. Just his luck to stumble across someone who was a bit of a lame duck herself.

"Hey, Kath--want to go to lunch?"

"It's three o'clock in the afternoon, Tex," Kathy told Simon. "On this planet, we try to hit McDonald's or Burger King around noon, give or take an hour or two."

"Hmmm. Guess that explains why I've always felt a little disenfranchised." Simon settled on the corner of her desk.

A fast-food pun. Now *that* was more like her Simon. Kathy slid the Internet print-outs on male depression under a stack of papers. "Haven't you eaten today?"

"Didn't feel much like it earlier. Besides, I'm having a late dinner, so eating now will work out fine."

"Who's the late dinner with?" If he was feeling better, he was going to pay for it with information. And maybe this woman, whoever she was, was the reason he was feeling better.

But Simon just smiled.

"Okay, out with it!" she demanded. "Who is she?"

"That's for me to know, and for you to find out," he said, still grinning.

"Now that's mature of you, Aamot," she said, poking him in the shoulder with a finger. "And, I might add, it's a dare, and you *don't* want to dare me."

"Ooh, I'm scared." Simon said, picking up the framed photo of Ned she kept on her desk. "Speaking of mature, when are you going to do the adult thing and marry this guy?"

She ignored the question. "I have to go down to the first floor. Want me to pick you up something?"

A convenience store on the street level of their building sold packaged sandwiches. But even Simon usually drew the line at bologna and processed cheese on gummy white bread. The offer--or threat--should be enough to divert him, though.

"Nah, I'm going run out to Harry's. Maybe get a cup of mushroom barley and a bagel."

He was <u>so</u> easy. "Then go next door to Connelly's and buy some clothes. Much as I love what you have on, I'd really hate to see it again tomorrow."

Simon set Ned's picture down. "You realize I can spend five hundred bucks on clothes and still come in tomorrow wearing jeans and a rugby shirt."

"Yeah, but they'll be different jeans and a different rugby shirt. Or maybe you'll get really adventurous, and splurge on a golf shirt or even..." she lowered her voice, "a Henley."

Simon gasped. "Go *collarless*??"

"If anyone can pull it off, Tex, you can." She sat back in her chair. "Seriously," she said, "I'm glad to see you smiling. I've been a little worried about you."

"My house did just burn down," Simon pointed out.

If his mood was that recent, Kathy wouldn't have been worried. But she'd noticed a gradual slide over weeks, not days.

"Don't I get a grace period," he was asking, "or make that an *ill*-grace period?" He grinned at her. "Do I always have to be Mr. Happy?"

Kathy cocked her head suspiciously. "That's one of those sex toys from your dirty book collection isn't it? Which one? *Tons of Lust*? *Nympho-Bavarian*?"

"Please," Simon said, getting off the corner of her desk, "some respect for the dearly departed, please. It's *Tongues of Lust* and *Nympho-Librarian*, though I have to say I think your sequels have real possibilities."

Kathy stood up and gave him a hug. "Now that's my old Simon. Go get yourself something to eat. I'll call you if we get results on the financial records or the piles of plastic formerly known as videotapes."

Simon laughed and started out the door, and she sat back down to sort through the stack of reports on her desk.

"Kath?"

She looked up. "Forget something, Tex?"

He pointed at the picture on her desk. "I know you changed the subject, but if you ever <u>do</u> want to talk about the doc, just let me know."

Kathy blinked and looked back down.

Harry's was around the corner and down the block. A neighborhood institution, the deli had great soups and the city's best corned beef sandwiches served on slabs of primo rye bread.

Simon had Dianne, his ex-wife, to thank for introducing him to the place. It had been the lunchtime hangout for her colleagues at her first law firm, where she'd worked before she landed the partnership with Lancaster and Franks. He doubted anyone at L&F would be caught dead there.

That's why he was so surprised to see Dianne.

He'd picked up his bowl of soup--real china bowls, none of that Styrofoam crap--and bagel and turned around to find a seat, when he saw her at a table dead in front of him.

Dianne was tall, almost as tall as Simon himself, and full-figured. Zaftig, one of Simon's friends had called her once, and it was a compliment. Long blonde hair, near-sighted baby blue eyes, full breasts and hips, tiny waist. She was all curves and wore clothes that accentuated her figure in colors like lemon yellow, lilac, peach and sea foam green. Everything about Dianne was soft and pastel and slightly out of focus, like a Monet painting.

Until she opened her mouth.

"Simon! Over here!"

She'd gotten the attention of everyone in the place with three words. And she hadn't even had to stand up or wave. That was the way she was in court, too. Magnetic. Dramatic. Electric. All those other -ics.

God, how he'd loved her.

And hated her.

Now he was drawn to her table. He'd say like a moth drawn to a flame, but it was such a cliché.

No, he was drawn to Dianne more like a fly drawn to a Venus Fly Trap. Talk about a metaphor that rises to mythical and pornographic proportions, he thought. Jake would like the word-play. Dianne would think it was juvenile.

He set his tray down on Dianne's table in order to give her a hug. "Are you alone?" he asked, because Dianne was seldom alone.

"Yes!" she said brightly. Because she was always bright. Except with him, usually. "Why don't you join me?"

Simon sat down, taking his soup, bagel and Mountain Dew off the tray to save space. As he set the tray on an adjacent empty table, he noticed his hand was shaking.

Dianne must have seen it, too. "Are you okay?" Her eyes were like a heat-hazy summer sky.

Simon stashed his hand in his lap. "Just tired," he said, "and I haven't eaten today."

Dianne took a bite of her Chicken Caesar Salad. "Busy?" She was doing that bright thing again.

He'd take care of that. "The house burned down last night."

She was pulling her roll apart and stopped mid-roll. "What house?"

"Our house." Then he corrected himself. "*My* house." He started to reach for his Mountain Dew, but his hand was still shaking. He buried it back under the table.

But he'd gotten her attention. "Our...your house burned down? How?"

"Arson."

"Who? Why?"

"What" and "when" were coming next. "Don't know."

"It's one of those perverts you put away. You know that, don't you?" Her voice was rising to the pitch it had sustained during what he thought of as My Marriage: The Later Years. Or "Year," actually. Bright had been replaced by brittle. Not that it was any excuse for what he'd done. "I don't know why you--"

"Can it, Dianne," he said quietly. "Please."

"There are so many other things you could do." She had that look on her face, the one that said scared and repulsed all at the same time. "You have such a good mind, Simon, but I worry about you."

"I like what I do," he said firmly, "and I'm doing fine."

"Are you seeing anyone?"

Ahh, the relationship question. It sounded patronizing no matter who asked it, but even more so coming from your ex-wife. Especially when that ex-wife was beautiful and successful. Simon balanced his desire for privacy with his desire to wipe the pitying look off her face. Wiping won. "In fact, yes."

Dianne looked up pertly. She did "pert" nearly as well as "bright." Sometimes she even combined them. "Really! What does she do?"

A lot of things, Simon thought, and most of them better than you. "She's at TV8."

"On-air?"

The status question. "She used to be, but now she's producing and directing."

"Really!"

"Really!" was to Dianne, what "No, shit," was to the common man.

"Really," Simon confirmed. "Her name is Wendy Jacobus." Because that would be her next question, and he wanted to save himself a "Really!"

"Really!"

Well, he'd tried.

"Wendy Jacobus." Dianne's hazy blue eyes were lasering in suddenly. Her firm, Simon knew, represented TV8. "Isn't she the one who--"

A cell phone rang then, and twenty people dug into their pockets or handbags to see if it was theirs.

Dianne won. "Dianne Aamot." She'd taken his name, and then kept it after the divorce. Both moves were puzzling to him in hindsight. "Okay, I'll be right there."

She stuffed the phone back in her bag and stood up. "Jury's back, I have to go."

That explained why she was at Harry's. The courthouse was just down the street.

She leaned down and kissed him on the cheek. "I'm really sorry, Simon. About the house. I know you loved it."

Her look said the "more than you're capable of loving a human being" part.

Simon watched her leave and then picked up his Mountain Dew and took a pull before looking down at his food. The soup had congealed and the bagel was cold and hard. The Mountain Dew was working its magic though, the shakes were going away.

Caffeine and sugar. Nature's building blocks.

FOURTEEN

Pat Firenze was listening to his mother.

"Little Pat," she said from the back seat, "I want that you should take..." Her words faded out.

"Ma, I can't hear you back there."

"Mamma," said Angela from the passenger seat next to him, "I told you that you should sit up here. I should sit in the back."

"No, no, Angela, you have the longer legs. Me, I'm little. I fit fine back here. Now Pat..."

A truck passed them, and her words were lost again. They were on the way home from St. Luke's, where his father's funeral would be held. At this time tomorrow it would all be over. His father's body would be cremated and--

"...tribute you hear?"

His mother's words came through loud and clear, her mouth being just inches from his right ear now. "Jesus, Ma," he said rubbing it, "you almost broke my eardrum."

"Little Pat," the voice was accompanied by a wagging finger. "How did I teach you? We do not use the name of the Lord Thy God in vain."

Angela captured the finger. "Mamma! You're going to poke out Pat's eye if he turns his head. You must sit back and put your seatbelt on. You're going to cause an accident."

"Well! If your father was alive--" Pat didn't have to look to know his mother was making the sign of the cross.

He glanced over at Angela. "Tudy says we have just enough stars for another blue sixteen-incher."

"Good."

Pat didn't answer.

114

"What is it? Why are you worried?"

Worried didn't cover it. Even the fluffy white cumulous clouds had black powder linings these days.

For reasons Pat couldn't quite figure out, he had not only received a check today for the balance owed on the Lake Days show, but also the fifty percent down on the Fourth of July show on Wednesday. He would have bet anything the mayor and Williams were going to try to replace them on that show.

Meanwhile, TV8 already was promoting the hell out of their broadcast. Pat had an uneasy feeling that everyone was just waiting for--even hoping for--Firenze Fireworks to blow something up. Something they didn't intend to, that is.

So what was Firenze Fireworks going to do? Make another big blue shell like the one that had killed his father, of course, and fire it at the end of the show. Like instant replay.

"It will be a tribute to the great Pasquale Firenze. You hear me, Little Pat?" his mother was yelling from the backseat.

"I hear you Ma." Pat said, and he did.

Maybe she was right.

Maybe they did need to finish what his father had started.

When Simon got back to the office, Kathy had a message for him. "Stephen Cruise in auditing wants you to stop by."

Cruise's "office" was more a cubby-hole amongst cubby-holes than an office. Simon stopped at the corner of the maze of cubicles, catching sight of the top of Cruise's head bent over papers. He knocked on the fabric-covered wall that separated Cruise's office from the next one over.

Cruise looked up. "Simon, I think I found something here."

Simon sat down in the chair next to the desk and snagged a glimpse of what Cruise was poring over. "That paper giving you problems, Steve? Want me to knock it around for awhile?"

Cruise laughed, flattening the crumpled paper with both hands. "It appears someone has already gone a few rounds with it. And I think I know why."

"Looks like a contract," Simon said. "For a fireworks show?"

"For *the* fireworks show."

"Lake Days?"

"Yeah," Cruise said eagerly. "You know how much they paid for that show?"

Simon was looking sideways at the paper, trying to read it. "$75,000?" He whistled. "That seems like a lot of money for a small-town event."

"A small-town event, but with a deep pocket sponsor. This contract is between Refresh Yourself and Firenze Fireworks."

"Okay," Simon said. "But why are we interested in it other than idle curiosity?"

"The first thing that caught my attention," Cruise said, flipping open the front cover of one of the ring binders Simon had given him, "is where I found it. Tucked down in the front pocket of this folder."

"Balled up?"

"No, like it had been crumpled, then straightened out, folded in half and slipped in. I didn't see it at first--only found it when I slid my fingers into the pocket."

Simon didn't ask why he'd slid his fingers into the pocket. Probably an accountant thing. "So maybe somebody had salvaged it from a wastebasket?"

"That was my thought," Cruise said. "So I checked the contract amount with the amount deposited. That's when I found the discrepancy.

"What kind of discrepancy?"

"A fifteen thousand dollar discrepancy. According to the contract, a fifty percent deposit was required at the time of signing. Half of seventy-five thousand is thirty-seven five, right?" Cruise waited.

Cruise was one of those guys who liked to spring questions on you like, "Is it legal for a man to marry his widow's sister?," so Simon answered warily: "Thirty-seven thousand, five hundred. Right."

"Nope."

Damn it. "Okay, I give up."

"In this case," said the auditor, pinching the bridge of his nose, "fifty percent of seventy-five thousand must be twenty-two five, because that was what was deposited."

Ahh, Cruise was being clever. It didn't become him, and Simon would tell him that the next time they had a beer together. In the meantime: "So you're saying $15,000 is missing? That's hardly enough to kill someone over."

"It is," said Cruise, "if it's only the tip of the iceberg. I'm trying to compare other contract fees with bank records, but some of the contracts are missing."

That was interesting in itself. Simon sat back in his chair. "So you think Guida may have been doing this long-term? But wouldn't someone have noticed?"

Cruise shrugged. "Family businesses are the worst, accounting-wise. They start out small and grow gradually, but eventually the books become complicated. Complicated enough to make it worthwhile to hire somebody, but no one wants to spend the money. So they let Cousin Billy do it and don't ask questions, because they don't want it dumped back on them."

Simon could see that.

"In this case," Cruise went on, "it might have been simple. Pasquale Firenze would have signed the contract, gotten the check from Refresh Yourself, and given it to Guida to deposit."

"And who's to know whether Guida deposited all of it or took cash back out of it," Simon said. Fifteen thousand, in cash.

"Exactly. Unless," Cruise said, holding up the crumpled contract, "somebody got suspicious and checked."

"Like Pasquale." Simon said.

When Jake got back to her office, there wasn't time to obsess about her confrontation with Gwen. It was nearly four, and she needed to get ready for the Five and Six O'Clock News.

Besides, what was the point of thinking about it--either Gwen would fire her or not. Censure her or not. Make her life a living hell, or not. See? Life was easy when you looked at it that way.

When she was safely through the Five and Six O'Clocks, Jake took advantage of the break before the Ten O'Clock to work on a feature dealing with fireworks accidents. She needed footage on explosions, but TV8's archives had turned up only the Firenze accident two years earlier. Not wanting to add fuel to that fire unnecessarily, she went on-line to her favorite stock footage website, instead, in search of out-of-state explosions.

She browsed the "F"s:

Fireworks: Festivals

Fireworks: Shells

Fireworks: China

Nothing even close to what she was looking for. She checked the clock. Eight-thirty, and she still had the Ten O'Clock News to get ready. Maybe a Google search would turn something up fast.

The Google screen popped up on her computer. She typed in: footage +fireworks +accidents. Then she clicked on Google Search.

The search turned up 890 items, but most of them were print references to video footage, not the footage itself. Only one of the listings on the first page held any promise:

Fireworks Accident
...exclusive footage...killed one...blast destroyed one building fireworks factory...
www.lbshotvideo/fireworks/accident

Jake clicked on it and read the description:

"Exclusive footage shot by first camera operator on the scene of a fireworks accident that killed one person. The shell blast also destroyed one building of the fireworks factory."

Below the description was a small still photo. Jake recognized the buildings immediately. It was Firenze Fireworks. This had to be footage of the same accident she had found in the station‘s own archives. Just exactly what Jake didn't want.

She hadn't been assigned to the story, since at the time she had been splitting her time between going through chemo on-camera and throwing up off-camera. She remembered it well, though, since her camera man had been called away to go the scene of the accident.

That camera man had been Luis Burns, just a month after he started.

www.lbshotvideo LB. Luis Burns.

Jake chewed on her left thumbnail. This would explain why Luis was running tape on the barge at Lake Days. In addition to sending footage via hardwire to the microwave truck and then onto Jake's production van, he also was recording on the tape in the his camera. That way, he had a duplicate of everything he taped legitimately to sell, plus he could tape other stock footage while he was out there. Stuff that would be generic and even easier to sell. And he'd been doing it for nearly as long as he‘d been at the station.

A great scheme and lucrative. Jake routinely paid fifty dollars a second for one-time use of broadcast quality stock footage. And because Luis was selling directly to the client via his website, he was pocketing the entire amount with no outlay on his part. TV8 was not only paying for the equipment, they were paying for Luis's time.

Geez.

Jake sat back in her chair and stared at Luis's Hot Video website.

Bless the Internet, it made research a snap.

What it couldn't do, though, is decide for you what to do with the information once you had it.

Angela woke up at ten-fifteen in her parents' guest room. She had lain down with a headache after dinner and had fallen asleep. She wasn't sure what had awakened her, but downstairs she could hear the news blasting on the television.

The noise just made Angela's still aching head hurt all the more. The telephone had been ringing all day with reporters. She and her mother had stopped answering eventually, since her parents' house did not have an answering machine and screening the calls was not possible. Her mother fretted, though, about missing an important one.

It was Angela who remembered that the computer in her former bedroom had telephone answering capability, so she'd simply slipped the telephone line dedicated to the Internet out, and the home-phone line in. The phone would ring three times, then the computer would pick up the call, answering with its mechanical voice.

The telephone was ringing now, and Angela realized it was the ringing that had awakened her. She pulled aside the bedspread and sat up, waiting for the computer to pick up. Two rings, three, four... And who knew how many before she'd awakened.

"Angela," her mother called up the steps. "You want I should get that?"

"No, Mamma," she said, folding the afghan and placing it neatly on the end of the bed. "I'll do it. Something must be wrong with the computer." She crossed the hall to her old room, but the ringing stopped just as she reached the door.

She was surprised to see her brother sitting at the desk. "Pat, what are you still doing here?"

Her brother turned from the keyboard of the computer. "I tried to go on-line while you were taking your little..." he looked at the clock in the corner of the computer screen, "three-hour nap. This thing is slower than slow, so I'm cleaning some things out. Dad's mailbox has 1,453 e-mails saved.

"Look at this." Pat read off the screen: "'Get Viagra, Coral Calcium On-line,' 'Benefits of huperzine A, phosphatidylserine,' 'Is it long enough for you?' 'Is it long enough for *her*?'" Pat turned back to his sister. "Just what do you think Dad was into?"

"Please, no more." Angela reached around him and switched off the computer.

"What are you doing?" Pat squawked. "I was in the middle of--"

"Remember the story of Noah in Sunday School?" Angela scolded. "We shouldn't be like Ham and look upon our father's nakedness. We should be like Shem and Japheth and cover him up."

"Do you think he--"

Angela pretended not to hear him. "The computer is slow because we do not have high-speed access. Using the modem--"

The ring of the telephone interrupted her, and she realized why the computer's answer phone wasn't picking up. "You've unplugged the house line," she said to her brother. "I had it running into the computer, so we could use the answering machine to screen calls."

"Oh," Pat said. "I needed to go on-line, and I didn't want to tie-up the home line."

"Then the least you could have done was to answer the phone, instead of letting it ring when you were right here."

She shook her finger at him. "And please, Pat, you know so little about computers, you are the last one who should be plugging and unplugging things. You call for help on every little thing. Even Pappa knows more, he--"

"Knew," Pat said, turning away from her and rebooting the computer.

"What?"

Pat swiveled back to face her. "Dad *knew* more. He's dead, remember?"

It was like her brother had plunged a knife into her heart. And it was true: she had forgotten, just for a moment. "At least I'm not erasing any trace of him." She nodded toward the computer screen.

"Angela!" her mother called from downstairs. "The phone! It could be someone important!"

Angela answered the still-ringing telephone, wondering why her brother really was on her father's computer.

It was a little after eleven when Jake got home.

True to his word, Simon had ordered Chinese: egg rolls, spicy beef, Hunan pork, chicken with peanuts, and sesame shrimp.

The display of food cartons reminded Jake of Simon's Great Wall of paint samples. "Couldn't decide, huh?"

"Variety," he said, handing her a glass of wine. "It's the five-spice of life. Besides, I've seen you eat."

"Good point."

He raised his glass in salut. "Thank you."

Jake raised hers, too, and smiled. She was feeling very mellow all of a sudden. "I was just going to thank *you*, and not just for getting me out of the fire. I'd forgotten how nice it was to have someone to talk to besides the plants."

Simon looked around. "You have no plants."

"Dead," Jake said. "Everyone of them. I'd watch out if I were you."

He clinked glasses with her. "To those who have come before."

"And gone," Jake said, laughing. "So how was your day, dear?"

"Well, now that you ask, it was very interesting."

Before Jake could inquire further, the phone rang. Simon set down his wine glass and made to answer it, but Jake got there first. "Hey, it's *my* phone. You want people to gossip?"

Simon held up his hands in surrender as she picked up the phone. "Hello?"

Five seconds of silence. It gave her just enough time to wonder if she really was afraid of gossip, or afraid that Simon--or Jake herself--would become too comfortable with the living arrangements. You start out ordering in Chinese and answering each other's phones, and pretty soon you're finishing each other's sentences and planning to grow old together.

"Someone you don't like?" Simon asked, as she hung up the receiver.

"Telemarketer, no doubt. They apparently didn't want to talk to me."

"Well, I want to talk to you." He kissed her on the nose. "Can I trust you?"

"That's what the plants asked, just before they died."

He laughed. "Okay, guess I'll take my chances, but first, can I offer you a little spicy beef?" He held up a carton.

After dinner, they took to the couch in the living room with the balance of the bottle of wine. Simon was tired, but he still wanted to talk to Jake about event contracts in general, and the Firenze contract in particular.

She made it easy. "Okay, so what were you going to ask me?"

"Say a contract was found between a fireworks company and a sponsor," Simon said, stretching. "And say that contract called for a certain down payment, but the money actually deposited was another, lesser amount."

"And two trains were traveling at..." Jake curled her legs up under her. "So you found a contract between Firenze and Refresh Yourself. For how much?"

Simon grinned. "Seventy-five thousand. That seemed like a lot to me."

"Not really. It's pretty much in line for a big show."

Okay, so Cruise was right on that, too. "The contract requires half down, or thirty-seven thousand five, but only twenty-two five wound up in the account."

"You're wondering what happened to the other fifteen thousand dollars?" Now here was a woman who could hold her numbers.

"My first take is that Guida took cash back from the deposit, unbeknownst to Pasquale and the rest of the family."

"That's a possibility," Jake admitted, "but it's not the only one." She sounded almost reluctant to say it.

"So what are the others?" Simon asked.

"Other. And it's Bryan." She wasn't looking at him.

"Bryan Williams?" Simon didn't get it. "You think he could have taken the money? How?"

"I'm not sure of that, or of why I'm telling you when I'm not even sure what I'm thinking." She took a gulp of wine.

Simon didn't bother to try to decode the convoluted sentence. He wanted to go to bed. Jake's bed. "Out with it."

"Okay, listen, this can get sort of complicated." She leaned forward. "Part of Bryan's job is securing sponsors. His fee is a percentage--usually thirty percent--of the amount the sponsor pays for the sponsorship."

"So if Refresh Yourself paid seventy-five thousand dollars for the fireworks, then Williams should have gotten twenty-five thousand, give or take."

"Give or take," Jake said. "But here's where it doesn't add up. Bryan's fee should have been part of the title sponsorship agreement, and that contract would be between Refresh Yourself and Lake Days. Then *Lake Days* would contract with Firenze for the fireworks themselves. If the contract you found is between Refresh Yourself and Firenze..."

"Williams wouldn't have gotten a cut?"

"No, and it's not like Bryan to do something for nothing."

"Well, you should know. You used to work for him." My God, was that a twinge of jealousy?

"If you think Bryan let me touch the money, you don't know Bryan," Jake was saying. "But I *have* heard that he's not averse to taking a little something under the table."

"A gratuity of sorts? Where did you hear that?"

"From Pasquale. Evidently Bryan asked him for a kick-back on a contract once, years ago. Pasquale never forgot it."

"Wait." Simon was confused. "So whenever this was, Pasquale signed a contract with a third party and Williams wanted him to funnel part of the fee back to him."

"Right," Jake said. "Bryan called it a referral fee, which is fine if everyone has agreed to it. But from what Pasquale told me, Bryan wanted Pasquale to pay him without Pasquale's end customer--Refresh Yourself in this case-- knowing about it."

Sounded like someone besides the fireworks company was getting the short end of William's shtick. "So what happens to the customer? They pay for a seventy-five thousand dollar show, but get a fifty-thousand one?"

"Yup. Plus the fireworks company takes a double hit. Not only is it paying the 'referral fee,' but its reputation suffers because shows start looking chintzy in comparison to its non-kickback-paying competitors."

"Unless all the companies can be talked into falling in line," Simon said thoughtfully. "Then 'chintzy,' as you put it, becomes the standard."

"Wait," Jake's face had gone white. "You're not thinking that Bryan set up the explosion to try to force Pasquale into going along?"

Of course Simon was thinking that. What else would he be thinking?

But Jake was shaking her head. "While I'm the first one to call Bryan a slimeball, I can't see him as a murderer. Besides, if the missing fifteen thousand really was a kickback to Bryan, shouldn't he be satisfied?"

Simon had been thinking about that. "Fifteen thousand dollars is still ten thousand less than what you say he normally should have gotten. Maybe the explosion was only meant as a threat. Williams had no way of knowing Pasquale would go back to relight--"

"Sixty-five hundred less," Jake interrupted. "It's thirty percent, not one-third, so that's twenty-one five, not twenty-five thousand."

"Whatever." Jake should get together with Cruise. "But, anyway, the sabotage of the shell was an inside job, so--"

Jake interrupted, looking puzzled. "Sabotage? So you're certain it wasn't an accident?"

Simon realized she hadn't been privy to his conversation with Pat on the porch...was it just last night? Seemed weeks ago now. He filled her in on that, along with the cause of the fire at his house, complete with broken bottle, and lighter.

"So," Jake summarized, "someone switched the black powder in the lift charge with silica sand, so it would explode in the mortar. And that someone burned down your house."

"Let's leave my house for another discussion," Simon said, shifting uncomfortably. "As for the shell, it had to be someone with access either at the factory or on the Lake Days grounds. That means a member of the family or one of their employees."

"Then that leaves Bryan out?"

Was she asking that hopefully?

If so, Simon had no aversion to crushing those hopes. "Not necessarily. After all, somebody had to give Williams his cut."

"Somebody inside." Jake tucked her feet up under her. "And Pasquale found out."

Luis had a dilemma.

And it wasn't a good kind of dilemma. You know, the do-you- get-the-Mustang-or-the-Corvette kind of dilemma. Sweet, either way you cut it.

No, this was more like take-the-bus-or-walk: Bummer. Or *major* bummer.

Luis got up from the couch in his living room and started pacing. He'd talked to Gwen, who'd talked to Jake, and sure enough, Jake had taped over the close-up of the old man getting blown up. And even though Gwen was pretty ticked at Jake, she said there was no way to recover the footage. Didn't seem all that broken up about it either.

Luis didn't get it. Yeah, the footage showed the old guy getting blown up, but there was no blood or guts. Besides, even if there was, blood and guts sells. If it bleeds, it leads, right? Right?

Wrooong. Luis picked up his bottle of Pacifica and took a hit. At least when you're dealing with Jake and Gwen, it was wrong. W...R...O...N...G...

Luis would give anything to be back in the old days, when newsmen were, well...men. And they actually reported, instead of reading press releases. Hell, sometimes they were right there in the thicket of things, making news themselves. What did Gwen and Jake know or care about the First Amendment and freedom of the press? Nothing, that's what. And there was something else they didn't know, either.

They didn't know Luis had a duplicate tape.

Luis had told Jake he started running tape *after* losing the link to the microwave van. He'd lied. He had been running tape all day. In fact, he had just filled one tape and stashed it in his bag when the explosion rocked the boat.

Setting the beer bottle down on a coaster, Luis started the pacing again. Up and down, from his five-disc progressive scan DVD, past the Bose speakers, to his plasma flat-screen and back again.

Okay, so he had the close-up footage right here in his apartment. But what could he do with it?

If he told Gwen, she'd tell Jake, and Jake would know he lied. And she'd want to know why. Then everything would come out. LB's Hot Video, the website, the whole thing.

And after all that work. Shooting the video and cataloguing it, creating the website, hooking up with a payment service so customers could pay him direct and not have to worry about security. He was an e-mogul, that's what he was, and now...

Shit, shit, shit. Why hadn't he just told Jake he was running tape the entire time? Let her think he was just being cautious out there on the barge?

Because he knew that *Jake* knew that Luis didn't "do" safe, that's why. She'd have known something was up, just like she would know something was up now, if he pulled the tape out of his butt.

Truth was, Jake saw right through Luis and it gave him the creeps. Like she was a mind-reader, like Professor Xavier in X-Men. Or his mom.

Focus, Man. *Focus.*

On the other hand, if he went ahead and sold the footage anonymously, Jake would recognize it the minute it showed up on CNN, or MSNBC, or Fox News, or....

Screwed.

That's what he was: screwed.

Stuck between a rock and a hard piece.

All those news outlets wanting his tape, and he couldn't sell it to any of them, no matter how much they paid. Not only that, he couldn't even give it to his own station and get credit for it.

Yup.

He was screwed.

And it was all Jake's fault.

FIFTEEN

Simon had asked Jake to wake him before she went for her swim. That shouldn't be hard, seeing as one of his legs was draped over her, pinning her to the mattress.

Dang, if he were staying for any length of time, she'd need a bigger bed. She tried to slide out from under the leg quietly, intending to go to the bathroom and take care of both her morning breath and bedhead before waking him, but she overbalanced and slithered off the bed and onto Irish on the floor.

The dog's indignant yelp worked better than punk rock.

"Wha!" Simon was up and reaching for something on the nightstand before his eyes were open. There *was* no nightstand on that side, which Jake figured was a good thing. Something told her that was where Simon kept his gun at home, and startling him when a gun was in reach probably wasn't a good idea.

Happily, he'd put the gun safely on the dresser next to the clock radio last night. She'd told him it was set to the punk rock station, so maybe there was some logic to that.

Now Simon stood bare naked on the other side of the bed. Irish was at the bedroom door, also bare naked, with a wounded look on her face. Jake was still on the floor. Yup, bare naked, too.

"Morning!" Jake said brightly.

Simon swiped his hand over his face. "Morning. Why are you on the floor?"

Jake considered telling him she had slept there, but thought the truth was better. "I fell out of bed," she said, getting up.

Simon came over and gave her a hug, not seeming to mind the morning breath. He looked down at her. "You fell out of bed?"

125

"It's not as tough as you might imagine."

He laughed and nuzzled into her hair. They stood like that for a minute before he said, "Pasquale's funeral is today."

"I know. One o'clock, right?"

"Yup. Are you going to be able to come?"

Jake tilted her head up--way up, gosh this guy was tall--and kissed him before letting go. "I'll be there for the service, but not the cemetery."

"There's nothing at the cemetery, since Pasquale was cremated. They're just having everyone over to Sadie's after the service."

"That's right, I forgot." Jake was pulling on her swimsuit. "But house or cemetery, I can't go either way. I should be home early tonight, though. Another producer is handling the Ten O'Clock News, since I'm working the holiday." Tomorrow was the Fourth of July, and the fireworks broadcast.

"When do you start broadcasting down there?" He reached over to untwist the shoulder strap of her suit.

She touched the strap self-consciously. Weird--they were acting like a real couple and all in the space of less than thirty-six hours. "Eight-thirty tomorrow night, but we'll be doing the Five and Six O'clock from Shore Park before that." She picked up her gym bag. "See you later?"

"Yup." Simon kissed her. Then he ran his hand slowly down along her side, over the curve at her waist and down to the notch just inside her hip bone. He paused to massage a small circle with his thumb. "Later."

Jake gave a quiver.

Weird, maybe. But very, very nice all the same.

Simon hung up the phone and looked at the sheet of paper in front of him.

Viagra. Huperzine A. Phosphatidylserine. Coral calcium.

Pat said he wasn't sure what they meant, but the very fact he'd called and told Simon what he had found on Pasquale's computer made Simon question that.

Problem was, whatever Pat knew or didn't know, Simon was most definitely in the dark. Sadie had said Pasquale was "all lusty and virile-like" and Simon had suspected then that the old man had discovered Viagra or its equivalent. But what were the other substances? Drugs? Additives? Nutritional supplements?

Simon pulled his laptop out of the drawer and fired it up. Opening the search engine, he typed in the four terms and hit "Search."

One hit: A "Natural Sex" site.

Well, that certainly fit, but…

He tried eliminating "Viagra"—the one item he knew—and hit "Search" again.

Seventeen hits. And the top two were: "Alternative Treatments for Alzheimer's."

Simon sat back. At dinner at the Firenze house, Sadie had talked about Pasquale and his "vitamins," and Pat had kidded her about the new "pots" Pasquale had bought her for her birthday. Simon knew there was a theory that aluminum—both in cooking pans and in other substances like deodorants and antacids—contributed to Alzheimer's. And then there was Pasquale's confusing the Teamsters with the Masons. That might have been quintessential Pasquale, or…

Could Pasquale have had Alzheimer's? Or known someone who did? Or both?

On a hunch, Simon typed in "Ohio +Masons +Alzheimer's."

And there it was, the place Angela had mentioned. The one her aunt had wanted Pasquale's brother Francesco to go: Pathways Center. It was located in the Ohio Masonic Home—and they specialized in Alzheimer's.

A knock at the door interrupted Simon's thoughts. Collins. "Let's talk."

Simon reluctantly followed him to his office and sat down, still thinking about Francesco and Pasquale Firenze as Collins put on his reading glasses and rifled through a mountain of papers before finding the one he wanted. "Here's the preliminary report on your house fire. Seems conclusive that it was arson, so we're taking over the investigation."

"Molotov cocktail, like Johannsen thought?"

"Yup, pretty low tech." Collins looked up. "What's your take on it?"

Simon leaned forward, resting his elbows on his knees. "I'm thinking it's most likely tied to the Firenze case."

Collins loosened his tie and leaned back. "You've confirmed that the fireworks shell was tampered with?"

Simon decided it was time to lay it all out with Collins—except, of course, for what he'd just learned. Simon wasn't sure, himself, how that fit in.

And then there was the niggling question—one he had no intention of sharing with his boss: Had Simon missed something during the investigation of Francesco's death? He didn't think so; but even if he had, what did it have to do with Pasquale's death?

Setting that question aside for now, Simon told Collins about the silica sand and the information Jake had given him, as well as the discrepancy Cruise had found in the books.

"Everything points to Ray Guida with or without Bryan Williams," he summed up. "I'm going to see Williams today. We'll probably have to subpoena his books…" He stopped.

"What?" Collins asked.

"The books," Simon said, feeling like an idiot. "That's why he burned down my house. He thought I had the Firenze financial records there."

"Why would he think that?"

"I left the binders in my car, but I carried in my briefcase and some videotapes. He probably mistook the briefcase for the black ring-binders."

"He followed you?"

"Apparently so." Simon thought about the rustling in the woods behind Sadie's house. "The Firenzes gave the binders to me the night of the fire," Simon said, skipping the part about dinner and a date. In fact, he had no intention of bringing Jake up at all.

"So all of the Firenzes knew you had them."

"Yeah, but if any one of them wanted to cover up something in the books," Simon pointed out, "they could have taken care of it before I got there."

"Doesn't the same go for Guida? Why wouldn't he have destroyed the evidence before he staged his death?"

Good question. And Simon didn't have an answer for that one either.

He hoped Bryan Williams did.

And just last week, Jake had been thinking she was about as exciting as paint drying.

She did the same thing every day. Got up, pulled on her swimsuit, drove to the Y, swam up and back thirty-six times and then went home or to work.

Now, all of a sudden, she had a lover. And a lover's dog. And an ex-lover who might be a murderer. And a subordinate who was a thief. Not to mention a funeral to attend.

Jake was dreading Pasquale's funeral, but then who didn't hate funerals? She agreed with Pasquale on the cremation thing: the service, visitation, and all that jazz seemed something best bypassed. Like death, in fact. Cryogenics, now that was the ticket. Right.

Jake was on her twentieth lap by the time she got to the subject of cryogenics. The Croc was swimming in the lane on one side of her and Cindy, another regular, on the other side. Jake paused to adjust her goggles and Cindy stopped, too.

"That guy," Cindy said, watching the Croc swimming away from them, "gives me the creeps. He doesn't take his eyes off you."

Well, at least Jake knew it wasn't her imagination. "You noticed, too, huh?"

"Noticed?" Cindy snorted. "You've got to be kidding. Do you know he switches the side he breathes on so he can look at you?"

Jake didn't understand. "What do you mean?"

"I mean most of us breathe to one side. You and I both breathe on our right. That means when you're going down the lane, you're looking toward the whirlpool. When you're coming up it, you're looking toward the windows.

"Watch." She gestured toward the Croc, who was just making his turn. "He was breathing on his right side when he went away from us, and now he's breathing on his left as he's swimming toward us. He's always looking toward your lane.

"And he only does it," she added significantly, "when you're swimming next to him. I wouldn't be surprised," she lowered her voice as the Croc got closer, "if he's whacking off in the hot tub."

Ugh. The Croc reached their end, paused to look at Jake, and then turned and swam back the other way.

"He's checking out my chest, and I'm flat as a board," Jake said.

Cindy laughed. "You know what they say, 'different strokes for different folks.'" She made a lewd hand gesture to suit her words.

Jake went back to her swim, trying to throw off the tension she felt in her shoulders and back. The guy was creepy, but he *was* just looking, after all. She tried to turn her thoughts to more pleasant things. Since she'd already covered cremation, cryogenics and stalkers, she moved on to Luis.

Criminy, what was she going to do about Luis? She should turn him in, but she really hated to do that. Maybe she'd have a talk with him. Yeah, that was it, a nice mother-to-double-dipper talk.

The locker room was deserted when Jake went in to shower and dress for the funeral. Normally, she'd be thrilled to hit the ebb-tide of locker activity when everyone was in Step class, but it felt a little spooky today.

Pulling her razor and shampoo--today's shampoo courtesy of the Hyatt Hotels--out of her gym bag, Jake tossed the bag back into her locker, and then padded into the shower room. Stepping into one of the narrow shower stalls, she quickly showered, shampooed, and shaved her legs, before turning off the water.

She had just popped open the door to reach for her "Welcome to Ensenada!" towel when she heard a noise. Wrapping the towel around herself, "Ensenada" side in, she stepped out peeked around the corner. The locker room was still empty--nary an ax murderer or soccer mom to be found.

She was towel-drying her hair when she heard it again. Psst! She instinctively started for the door, but stopped when she realized she was dressed in a towel and a pretty tacky towel at that. While Jake wouldn't hesitate to run out into the lobby if she were truly in danger, was she? Or was she having a Croc-induced episode of paranoia?

Psst! The noise had come from the wheel-chair accessible shower two stalls down, she was sure of it. The stall didn't have a door, just a shower curtain so users could roll right in. That shower curtain was drawn now, but she hadn't seen anyone pass by and the water wasn't running.

Psst!

Oh, shoot. This was stupid. She marched over to the accessible shower curtain, and yanked it aside.

Nothing. Nobody.

Neither.

Just what in the heck--

Psst!

Startled, Jake looked up to the source of the noise. A small white box with a glowing orange light was mounted near the ceiling.

No Tony Perkins. No knife. No blood--in black & white--circling the shower drain. Just a little white box.

And Jake had been in more danger in the shower trying to shave her own legs than she was from either the box *or* the Croc. Still, having come this far, metaphorically, she wanted to know what the stupid white box was, and why it was "psst"-ing at her.

Not quite able to make out the printing, she pulled over a stool and climbed up to look. "FreshAir--," she read.

Psst!

She should really learn to read with her mouth closed, Jake thought as she dressed. On the bright side, her breath was now "freesia-fresh."

What an idiot, getting all worked up because of a little noise. At least she'd confronted the air freshener, instead of running screaming and naked into the lobby for help. But then, the twelve-year-old at the desk wouldn't have been much help anyway. Probably would have asked her name and handed over her membership card so she could leave.

Nuts, Jake thought, she really had to get a grip. She slipped on her shoes and went to the full-length mirror to make sure everything was on straight, properly buttoned and fully zipped. Instead of her usual sweats or jeans, she was wearing her go-to-funeral clothes. A white sleeveless turtleneck, navy skirt, and heels. And a piece of toilet paper on her knee, where she'd cut herself shaving.

Doug walked right past her when she was waiting for her card at the membership desk in the lobby.

"Doug!"

He stopped. "Jake? Is that you?"

She moved aside to let the blonde guy from yesterday retrieve his card. "Jenson," he told the kid at the desk, and then gave Jake the once-over while he waited.

Maybe she should get dressed up more often.

"C'mon," she said to Doug, as she discreetly swiped at the toilet paper. "You've seen me dressed up before."

"I've never even seen you *dressed* before, much less dressed up." He nodded toward the blonde guy, who was walking out the door. "And neither has he, from the way he's looking at you."

"Who is he?" Jake asked, smiling. Okay, so she was flattered.

Doug gave her an odd look. "You're kidding, right?"

Jake felt the smile drain away. "What do you mean?"

130

"You don't recognize him?"

"Should I?" Jake looked out the front window at the man, who was getting into a blue SUV.

"That's the guy who swims with us. The one who stares at you."

Jake had a sick feeling in the pit of her stomach. "But this guy is blonde. The Croc has dark hair." This guy did look familiar, though, she had to admit.

Doug laughed. "You ever notice hair is darker when it's wet?"

"Good point." Jake was still staring after the SUV as it drove out of the parking lot. "But this one's hair isn't starting to thin on top."

Doug took two hands and flattened down his hair on both sides. "We're all thinning on top when our hair is slicked down."

"Some more than others," Jake said, forcing herself to smile. "Pretty soon you're going to need a filler there, Doug."

"I prefer to go *au naturel*," he said. "Besides, I'd have to superglue it when I swam, so nobody'd think a squirrel got loose in the pool." He smacked her on the back and continued into the locker room before she could ask him about his doctor's appointment.

Jake walked to her car, thinking hard. It bothered her that she hadn't recognized the Croc on dry land.

But what bothered her even more, was that she had seen the same man leaving the Y yesterday morning, fully dressed, as she came in. And half an hour later, he--the Croc, as it turned out--had been swimming next to her.

Now *that* was weird.

Bryan Williams' office was located in a two-story building on the west side of the city. Although the building held other businesses, Festivities took up half the first and second floors, with a private circular staircase connecting the two.

Everyone in the place was young and female, and everything about the place said "chic" and "artsy." The receptionist, who was chic, artsy and wearing a very short skirt, said she'd let "Bryan" know Simon was there.

As Simon looked around, Williams descended the circular stairs with Lillian White, his assistant. From Simon's vantage point he could see right up Lillian's skirt. Which was also chic, artsy and short. She was wearing those high platform shoes, and seemed to be trying hard not to look at her feet as she negotiated the steps like a little girl playing Cinderella at the ball.

"Simon," Williams said as he hit the last step. "What can I do for you?"

Simon explained he had some questions about the Firenze's contract for Lake Days. "Is there somewhere we can talk?"

"Certainly." Williams led the way into a conference room with a wide mahogany table. "If you don't mind, I'll have Lillian join us."

"May I get you something to drink, Mr. Aamot?" she asked.

"No, I'm fine." Simon took the seat across the table from Williams and set his notebook on the table. Lillian sat next to Simon and tugged on her skirt.

Simon opened the notebook and took out the Firenze contract, straightening it before he slid it across the wide table to Williams. "Is this the contract for the Lake Days Fireworks?"

Williams pulled it toward him and looked it over. "I believe so, though the contracting for this show was done directly between the vendor and the sponsor.

"Lillian?" He sailed the paper across toward his assistant, who made a good grab to keep it from going over the side. She glanced through it. "Yes," she said, looking to Williams as she answered. "This looks like the Lake Days contract between Refresh Yourself and Firenze Fireworks."

"Your office didn't draw it up?" Simon asked.

Another glance toward Williams before Lillian answered. "No."

Seemed like a lot of hesitation for such a short answer. "Is that unusual?"

Lillian opened her mouth, then looked at Williams again.

"Lillian, why don't you get me a cup of coffee," Williams said. "Are you sure you don't want anything?" he asked Simon.

Simon declined and Lillian stood up, still pulling on her skirt. Simon didn't get why women wore things that were so much work.

He watched her leave before he turned to Williams. "Okay, so *you* answer the question."

Williams shrugged. "It is unusual, which is why Lillian was twitching like a cat on a hot tin roof. She knows I didn't like the arrangement, but probably didn't want to tell you that.

"You see, Simon," Williams straightened his tie and leaned forward, trying to project "earnest," while maintaining "chic" and "artsy." "Short" he already had in the bag. "A company like mine normally takes a percentage of the sponsorship dollars it generates. A direct deal like the one between Refresh Yourself and Firenze cuts us out."

"So why did you do it this way?" Simon asked.

"Pasquale Firenze insisted on it. 'The customer gets what they pay for,' Firenze kept saying."

If Pasquale had Alzheimer's, it apparently wasn't affecting his sense of fair play.

Williams was smiling wryly. "He said it in front of the Refresh Yourself people. Refresh Yourself was already concerned about an ambush attempt by CoolSplash, and Firenze made it rather difficult for me to refuse."

Cut-throat business, this sponsorship stuff, Simon thought. Williams better watch it, or he'll wake up one morning with a giant beaver head in his bed. Still, much as Simon hated to admit it, Williams seemed to be leveling with him. "So how are you being compensated? Is Refresh Yourself paying you separately?"

"No, no, no," Williams said, waving his hands. "Let me explain how event sponsorship works. We're actually hired by the event. In this case, that would be the city of Liberty, which puts on the celebration. Our job is to bring in sponsors to pick up the cost of the event. In exchange, those sponsors get positive exposure from being associated with a quality event. Our job is to make sure they get that exposure, so they'll want to do it again."

It matched up with what Jake had told Simon. "So in lieu of your normal percentage of the fireworks contract, Refresh Yourself isn't about to pay you for taking their money, correct?"

Williams nodded, pleased. The "in lieu of" thing must have impressed him. "Absolutely correct, but we do have to be paid for our services, as I told the mayor. I have overhead." He gestured toward the outer office, where the receptionist was now climbing the circular staircase. Simon wondered whether Williams had them on rotation.

"And very nice overhead, indeed," Simon agreed dryly. "So what did you work out?"

"We're taking a percentage of the sales on the Lake Days grounds-- vending, T-shirts, and so on." Williams shrugged. "Essentially, the city is passing their cut from the vendors on to us. Frankly, it's better than nothing, but just barely."

"So why are you involved with Lake Days at all?" Simon asked. "Out of the goodness of your heart?"

Williams laughed outright at that. "I have no heart, ask anyone. Ask our friend Jake."

Simon didn't respond, and Williams cleared his throat, seeming to sense he'd made a misstep. "No, I agreed to stay on, because it would have damaged my relationship with both Refresh Yourself and the city to pull out. I'm looking at it as prospecting."

"Prospecting?"

"Looking toward prospective business. The mayor controls both Lake Days and tomorrow's Fourth of July celebration."

"And what about tomorrow's fireworks?" Simon said. "Is there the same arrangement between Firenze and Refresh Yourself? Are you being cut out again?"

"No, thank the Lord," said Williams. "Refresh Yourself has a title sponsorship agreement with the city--through us--that covers the entire celebration. Firenze is being paid by the city out of that sponsorship money, *after* we take our percentage."

"Seems straight forward enough," Simon said, though he still wasn't quite clear on the concept. "But back to Lake Days. Any idea why the contract indicates that Refresh Yourself made a down payment of thirty-seven thousand five, but Firenze financial records indicate they only received twenty-two five?"

Williams sat back, looking stunned. Or, maybe, feigning looking stunned. "No. As I said, we weren't involved in that transaction."

"Even after the fact?"

"What do you mean?"

Williams was getting defensive, which pleased Simon to no end. "I've heard that kick-backs aren't all that unusual in your business."

"I'm sure I don't know what you mean." Williams was sitting so straight that the term "a stick up his butt" came to mind. Pretty soon he'd be tut-tutting.

"Of course you do," Simon said. "Kick-backs, in lieu of payment?" Williams didn't look as impressed this time.

Simon pressed on. "You know, where you suggest that a customer hire a particular company, and that company...rebates you? I understand that you approached Pasquale Firenze, and he refused."

As Williams opened his mouth to object--strenuously, no doubt--Lillian White re-entered the room with his coffee.

"I'm not sure who your source is," Williams said, as Lillian set it down, "but I assure you I did no such thing."

"Just this time? Or ever?" Simon said, smiling pleasantly.

Williams turned three shades of red. Magenta, Aztec Rouge and Vermilion, by Simon's reckoning.

Lillian took one look at him and interrupted smoothly. "Excuse me, Bryan. Kimberly asked me to tell you that your eleven-thirty is here."

What a good girl Lily White was. Simon wondered if Williams routinely had an "out" set up--a phone call he had to take or an appointment--or if his assistant had done it on her own initiative.

Either way, it worked. Williams stood up. "I'm afraid we'll have to continue this discussion another time. I need to take this meeting, and then I have a funeral to attend."

Simon allowed Williams and White to escort him into the lobby, which was devoid of visitors, including the "eleven-thirty." In the bathroom probably.

"The Firenze funeral? I'll be there, too," Simon said, extending his hand. "We can 'continue this discussion' then."

Williams shook his hand. Wussy little grip. The guy really should work on that.

SIXTEEN

Jake arrived at St. Luke's about quarter to one. There was a crowd in the narthex of the church, the jam was caused by people paying their condolences to the family.

Sadie and Angela stood side-by-side next to the door, book-ended by Pat and Tudy. Both of the men wore black suits and sunglasses. Both of the women wore black, too: Angela's dress accessorized with Coach's red Ergo Small Zip handbag; Sadie's, a crumpled white cotton handkerchief. Angela's scent was "Ethereal," and Sadie's, a mere whisper of "Cashmere Bouquet."

The resemblance between the two women was striking, though. Funny. Jake hadn't noticed that before. Angela's cheekbones definitely were her mother's, and the hair, too, though Sadie's was now steel gray and caught in a bun behind her head. Still, it remained every bit as thick as Angela's, which flowed glossy and black halfway down her back.

That must have been how Sadie looked when Pasquale had met her, Jake thought. Young and beautiful. Pasquale had told Jake once that his wife was still the most beautiful woman he had ever laid eyes on.

How sad to lose the one person who would forever see you that way.

Jake edged past the group and took a seat on the aisle. At the front of the church, an urn had been placed on a blue-draped table. On each side of the urn was a bouquet of what Jake's mother had called "firecrackers" because the blossoms looked like miniature fireworks bursts. A nearly life-size photograph of Pasquale sat on an easel next to the table. In it, he was smiling up at the camera as he lowered a shell by its fuse into the mortar.

Jake guessed that honoring Pasquale's without honoring his life's work-- even if it was also the means of his death--would be unthinkable to the Firenzes. She wondered if she could be as forgiving.

As the first bars of "On Eagle's Wings" sounded, the family took their places in the front pew and Jake opened her hymnal.

Not that she didn't know the words by heart.

Simon arrived at the funeral just as the congregation started singing the Eagle's Wings thing. God, how he hated that song.

He propped himself against the wall at the back of the church and surveyed the crowd. Pat, Angela, Sadie, Tudy, and a woman he assumed was Tudy's wife were seated in the first pew on the right. Pat glanced around and, catching sight of Simon, turned back to say something to Tudy, who also looked. Both men were wearing sunglasses, even in the dimness of the church. Not that Simon could have read their eyes from this distance anyway.

Was Pat thinking that Pasquale—like his brother, apparently--had Alzheimer's and it had contributed to his death somehow? Could the old man have mistaken sand for the black powder in the lift charge? Seemed improbable, especially since the sand had been in the storeroom, not in a magazine like the black powder.

The woman who had been slicing stars in the process building, passed by Simon to quietly take her seat next to Maxie, who had assembled the eight-inch shell at the shop. Simon didn't see some of the others he had expected. No sign of the mayor, or Martha Malone, or George Eagleton.

And where was Williams? Maybe they were all distancing themselves from the Firenzes and their "carelessness." Simon felt badly about that. Pasquale deserved his due. Maybe Simon *should* release as much as he knew about the sabotage.

Jake, the sole TV8 representative, sat about two-thirds of the way back on the aisle. And as Simon looked on, Williams hurried down the center aisle and shoehorned himself in right next to her.

On the second chorus of "On Eagle's Wings," Bryan had slipped into the seat next to Jake. There actually was no seat, it being a pew and all, but he managed to wedge himself in between Jake and the woman next to her. The woman looked like a young Sophia Loren, so Bryan's seating choice didn't surprise Jake.

But Bryan ignored "Sophia" and turned to Jake, planting one hand on the hymnal rack in front of them, and the other next to her head on the back of the pew.

"I need to talk to you," he whispered in her ear.

"Amen," Jake sang.

"What did you tell you Aamot?"

Jake slid her hymnal back into the rack, nearly taking off his fingers. "Quiet."

"Nobody can hear." They stood up with the rest of the congregation. "What did you say to him?"

"Who?"

"Aamot." Bryan seemed perturbed.

"About what?"

"Firenze!" Bryan said it louder than he probably intended, and heads turned in their direction.

"I don't know." Abbott and Costello had nothing on her. She turned and whispered in Bryan's ear. "But I do know that this is Pasquale's funeral, and you will show respect for him."

Bryan pulled back and looked at her. Apparently he wasn't used to being talked to like that.

Jake faced forward. "We'll discuss this later," she said, getting the signal to sit down.

Bryan was a half-beat late lowering himself to the bench.

SEVENTEEN

Simon, seeing as he'd never actually sat down, managed to be the first one out of church after the family, and the first one in line to talk to them.

"Simon, thanks for coming." Pat shook his hand. He'd had his sunglasses off and was wiping at his eyes, but he slipped the glasses back on as Simon approached.

Simon could see his own reflection in them. It was like talking to twin miniatures of himself. "Nobody will think less of you if your eyes are red, you know."

Pat sighed, and pulled the glasses off. He swiped at his eyes again, then put the glasses right back on. "Everyone's staring, and this just makes it seem less..."

"Intrusive," Simon finished for him. "How are you holding up?"

"Okay. Have you found out anything?"

Many things, Simon thought, but the line was backing up behind him. "Yeah, but we can't talk about it here."

"You're coming over to the house after this, aren't you? We're having food, wine and then fireworks at dusk."

All the elements of a fireworks wake.

Simon nodded and was shouldered aside by an elderly Italian lady eager to pay her respects.

Jake was trapped in the sea of people trying to exit down the center aisle of the church. She didn't know what the back-up was, but she had to get to work. She also wanted to avoid Bryan. Turning around, she saw him three bodies over, chatting up Sophia.

Jake made her move, taking an abrupt right through an already vacated pew to reach the side aisle. A door three-quarters of the way down the aisle

138

led her into a dim corridor lined with classrooms, but the lighted "Exit" sign was as good as its word, and Jake found herself outside in the parking lot.

Cool.

Until Bryan caught up with her.

"Wait! Jake!" Huffing and puffing, he grabbed her arm.

She gave his hand a dirty look. "You must be out of shape. The corridor wasn't that long."

He ignored the insult, but removed his hand. "So it's later. Let's talk. What did you tell him about Firenze and kickbacks?"

"Who?"

"Don't pull the "Who's on First" crap with me, Jake."

Crap? From the urbane Bryan Williams? But then Jake had seen this plainspoken side of Bryan before. And liked it better usually, than his social persona. Unless he was threatening her.

Jake took her keys out of her purse and walked toward the Jaguar.

Bryan followed. "Listen, Jake. I did *not* ask Firenze for a kick-back on Lake Days."

Jake stopped next the car. "Of course not. You knew he wouldn't give you one. After all, you'd been through this with him before. Years before."

He grabbed her arm again. "You mean when you were working for me? Or maybe later, when we were sleeping together? When we said we loved each other?"

Fine time to pull *that* one out. "Oh, please. Are you trying to make me feel guilty or are you claiming non-spousal privilege? Now let me go."

They were standing very close, practically toe to toe. He let her go, but he didn't step back. "I just want to remind you that you were there, too."

"I had nothing to do with the money side of the business, Bryan, and you know it."

"I do, but..." He let it hang.

What a jerk. She pushed the remote key to unlock the door.

Bryan tried another tactic. "Whatever you thought of me then, Jake, whatever you think of me now, I assure you I did nothing illegal with the Lake Days sponsorship or the Firenzes."

"What about immoral? Did you do anything immoral?" She laughed and touched his face. "Don't worry, Bryan. I didn't betray any confidences...from you."

The truth, she thought as she drove off. It really will set you free.

As Simon left the church, he saw Jake and Bryan Williams in the parking lot. They were standing very close, and seemed in deep conversation. Jake reached up and touched Williams' face before getting into the Jaguar and driving off.

Simon was.... Stunned was too grandiose a word. Bummed, maybe. Jake said she'd "worked" for Bryan, but was there still more to the relationship? Like a "relationship"?

The Jaguar. Why was it easier for Simon to imagine Williams buying it for Jake, than Jake buying it for herself?

He gave that some thought.

Maybe because Williams had a big, impressive office, and Jake lived in a little house.

Maybe because Williams owned his own company, and Jake worked for a television station, which usually meant more prestige than money.

Maybe because Williams struck Simon as someone who would spend seventy-five grand on a car, and Jake didn't.

Maybe.

Or maybe Simon was just a jealous, sexist asshole.

Yeah, that was it.

Kathy held up a telephone message as Simon walked in the door. "I have something for you."

Simon stuck out his hand. "Lay it on me, Sugar."

"You're going to like this." She dangled it just out of his reach.

"You're a brat, you know that, don't you?" He snatched the message. "It's why your brothers won't speak to you anymore," he said over his shoulder as he walked into his office.

"I don't have any brothers." She followed him in and plunked herself down in his guest chair. "Why aren't you at the funeral?"

"Already went to the funeral," Simon said, reading the message, "and I'm on my way to the funeral lunch or dinner or whatever you call a meal served at three in the afternoon."

Kathy smiled. "You should know: What did you call *your* meal yesterday afternoon?"

"Hell."

Ah-hah. "Dianne called here this morning."

Now she had his attention. "Dianne? Why?"

"She said she saw you briefly at Harry's and wanted to make sure you were all right." Kathy tried to keep the skepticism out of her voice. Simon's ex-wife had sounded more curious than concerned.

Simon squirmed like a man who had been caught cheating. Why was it the innocent ones who acted guilty? "Dianne was there, waiting for a verdict to come in," he protested. "I just told her about the house burning down."

Kathy reached over and patted his hand. "You don't have to explain to me, dear. I'm not your mother or your wife."

"I think of you more as my bossy baby sister, and I bless you for that," Simon said, looking up from the telephone message. "For this, however, I bless the Safe Explosives Act." He waved the slip of paper.

"Me, I can understand," Kathy said, lifting her eyebrows, "but the Safe Explosives Act?"

"Yup. It requires fingerprints and photos of anyone who works with fireworks. Including Ray Guida. And," he said, getting up and adjusting his necktie, "since you read all my messages, you know that Guida's fingerprints are on the cigarette lighter they found outside my house."

"I write all your messages, you stooge, so it's a little tough not to read them."

She stood up and retied the tie, then straightened his collar. "Where did this suit come from?"

"It's the one I keep here for court appearances."

Kathy nodded. "I thought I recognized it. Ten years old and doesn't look a day over nine." She flopped open one side of his jacket. "These pants look a little big, are you losing weight? Maybe you should have them taken in."

Simon kissed her on the top of the head. "I love you, you know that, you little snot?"

"I know." Kathy stepped back. "Collins already has people looking for Guida, but you be careful out there, you hear me?"

Simon saluted her dutifully and left, still looking a little rumpled despite Kathy's best efforts.

She had to give Simon's ex credit for one thing. Dianne had cut him loose fast once she realized he wasn't going to be the trophy husband her career required. Good thing, too, because Simon would have hung on and tried to make it work, just like he had hung onto that old suit.

Alterations--of any kind--didn't come easily for Simon Aamot.

The family hadn't made it to the house by the time Simon arrived, but a woman who looked a lot like Sadie welcomed Simon at the door. "You come and eat. My sister Sadie and her family will be here very soon. You want some wine? Some manicotti?"

This must be Marie, of the Italian Wedding Soup. She may not make tiny meatballs for her soup, but she said manicotti "man-i-*got*" like Sadie did, so Simon knew he was in good hands, gastronomically speaking.

After he'd filled a plate to placate Marie ("You eat now, you understand?"), Simon wandered through the assorted Firenzes. He wondered what it felt like to be a part of a family like this: big, boisterous, wearing their feelings on their sleeves or, in the case of Pat and Tudy, behind their sunglasses. Around him people were laughing and people were crying and no one seemed to be embarrassed by either.

Simon wondered what their reaction would be if he told them Ray was alive. And--either in tandem with Bryan Williams or alone--had caused Pasquale's death. For Simon's part, he was relieved. The Alzheimer's had muddied the water, but this was a simple case of greed. And greed, Simon understood.

Still, he wasn't quite sure what to make of Williams. Normally Simon had a sense of whether a person he was interviewing was lying. In this case, his intuition was telling him just the opposite of what he wanted it to.

While Simon wouldn't be surprised if Williams had taken kick-backs, the man seemed to be telling the truth about Lake Days. But then, Simon hadn't gotten the chance to ask him the $15,000 question: whether he had paid Ray to sabotage the show.

Simon was itching to subpoena Williams' financial records, but there were no grounds. What Jake said that *Pasquale* had said, sure wouldn't hold up with a judge.

And speaking of Jake: What was the little scene between her and Williams?

Simon had wandered out onto the porch looking to stash his still full plate where Marie wouldn't catch him, when he heard a dog bark and the crunch of tires on the gravel drive.

Pat was driving, with his mother in the front seat and Angela and Tudy in the back. When they stopped, Angela helped her mother out of the car and led her toward the house. The two men, still wearing their sunglasses, fell in behind them. There was no sign of Tudy's wife. Pat raised a hand in greeting to Simon.

As the group made its way to the house, Bela looped an expanding figure-eight, with the car on one end and the Firenzes on the other. At one point, he very nearly knocked Sadie over.

"Bad dog!" Pat scolded and lunged at him. Bela ran off into the field, howling like he'd been hurt. Pat held up his hands to show he hadn't touched the dog.

"Don't scream at poor Bela," Angela said, supporting Sadie's arm as they climbed the steps together and entered the house. "He's missing his friend."

Simon thought at first that she was talking about Pasquale, then realized he didn't see Lugosi around. "Where's Lugosi?"

"At the vet," Tudy said, mounting the steps slowly. "He got sick yesterday. Probably ate a bad rabbit, the dumb bunny." The old man mustered up a smile at his joke.

"He's lucky he can still catch rabbits," Pat said. He had followed Angela and his mother into the house. Now he came back on the porch with a bottle of wine in one hand and three stemmed plastic wine glasses in the other. He handed Simon the bottle and set the glasses on the porch railing, careful to push each stem firmly into its plastic base. Simon filled the glasses and handed one to Pat, one to Tudy, and took one himself.

Pat lifted his. "To my father."

They all clinked plastic glasses and drank. Pat removed his sunglasses, this time finally leaving them off.

Tudy looked off into the field where Bela had disappeared. "You remember Pat, the way your father called that dog *Leg*-osi? And Angela and Sadie would yell--ooh, you never heard such a scolding they'd give him."

"This was after Lugosi had the run-in with the Cougar, I assume?" Simon asked him, but it was Pat who answered.

"Oh, yeah. My father: Mr. Sensitivity." Pat stopped. "But you know, he never meant it mean. He loved that dog, wouldn't hear of putting him down."

"And now Pasquale is the one who's gone," Tudy said. He turned purposefully to Simon, like he was about to confront his devils--and Simon was them. "And what about my son? Is there any news?"

Simon wasn't sure how to answer and Tudy misinterpreted the hesitation. "I know, I know. The lake is deep and dark and cold. One person, one body..." The little man shook his finger at Simon. "But I want to bury my son, you understand? I don't want to leave him down there with the fishes."

"I know, Tudy, and I need to talk to you about something." He drew the old man away from the door as a cluster of late-comers mounted the porch steps. Pat greeted the group and then moved over to join Tudy and Simon.

Simon didn't know if what he was about to tell Tudy qualified as good news or bad news: Your son is alive. But he's likely a thief and a murderer.

On the other hand, the family had a right to know that money was missing, and that Ray was still alive. And as far as his investigation was concerned, they also might be able to tell him where Ray would run.

Simon glanced around, not wanting to be overheard. He had to tell Angela, too, about her husband, but he could hear her inside the front hall, talking to her mother and her aunt. Best to start with Pat and Tudy, so they would be there when he told Angela. And Sadie.

"At the church you said that you'd found something," Pat prodded him.

Simon hated breaking bad news. And he was really bad at it, tending to back into it rather than plunging straight in. "Our accountants went through your financial records."

"They found something was wrong." It wasn't a question.

Simon did a "who-knows" with his hands. "You'll have to tell me. Maybe there's a simple explanation I haven't thought of. We found a copy of the Lake Days contract. It was for seventy-five thousand."

"Okay." Pat was waiting.

"Was that the amount you were paid for the show?"

"Yeah. We just got the balance."

"Biggest show we've done so far," Tudy added.

"Did either of you ever see the contract? Or the check for the fifty percent down payment?"

Tudy looked Pat. Pat looked at Tudy. They both looked at Simon.

"My dad normally handled the contracts, and Ray handled the money."

"Can you think of any reason why only twenty-two five of the thirty-seven five down payment that the contract stipulated was deposited?"

Pat looked at Tudy.

Tudy looked at Pat and shrugged. "Don't know. You boy?"

Pat shook his head. "No, but Ray..." he started, then stopped himself.

They all stood silent.

"My house was burned down," Simon said finally.

"I'm sorry, Simon, we should have called--" Pat looked embarrassed.

Simon should have been the one who was embarrassed. He was botching this. "I didn't mean that, Pat. The reason I brought it up is that it was arson. Somebody broke my basement window and tossed in a Molotov cocktail."

Tudy looked confused. "Is that one of those Russian drinks?"

"No," Pat said, laying his hand on the old man's back. "It's a bottle filled with gasoline. A rag is stuffed in the neck like a wick and lighted. When the bottle is thrown, it smashes and sends gasoline and fire all over the place."

"And somebody did this to your house, Simon?" Tudy asked.

Simon felt a fine sheen of sweat break out on his face. "They found a cigarette lighter outside my house."

"It was probably used to light the rag, right?" Tudy asked.

Pat had it now. "You think your fire had something to do with my father's death and with Ray's?"

"The lighter had Ray's fingerprints on it," Simon said.

"Was it silver? A Zippo?" Tudy asked.

Simon nodded, surprised. If he'd needed any further confirmation that it was Ray's lighter, he'd just gotten it.

"That was my Zippo, you remember Pat? Both your dad and me, we had them. I gave that lighter to Ray when he turned eighteen." Tudy set his wine on the porch railing as he spoke. The round base had fallen off and the glass toppled into the bushes below.

Pat watched it go and turned to Simon. "But your house burned down the night *after* Dad was killed. Ray was already--"

"You think my son had something to do with this mazeltov cocktail of yours?" Simon could practically see the wheels turning inside Tudy's head as he tried to comprehend this. "You accuse him when--?"

A crash and the sound of broken glass from the house stopped Tudy, and they all turned to look.

Framed in the kitchen window was Sadie. Simon wasn't operating at peak efficiency or he'd have remembered the kitchen sink was located under that window.

"Are you saying that Ray is alive?" Sadie demanded through the screen. "Are you saying Tudy's son stole money from my husband and burned down your house to hide it?" Sadie had a keen mind. She also had an aging body, and that body was giving out. She started to sag.

Pat already was in the house and Simon could hear him rounding the corner to the kitchen to catch his mother. Simon turned back to Tudy.

The little man was hanging over the porch railing throwing up into the bushes.

God, Simon thought, I really do suck at this.

Jake fired up her computer when she got into the office. He'd actually threatened her, the jerk.

The phone rang, and she picked it up. "Production!"

Breathing. A man's breathing.

"Production!" she screamed into the phone. She figured anybody with a lick of sense would hang up.

He did. She slammed the phone back down on the cradle.

Dang. So what was Bryan planning to do? Claim she was in cahoots with him? If it was a crime being too stupid and too much in loooove to see what a slime ball a man is, then she was guilty. What an idiot she'd been, not to see how shallow he was. How self-centered and materialistic. How conniving, how, how...

The phone rang again, and again, Jake picked up. "Production!"

A hesitation, and Jake was ready to hang up when she heard the unmistakable click of a handset being lifted. "This is Dianne Aamot. To whom am I speaking?"

Dianne *Aamot*? Like in Simon's wife, Dianne Aamot??

Jake panicked and almost hung up. Steeling herself, she said, as calmly as she could muster, "This is Wendy Jacobus."

"Excellent," the voice on the other end of the line said. "Just the person I was looking for."

Jake just listened, wondering what was coming next.

"Ms. Jacobus, I'm with the law firm of Lancaster and Franks, which, as you probably know, represents TV8."

"Yeees." Lawyers were always bad news from Jake's perspective. What she didn't know was *which* bad news Attorney Aamot was calling about.

Liability for the sunken microwave van? Jake's destroying Luis's videotape, which, even though it was a smaller chunk of station property, was a lucrative one? Or maybe the lawyer was merely calling to ask Jake if she was fooling around with her ex-husband.

Choose any door, Jake thought. There's a lady tiger behind all of them. "What can I help you with Ms. Aamot?"

The sound of a pen--most likely a Mont Blanc--tapping on a wooden--most likely mahogany--desk. "I'd like to set up a time to meet. Perhaps today?"

Uh-oh. "I'm really sorry," Jake tried, "but today is impossible. TV8 is televising the fireworks tomorrow night and I'm the producer. I don't have a spare second between meetings." A bit of an overstatement, but Dianne wouldn't know that.

"And you'll be on the fireworks grounds tomorrow?"

"I'll be tied up there all day, I'm afraid," Jake said, pseudo-apologetically, "in the production truck."

"Good." Jake heard papers flutter, like a page had been turned on a calendar. "I'm meeting the station's insurance underwriter at the park tomorrow night. I'll come by."

Double "uh-oh." Jake gave in, but not gracefully. "It would have to be well before eight," she warned. "The broadcast starts at eight-thirty and I--"

"Eight it is," Dianne Aamot said airily, and hung up.

The Internet Explorer home page came up on Jake's screen, with a beep.

Jake typed in <www.lbshotvideo>.

If lawyers and insurance agents were sniffing around, maybe it was time for Jake to protect *herself*, for a change.

She hit "Print."

Pat caught his mother before she hit the floor, and sat her down on a kitchen chair. "Angela!" he yelled.

Angela came running, along with Aunt Marie and, behind her, half the female population of the family.

"Mamma, what's wrong?" Angela knelt down next to their mother's chair.

Words starting pouring out of their mother's mouth, only a few intelligible. Unfortunately, they were things like "Ray," "steal," "kill" and "blow up."

The rumble of conversation from the crowd in the doorway grew. Thank God for Aunt Marie. She herded Angela and their mother up the stairs, along with Tudy and Simon, who had just come in.

"You talk among yourselves, you understand?" Pat heard Marie instruct their guests as he followed.

Angela led them into Pat's old bedroom or the shrine, as Pat called it. The wallpaper, the picture of JFK, the twin bed, the cross that hung square over his headboard threatening to impale him if he was bad. It was all there, including the Catholic guilt. Nothing had changed since Pat was ten.

No, that wasn't quite right. His mother had added a white fuzzy bedspread. Tudy sat uneasily on it now, holding a pink ruffled pillow--another addition--like a security blanket. He looked so ridiculous, Pat was tempted to pull the GENERAL LEE pillow out from under the bedspread and give it to him instead.

Pat's mother was sitting in the rocking chair across the room.

"Is this true, Tudy? Did your son kill my husband?" Leave it to Sadie Firenze to cut to the chase, Pat thought. She'd done it with his father more often than Pat could count. Pasquale would be waxing eloquent about something and--

"Sadie." Simon was crouching in front of the rocker. "Right now we're not sure of anything."

"But the lighter..." Pat started to say, then shut up.

"Why is he still here?" This from Angela, who stood in the middle of the room facing Tudy.

Simon pivoted to look at Angela.

"Lay off, Angela," Pat said to his sister. "Tudy--"

Simon interrupted. "Do you mean why is *Ray* still here?"

"Yes." Angela turned and held out her hands to Simon. "If he did these things, why would he stay here? If he stole money. If he tampered with my father's shell. Why is he still here? Why would he burn down your house? He has his money. Why wouldn't he just go, and leave us to live our lives?"

"I hear Ray and my husband, they argue," his mother piped in before Pat could.

"Argued about what?" Simon asked.

"It was about money, I think."

"When was this, Ma?" Pat asked.

"Last week. Maybe Wednesday, maybe Thursday." She searched the pocket of her apron and came up with her handkerchief.

"Do you remember anything else about it?" Simon asked, standing up. "Where were they?"

"In the office. My husband, he was sitting at the desk by the computer. Ray was standing above him." His mother's face crumpled, and she blew her nose loudly into the cloth. "Maybe he was threatening Pasquale. Maybe I should have said something."

Pat glanced over at Tudy. The little man had gotten even smaller. He was kneading the silly pink pillow like dough.

"No, Mamma," said Angela, going to their mother. "You didn't know."

Sadie tucked the handkerchief back into her apron and looked up at Angela. "Your father, he saw me. He tells me everything's okay, and to close the door." She shook her head. "I didn't know...I didn't know..."

His sister put her arms around their mother. "Ray was very angry at Lake Days. He was angry at my father. And he was angry at my brother, and angry at me," Angela said to Simon.

That was news to Pat, though it fit perfectly with Ray being a thief and a murderer. Especially, if--

"Do you know why?" Simon asked.

Angela shook her head.

Pat spoke up. "My father caught on to him. That's why."

His mother looked at him sharply. "Do you think Ray is still angry?" She asked, crossing herself.

Pat thought of the show tomorrow, and the thousands of people who would be there. But it was Simon who said what they all were thinking:

"God, I hope not."

Well, that had gone well, Simon thought on the way back to the town. Granted, he'd picked up some good information, but the whole experience had felt out of control. Like being on a freight train you couldn't steer or stop. And forget about changing tracks.

Simon had decided against staying for the fireworks show the Firenzes were going to stage in Pasquale's honor, but before he left, he sounded the family out about Pasquale's health. To a person, they'd sworn the old man was in good health. Meaning either it was true or Pasquale was hiding his condition.

Or, the Firenzes were very good liars.

Simon had also asked where Ray might hide. No one had any ideas, though everyone agreed it wouldn't be with family. There really wasn't any. Ray had no siblings, and Tudy was an only child, too. Tudy's wife had just one sister, living in Michigan.

Simon would check with her there, but he thought Ray was closer to home, possibly even on the factory grounds. Simon would need people to search.

Meanwhile, he'd best get hold of Longenecker and call off the Coast Guard search for Ray's body. He pulled out his cell phone, thinking of Tudy.

When Simon had voiced his suspicions of Ray, Tudy had seemed more angry than shocked.

It made Simon wonder how much Tudy knew.

Or Ray, for that matter.

148

EIGHTEEN

Jake put the color printout of the homepage for LB's Hot Video--or was it LB *Shot* Video?--on Luis's desk.

She didn't sign it. She figured she didn't have to.

She was right.

Jake had finished with the Five and Six and was packing up to go home when Luis knocked on the door of the editing suite.

The polite knock was the first sign that he was treading carefully. "Hi Jake, can I come in?"

"Sure--what's that you have with you?" Jake leaned back in her chair and stretched. It was kind of nice having the upper hand. Not that she knew what she was going to do with it.

Luis put the sheet on the console in front of her. "C'mon Jake, you know what it is. You put it on my desk."

He pulled over another chair and sat down heavily. He didn't even swivel it around and sit backwards on it. The kid really was feeling down. "What are you going to do?" he asked.

"I should give it to Gwen."

"She'll fire me." His chin was buried so deep in his chest she barely heard him.

"She should." Jake said it calmly, like she didn't care. And maybe she didn't. She was tired of protecting people. Or just plain tired.

Luis's head jerked up. Mom Jake hadn't answered the way he'd expected. "Listen, Jake, this job doesn't pay squat and--"

"Then you shouldn't have taken it." Amazing how easy it was to be logical when you didn't give a rat's butt. "How long have you been doing this?"

"Just the last few months, I--"

"Don't lie to me, Luis."

149

He sat and fidgeted in his chair like a little boy. "A little over two years."

"Good. Now I want you to tell me one more thing," Jake said. "I want you to tell me if you had anything to do with the Lake Days' explosion."

Jake didn't want to ask it, didn't even want to think it, but the question had been rattling around her subconscious since Saturday morning, and her conscious since yesterday.

Luis stared at her, trying to figure out what she was talking about. When it finally clicked, he jumped out of his chair. "No way, Jake. No *way*. Okay, I admit I wanted to shoot some freelance stuff out there. You know how much stock footage goes for. Lots of guys freelance."

It was an open secret in the industry that camera operators--who took cameras home with them so they could go right out if they got a call-- sometimes freelanced using station equipment. It drove the true freelancers, the ones who were paying for their own equipment, crazy.

"Freelancing with the station's equipment and tapes is bad enough," Jake said, "but you were doing it on company time, too."

"It wasn't like I wasn't doing my job out there..." He let it trail off. He looked like he was going to cry. "But, Jake, you can't believe that I would hurt someone, that I would go that far to get good footage. My God."

He started to sob into his hands.

And calm, disinterested Jake cried right along with him.

Simon was ready to make dinner whenever Jake walked in.

Boxed pasta to boil, jarred sauce to microwave, bakery bread to slice, and bagged salad to dress. The bottled wine was already opened, and he was drinking it. He set down his glass when he heard the Jaguar pull into the driveway and met Jake at the door.

They hugged and stayed that way for awhile. Finally Simon pulled back and kissed her on the forehead. "I had a shitty day."

"I was going to say the same thing," Jake said, looking up at him.

"Except you wouldn't say 'shitty,' would you? Did anyone ever tell you, you swear like a five-year-old?"

She laughed. "It's a part of a deal I struck with God awhile back. Though I have to say, today I might have gone as far as 'stinky,' and taken my chances with divine retribution."

"Then," Simon said, "you *are* upset. Let me get you some wine, and you can tell me all about it."

"Sounds good." She curled up on the couch as he poured. "Assuming you'll also tell me about yours."

Simon sat down and clinked glasses with her. "Deal. But first, I have a confession. I answered your phone a few minutes ago by reflex. I'm sorry."

A shadow crossed Jake's face. "Who was it?"

Simon held up his hands. "Don't worry, it wasn't your mom or anything. Just a hang-up, like last night. You get a lot of them?"

"More lately," Jake admitted. "Though sometimes I prefer those to the ones who *don't* hang up." She chewed the inside of her cheek, then caught a glimpse of his face and grinned. "You have your cop face on. So tell me about your day."

Simon smiled back, wondering what she wasn't telling him. "You go first."

"You want it chronologically, or by order of importance?" Jake asked.

"Chronologically," Simon said. "Importance can only be judged in retrospect."

"Ahh," Jake said, "a thought worthy of Confucius."

"And likely stolen from him, or from someone else. So let's see, chronologically. You swam first thing, right?"

"Yeah, and that was fine, except..." She set down her glass. "There's this guy who has been giving me the creeps."

"Why?" Simon asked, thinking this might be what was bothering her. "What's he doing?"

"He stares at me."

Simon kissed her on the nose. "Can't blame him for that."

"No, I mean all the time. And remember, I'm not exactly Pamela Anderson in a swimsuit."

"Only boob-wise. So how does he stare at you?"

"Like," Jake hesitated, "like he's thinking. He's staring at me, but he's thinking while he's staring. I don't know how else to explain it."

Simon thought she was doing a pretty good job. "Has he tried to talk to you? Does he talk to anyone else?"

"No. Just walks in and gets into the lane next to me, if it's open. The thing that really spooked me is that yesterday I saw him leave as I was coming in. Then the next thing I know, he's swimming next to me."

Simon didn't like the sound of that. "He came *back*? Are you sure it was him leaving?"

"I have to admit, I didn't recognize him myself. Somebody else--another swimmer who was in the lobby--pointed him out." Jake seemed embarrassed. "I usually see him wet. I mean, swimming, so I didn't even know the color of his hair. I could probably identify his feet better than I could his face."

"Actually," Simon said, "a walk is one trait that's tough for most people to disguise."

"Maybe, but it seems to me that people walk differently when they're padding in barefoot to swim at a pool, than when they're walking down the street. Not that I ever watch him come in, anyway," she said, running a finger around the rim of her wine glass. "I honestly try not to look at this guy, because I can feel that he's looking at *me*. I don't want to make eye contact." She shook her head. "Sort of wimpy on my part, huh?"

"It's probably more instinctive than wimpy," Simon said. "You don't look an aggressive dog in the eye, because he takes it as a challenge. In a way, you're doing the same thing."

"I guess. Though it still makes him the alpha dog, and me subordinate." She picked up her wine glass.

The woman knew her pack mentality.

"Well," said Simon, "he's likely harmless, but have you talked to anyone about him?"

"A couple of other swimmers have noticed him watching me, but I haven't reported him to management, if that's what you mean."

"Maybe you should. They can keep an eye on him, or talk to him."

Jake shifted uncomfortably. "But, maybe I'm making too big a deal of it. And even if I'm not, this is still a free country. People can look at other people if they want."

And God bless America for that, Simon thought. "Okay, but if he keeps bothering you, let me know and I'll go beat him up, okay?"

"Yeah," Jake said, perking up. "That'll be good." She hesitated, then seemed about to say something and stopped again.

"Something else that's bothering you? Someone else I can beat up?" he prompted.

But she just smiled. "Nope. Your turn. What's going on in your world?"

Simon considered telling her about Pasquale's possible Alzheimer's and his brother Francesco's probable case. But that discussion might take a turn toward the explosion that killed Francesco's and Simon's investigation and-- much as Simon trusted Jake--he didn't feel like reopening the same can of worms Martha Malone had been sniffing around earlier. Especially after the scene he'd made with Jake about it.

So, instead, he told her about Ray's fingerprints on the cigarette lighter and the fiasco at Firenze's. Jake listened avidly. "Whoa, you win the 'bad day' competition. So we know Ray is alive?"

"Explains the Coast Guard not finding the body, doesn't it?"

Jake didn't answer, and Simon thought maybe he'd been too flippant. "I saw your friend Williams at the funeral," he tried. Yeah, that was *much* better.

She wrinkled her nose, apparently not sure what to make either of the abrupt change in subjects, or of Simon calling Williams her "friend." "Yeah, me, too. He wanted to know what I had told you."

"I didn't tell him that we'd talked. He must have just assumed. What did you say?"

Jake laughed. "I patted him patronizingly on the cheek and said I hadn't betrayed his confidence. Which I hadn't. I betrayed Pasquale's, if anyone's, and he's past caring."

The cheek-patting explained, Simon felt better. But Jake was looking a little worried. "You do have him spooked, though," she said.

"How do you know?"

"Because he implied that if you found anything hinky back when I was working for him, he'd involve me."

"Was that what he implied, or what you inferred?"

Jake tilted her head and studied him. "You have way too good a vocabulary, you know that?"

"For what? A cop?"

Jake turned red and opened her mouth to reply.

Simon waved it off. "No, don't answer that. As for Williams' implication or your inference, you don't have anything to worry about. Assuming you weren't involved."

Jake grimaced. "I wasn't, but I can't help thinking that I should have known what was going on. Or that maybe I knew in the back of my head, but didn't do anything because I had a thing for him back then."

"You had a 'thing' for Williams?" Even though he'd been thrown momentarily by the cheek-patting, Simon had trouble picturing what-you-see-is-what-you-get Jake falling for Mr. Suave.

"Surprised, huh?" Jake hung her head. "We actually dated for a couple of years, but not when I worked for him. Believe it or not, even though Bryan loves surrounding himself with all those pretty girls, he doesn't date 'in-house,' as he calls it."

"Wise, given he's the boss."

"Appropriate, even," Jake said, with a little smile. "But for Bryan it was more that it would be, in his words, "like shooting fish in a barrel." The hunt is what excites him. He only got interested in me when I was on-air at TV8. He likes dating reporters. Anchors are even better."

Simon couldn't remember if Jake had said she'd been an anchor, but he didn't want to admit that. "So what happened?"

"He dumped me when I got sick."

Simon searched for the just the right thing to say. "Titty man, huh?"

Jake laughed. "You're totally insensitive, you know that?" She leaned in and kissed him. "And darned if I don't find that refreshing."

NINETEEN

Jake needed to be at the lakefront by noon, so she crawled out from under Simon at nine-thirty. As she pulled on her swimsuit, she thought about the night before. She'd started to tell Simon about Dianne Aamot's call, but had caught herself just in time. Nothing like injecting the ex-wife into the conversation to ruin a relaxing evening.

Not that it had stopped them from bringing up psycho-swimmers, ex-lovers, and others stranger. But still, former spouses were a special category and uncharted territory for Jake. She grabbed her gym bag and turned.

Simon was sprawled on his back on the bed, Irish curled up between his legs. "Slut," Jake said to the dog affectionately, as she leaned over to give Simon a kiss.

"Where ya' going," he said, grabbing her hand.

"To the Y," she said. "I have just enough time to swim before I need to be at the production van at noon."

"The Y is open on the Fourth of July?"

Dang. Another one of those pesky holidays. She plunked herself down on the side of the bed. "You know I did this on Christmas Day, too."

"You wanted to swim on Christmas Day?" Simon pulled her down to lie next to him, dislodging Irish.

"Well, I'd already opened my presents," Jake said. Nothing like admitting you spent Christmas Day alone.

"I patched drywall and painted on Christmas Day," Simon said. "But that was after I went to church."

"You're right," Jake admitted. "I should have gone to church. *Then* I should have gone to swim."

"I sing in church," Simon said, staring up at the ceiling.

Jake patted his arm. "That's nice, dear. We should all sing in church, shouldn't we?"

Simon laughed. "No, I mean I sing in the church choir."

Jake sat up and looked at him. "Really?"

"That surprises you?"

"Well, no, I guess not." Jake said, settling back down.

"Liar."

"What voice are you?"

"Baritone."

"I'm a soprano."

"I know."

"How do you know?"

"I can tell from your speaking voice."

"Oh." It was an unsettling thought. Jake had always suspected she sounded like Minnie Mouse. "I used to sing in church, too."

"You don't anymore?"

"No."

Simon propped himself up on one elbow. "Well, why not?"

"I sort of...left. When I was sick."

"Isn't that when people start going to church? When things are bad?" He ran his finger gently down the side of her swimsuit. Going for that notch by her hip bone again, she hoped.

"I've always thought that was wrong. Like being a fair-weather fan."

"More like a foul-weather fan, but I get your point. You're saying people go running to God when times are tough, but ignore him the rest of the time."

"Exactly. I mean, do they think God's stupid and doesn't notice? Well, duh."

"Well, duh?" He was laughing at her. "But that still doesn't explain why you stopped going to church."

"My pastor and I had a falling out." She sat up and pulled her knees up to her chest. "I had a good friend, Linda, who went through treatment with me. She died."

Simon just waited.

"I needed to talk to someone about it, so I went to see my pastor. He said that God couldn't save everyone, but that I was faithful and had lots of people praying for me. That God was going to take care of me. I think he meant to be reassuring."

"And it wasn't?"

"Heck no. In my mind, he was saying that it was Linda's own fault that she died. That her faith wasn't strong enough, or her friends didn't pray hard enough. Like there was something she could have done, in order to stop dying.

"And it's not just church." Jake was on a rant. "The songs say 'faith can move mountains,' the books talk about 'the power of positive thinking.' We're taught that we are in control of our fate, that we can do anything if we just 'believe.'"

"You don't buy that?" Simon traced a line down the inside of her arm and down to her palm.

"Heck no," Jake said, flopping back down on her back and closing her eyes. "The first time you try to fly when you're five, you figure *that* one out."

She heard Simon snort. "Don't tell me you were one of those kids who tied a sheet around her shoulders and jumped off the roof thinking she was Superman."

"Please," Jake said, opening one eye to see his face hovering over hers. "It was a pillowcase, and I launched myself off a swing. Even at five I was a cynic."

Simon smiled. "Sometimes," he said, reaching down to cup her cheek, "people just die."

Jake cracked a smile. "See? That's all I really wanted to hear. Sort of a clergy-version of "shit happens."

"You said 'shit,' you know."

"I know," she said, kissing the palm of his hand. "You're a bad influence on me. We have to talk about that sometime."

"I know," Simon said, "but not now."

Simon and Jake stayed in bed awhile longer, then ate breakfast together and went their separate ways. Both of them would end up at Shore Park eventually, but Jake was going directly there and Simon was stopping by the office first.

Even though it was a holiday, ATF's office was fully staffed. Simon and Collins had agreed they not only needed their own agents on the fireworks grounds, but all the help they could muster from the police and sheriff's departments, as well. And even though the display was going to be fired from land this time, it was still considered a marine event. Longenecker and the Coast Guard would be down there patrolling the water, too.

Kathy wasn't at her desk when Simon came in, but Ed Collins was in his office.

Simon picked up his messages and then knocked on Collins' door. He held up one of the phone slips. "They found an extinguished campfire in the Firenzes' woods."

"Can they connect it to Guida?" Collins waved him in.

"Cigarette butts. Ray's brand."

"Let's hope they prove hazardous to his health."

Simon smiled at his boss's unexpected flash of humor. "Any luck with the subpoena of Williams' records?"

156

Collins shook his head. "We don't have enough to get one. Firenze's word, posthumous and second-hand, won't do."

Posthumous and first-hand would be even tougher, Simon thought. He glanced out Collins' window as he sat down. The day was sunny, with a bit of a haze out on the lake. He checked his watch. Two. "I haven't heard a weather forecast, have you?"

"Hoping for a rain-out?" Collins asked.

"I don't like the fact that Guida is still in the area." Angela's question yesterday had been a good one. Why hadn't Ray taken off? Simon didn't want to get the answer tonight, amidst a half-million people and two tons of explosives. The fireworks were going to be fired from what locals called the landfill, a man-made peninsula that formed the northern-most side of the breakwater. The idea was the area would be more easily accessible than the barges for law enforcement personnel. Admittedly, though, that would be true for Guida as well.

Kathy walked past the door and Collins hailed her. "Do you know whether they're predicting rain for tonight?"

Kathy shook her head. "Last I heard, it's supposed to be perfect."

Kathy was wearing white shorts and a red, white and blue T-shirt. She looked great. "You heading out?" Simon asked.

She nodded. "Ed said it was okay. All the agencies have been alerted, and they have photos and descriptions of Ray Guida. Is there anything else you need before I go?"

"Nah, go have a good time. You going to be working on the cardiologist's heart today?"

Her face changed and, just for a second, Simon thought she was going to cry. Then she flipped her light-switch of a smile back on. "Nope, Ned's with a patient. I have a date with the girls." She skipped off. Literally. Skipped.

Simon wasn't buying it. As he got up to follow her, Collins slipped his reading glasses on. "Get this guy," he said as Simon left.

"Oh, I'll get him," Simon muttered. "The sonofabitch burned down my house."

"Kath! Wait up!"

Damn, she'd almost made it. The elevator pinged and opened its doors. "Thanks for nothing," she told it, as the doors slid closed again and Simon reached her.

He stopped a little too close, like he did when he wanted to intimidate someone and stared down at her. Kathy, at 5'9", wasn't usually cowed by his height, but she could swear the eyes were lasering holes in the top of her head.

She stepped back and held up her hands in surrender. "Okay, okay, I give up. I'm not seeing Ned anymore. He was cheating on me with the mother of one of his patients. Now you know. Happy?"

Simon didn't look happy.

He looked surprised, like he'd gotten way more information than he'd wanted. It reminded her of the time he'd asked her what was wrong one too many times, and she'd explained menstrual cramps to him in explicit detail. With charts and graphs. Served him right.

And this served him right, too. Men always wanted things. Information. Success. Women. Whatever. Then when they got them, they decided they didn't want them anymore. She stifled the sob that rose in her throat.

Simon put his arm around her. "Aw, geez, Kath. I'm really sorry."

She sniffled.

"Isn't that unethical though?" Simon asked, after a moment. "To fool around with a patient like that?"

"A patient's mother--he's a pediatrician not a pedophile." Kathy backed away. "And, sure, maybe the bimbo can file a complaint when he turns around and dumps *her*. But is that supposed to make *me* feel better?"

Simon shrugged and spread his hands wide. "It would me," he confessed.

"You only think so now because you've never been cheated on."

Something flickered in Simon's eyes, and for a second Kathy thought he was going to tell her something. Like maybe he had been cheated on. That maybe old What's-her-name had--

"Sometimes, Kath," Simon was saying, "love and sex are two different things for guys."

Kathy rolled her eyes, but Simon kept rattling on. "No, really. Guys can be just plain stupid, and make a mistake--"

"This was not one mistake," Kathy exploded. "He says he loves her, and that he never--" Just in time, she shut up.

Happily, Simon finished the sentence in a different way than she would have. "If he didn't love you, then he's a fool." He kissed her lightly on top of the head, then pressed the down button for the elevator. "Now go set some sparklers on fire and pretend they're him."

The elevator arrived and Kathy stepped in, leaving Simon in the corridor. "They'll have to be really little sparklers," she muttered as the doors closed.

The sound of Simon laughing followed her all the way down to the ground floor.

TWENTY

July 4, 2001
20:18:45

It wasn't hot, not like the other night less than a week ago, but Jake was sweating bullets. The crew was jumpy, too, but more in an "anticipating the best, hoping for the worst" sort of way.

At least that's the way Jake saw it, as she went over the station's contingency plans, or the so-called "Operations Conditions." Unlike the normal Operations Conditions associated with a live event--things like, "If fireworks are canceled because of rain between 8:30 and 9, JIP NETWORK"--these had a more ominous ring:

"If major incident disrupts display, fireworks anchor desk by Eagleton. Cravens emergency personnel. Martin scene. Malone swing." "If grounds are evacuated between 8:30 and 9:30..."

And so on. That same mixture of pent-up anticipation and guilty dread blanketed the crowd. Only people who have never been touched by disaster could feel that way, Jake thought.

For herself, she couldn't throw off the sense of impending doom that had been growing all afternoon, like the ridge of fog out on the lake. The west wind was keeping the fog out there, but if the wind changed direction and came from the east, it would blow the fog in and ruin the show. Perhaps even cancel it.

That wouldn't bother Jake a bit, but Gwen and Bryan had been having conniptions all afternoon. A fog-out would result in a major loss of ad revenue for the station and make Refresh Yourself very unhappy. Especially because the fireworks couldn't be rescheduled. A circus was supposed to take over the park tomorrow. A three-ring circus.

Not that anyone would notice the difference. Jake and her crew had been running around all afternoon and evening: did the Five, did the Six, ate a quick dinner at seven, and now here they were. Waiting.

Twelve minutes to air time. Jake hadn't heard from Simon since she'd left him this morning, or from the other Aamot--Dianne--either. Jake was torn between a rising sense of relief and a sinking certainty that Dianne Aamot would show up during the broadcast itself, demanding to talk to her.

Jake spoke into the microphone. "Pete, how's the fog out there?" Poor Pete was running camera for Martha on the boat, an assignment Jake could only equate to a wild-life photographer filming a she-bear defending her young--though in Martha's case, it was her career she was protecting.

"Not bad enough," Pete said, grudgingly, "but I'm still praying."

The camera operator had been hoping for a last-minute reprieve. Right now, though there was a marine warning further out on the lake, he was stuck on the boat inside the breakwater. With Martha.

Camera Three was set up on the seawall, and the monitor showed the crowd streaming by. Jake found herself coming back to that monitor, like she was going to catch sight of Ray somehow. Amongst half a million people. Right. She moved to Pete and Callie on the set.

"Callie. Are you set?" She could see George being miked through Callie's camera lens.

"Yup, Jake, I--"

George interrupted. "Jake, excuse me, but are we still a go?"

"So far, George. How's the wind?" She could see the American flags behind the anchorman rippling.

"I think we'll be fine if it stays like this."

Neal piped in from the seat next to him. "I'm concerned about this rundown, Jake. Only eight minutes between breaks four and five?"

"I know, Neal, but we have a lot more spots than last week and we needed to get that last break in before--"

Jake cut herself off with the flick of a switch. Oops. It was the one lesson Bryan had taught her at Festivities that was worth the price of admission: If you need to hang up on someone, do it when *you're* talking, not them. *Gosh I'm sorry, were we disconnected?*

As far as Jake was concerned, the time to discuss the rundown was the production meeting, not five minutes before going on the air. Out of the blue, Neal had become a prima donna, or *don* in his case, and she didn't have the time or the patience right now.

"Dave, are you and Luis set?" Dave, who just five days ago was Luis's colleague, was his camera operator today. Jake still wasn't sure what she was going to do about Luis, but first things first. They needed to get through this show.

"Yeah, we're here, Jake," Dave answered, sounding none too pleased about it.

"Give me your shot."

The monitor came to life, showing Luis standing in front of a row of mortars, futzing with the earpiece in his ear. You could always tell if someone was new to live remotes, because he couldn't keep his hands off the earpiece. The darned thing felt like it was going to leap right out of your ear and dash itself to the ground. It wasn't, and Luis had probably explained that from behind the camera, to hundreds of people. No matter, here he was doing it himself.

"Luis. You doing okay?"

He looked up, startled. "Sure, Jake. Um...we're at the top, right?"

Jake checked her rundown. "Three and a half in. Right after the 'Only Show in Town' package."

"Roger." Luis was checking his script, one finger in his ear, but at least he was back to his old hammy radio lingo.

Jake shook her head and continued down her checklist.

Simon was monkeying with his earpiece, too. Damn thing felt like it was going to pop out. As he made his way through the crowd to the snow-fencing that divided the spectator space from the firing area, he took a good look around.

There were a couple dozen agents on the grounds, dressed casually to blend in. A woman throwing a Frisbee here, a couple on the seawall there. That homeless guy with a shopping cart over there.

Simon stopped to watch as the agent tried to steer the cart through the dense crowd and over the uneven grass. The shopping cart routine probably played better in downtown Chicago than in Liberty.

Besides the ATF presence, uniformed officers and sheriff's deputies also were circulating. All of them had Ray's photo and all of them had been told to watch for anything suspicious from Ray or anyone else. An impossible task in a crowd this size and this diverse--everyone looked like they had something to hide. In most cases it was illegal fireworks or spiked lemonade.

As he followed the fence line, Simon monitored the chatter on the radio and tallied the officers stationed along the way. When he reached a makeshift gate, an officer checked his ID and peeled back a section of the fencing so he could slip through. The breakwater was shaped like an arm bent at the elbow, with the Firenzes set up on the wrist.

Simon had just reached the armpit, which, appropriately, was a depression where neither his cell phone or radio worked.

He kept walking.

Jake checked the time on her console. 20:29:46. "Showtime, people, in ten, nine..."

George: *"Welcome to TV8's presentation of the Refresh Yourself Fourth. I'm George Eagleton and with me is Neal Cravens. Martha Malone is out on the Lake Mist, and she's lucky to be there because we're told that by boat is the only way to get here, Neal."*

Neal: *"That's right, George, the sheriff's department has closed the roads leading to Shore Park, because of crowding. . ."*

Speaking of crowding:

"Kate," Jake said to the floor director, "watch Neal's side, we have people pressing into the shot. Luis, stand by."

As Jake waited to give him his cue, she glanced back at the monitor for the seawall camera. Now, in addition to the hordes passing by in search of someplace to sit, there was another line heading the opposite way, toward the portable toilets. People waiting for porta-potties didn't make for good video.

"Camera Three, can you reset your shot? Try to keep the toilet lines out of it."

"I'm trying, but it keeps growing." The camera operator backed up and to the right a bit. Just as he was set again, a man walked into the shot and stopped.

Jake sighed. "Luis, in five, four, three..."

Pat Firenze was checking the connections on the squibs, the small electric igniters that would detonate the lift charges. Tonight's show was going to be fired electronically, so if the damn shells exploded in the mortars, it wouldn't much matter. None of them--not him, not Tudy, not Angela, not any of their guys--was going to be near enough to get hurt.

After making sure the squibs were secure in the lift charges, he straightened up. Beyond him, to the west, he could see TV8's camera, but he was leaving that all to Angela. This time, Pat wouldn't concern himself with anything but shooting the show, and shooting it safely.

After checking out his father's computer, Pat didn't know if Pasquale's death had destroyed the company or saved it. Or maybe something in between. But Pat had turned over what he'd found to Simon—let him decide. In the meantime, it was Pat's job to pick up the pieces and rebuild Firenze Fireworks.

Pat followed the black electrical wires from the squibs to the control board behind the barricade they'd erected. A half-inch of plywood didn't sound like much, but it was enough to protect them from flying debris.

Tudy came back from checking the far mortars. "We're good, kiddo. Can you give me a hand with Big Blue?"

The old man was looking better, probably because he was busying himself with fireworks the way Pat's mother busied herself with cooking.

"How about Security," Pat asked, as they walked toward the end of the finale. "Are those guys staying back?"

"Yeah, yeah, I told them. They said they don't want to be no closer than we want. Some'll stay here with us, and some out by the lake. I chased that camera guy out, too."

Pat nodded. They needed the security, but you had to make sure people didn't come clomping through, disconnecting wires. If Ray...

Tudy gestured toward the lake. "I'm worried about that fog, boy."

Pat looked. The haze was getting thicker as the light died, but it didn't seem to be moving inland toward them. "I don't know, it looks to me like it might stay put."

"Do we make the call, go or don't go?"

Pat was really hoping no one would have to make that call, he wanted to get this over with. "Bryan Williams. He's making the call."

"Yeah, like that *stonato* knows anything about fireworks or weather," Tudy said. "All he knows about is money."

He shook his head and stopped at the last mortar. "You just never can tell on this lake, your dad always said. The weather blows in, the weather blows out. You just say your prayers, and you light your fuse."

Amen to that, Pat thought. He and Tudy had dug in the mortar for the last shell--Big Blue, as Tudy called the shell Pat's mother had insisted they make as a tribute to his father--so all but a foot of the cardboard casing was safely below the ground. Despite Pat's misgivings about the shell, he figured the setup was as safe as fireworks and explosives could ever be.

Which wasn't all that safe.

"C'mon, boy," Tudy said, standing above the sixteen-inch shell. "Let's load this."

And, together, they lowered Pasquale Firenze's shell into the ground.

Angela was running late, but she was very nearly finished. Using the hood of her car as her table, and a blanket as the tablecloth so nothing would get dirty, she carefully rolled a sheet of white stationery and tied a blue ribbon around it. Fastening the other end of the ribbon to the neck of the wine bottle, she ran the edge of a nail file down the length of the ribbon to curl it, and she was done.

Angela checked her watch. She was due soon at TV8 to talk about her father. Or so they wanted her to believe. But Angela was no fool. She knew that once she got there, that Neal Cravens would ask her about Ray over and over again, until she was forced to leave.

That was why she'd written the tribute to her father and attached it to the wine bottle. So they could read it for her if she ran out of time.

She had made the wine with her own hands, and it was her father's favorite until he had decided the red would be better for his health. Angela had helped her father in that, as she had in everything else. She'd kept his secret until now, when it was no longer necessary to keep.

Angela stepped back from the hood of the car and surveyed her work. Perfect. Along with the words on the paper and the shell Pat and Tudy would fire, it would be a fitting memorial to Pasquale Firenze.

Angela tucked the bottle into her bag, careful not to crush the note. Then she folded up the blanket and placed it neatly in the trunk, before setting out for the TV8 stage.

As she went, she pictured the display in her mind. The finale would go, all noise and white light. The strobes so rapid and so bright, the salutes so loud and so long, that the people would be stunned into silence.

And before they could catch their breath, before they could start clapping and cheering, there would be one final shell.

A blue shell, a blue so pure and so brilliant, it would be like the heavens had opened up above them.

The trek from the armpit to the wrist had taken Simon longer than he'd expected. Right above the elbow, his radio had kicked back in.

The sun had set so Simon was taking the long way around, following the seawall, so he wouldn't trip over the firing wires in the dark. He had no intention of either breaking his neck or dislodging something essential to the show.

The Firenze workers didn't have the same qualms, they were crossing and re-crossing the wires as they made final adjustments.

Simon saw Angela coming his way, and looked around uncomfortably for an emergency exit. None was forthcoming, other than the one over the seawall into the lake. He'd have to stop and talk to her.

"Simon, is everything all right?" Angela asked, her eyes scanning his face.

"Fine," he assured her. "I just need to check in with Pat and Tudy."

"You must hurry," she said, laying a hand on his arm. "The show will start very soon. And I must hurry, too. I am to be on TV8 in less than twenty minutes." She looked out over the rapidly darkening park. "Jake said to come to the stage, but I can't quite..."

"See the lights on the bluff?" Simon pointed, turning away from her as he did so. "Head for them."

Angela thanked him and started off in the direction he'd indicated. Simon, relieved the conversation hadn't needed to go beyond the mundane, to Ray and all the rest of it, had already begun walking when he heard her call his name.

He turned back to her.

Her eyes were big and dark and, Simon thought, hopeful. "I would like to talk to you tonight." He started to shake his head no, and she just said, "Please?" and waited.

"Angela, I--"

"It's about my father and about Ray. He knows." The last words were barely a whisper.

Before Simon could respond, Angela looked at her watch. "I need to be back here at ten o'clock for my father's shell. Please meet me where the snow fencing joins the seawall."

She squeezed his hand, and then she was gone, picking her way expertly over the wires as she ran.

Simon continued in the opposite direction, taking in the thick black cables that led to the truck-size generator dead ahead. It would be ridiculously easy disrupt the electronically fired show. Disconnect the right cable--the equivalent of pulling a plug out of an economy-sized outlet--and everything would stop.

But if that was all Ray Guida had in mind, Simon wouldn't be that worried. The fact was, though, Simon didn't know what Ray had in mind.

Nor Angela, for that matter.

George: *"We are less than twenty minutes away from the start of these fireworks..."*

Forty minutes into the broadcast, and Jake was still having trouble concentrating. She was directing on autopilot, following the rundown and calling shots more out of habit than anything else.

Most of her attention--her conscious attention--was on the monitors. The Ray watch. Would he show up in the porta-potty line, or in Callie's lens, or in Dave's, or out on the boat with Pete? Would he sneak up behind the backs of the police and the ATF and in front of the camera lens? Maybe remove a lift charge? Or light a fuse? Nonsensical as it was, she kept watching and waiting.

She picked up her cup of coffee and took a sip. Stone cold, perfect for clearing her head. It was almost fireworks time and she needed to get back into the game.

She set the coffee down, and thumbed the switch on the radio, thinking about Luis. "Dave?"

"Yeah, Jake?"

"Assuming we have time, we're going to be coming back to you and Luis just before the first shell. Make sure he's prepared okay?"

"Hey, that wasn't my fault--" Dave protested.

"I know. Just do me a favor, and keep an eye on him."

Jake had believed Luis yesterday, when he'd sworn he had nothing to do with Pasquale's death, she really had. But tonight, with the fog crouching out on the lake, and the crowd restless and expectant on the shore, anything seemed possible.

They were coming out of the break. Jake checked her rundown. Next up was an interview with the father of the family Neal had interviewed last Friday. Twice. And here he was back for more. These people were gluttons for punishment. Or publicity.

Jake could hear Callie give the countdown, and then Neal, George and Mr. Jenson were on-camera.

Dang.

Mr. Jenson. And the blonde guy Jake had seen coming in and going out of the Y. And the Croc.

All the same person.

Now what were the chances of that?

Luis was standing just inside the restricted firing area, where the line of fencing met the lake.

"So what do you think, Dave? That first one went pretty good, huh?"

Dave, who was on his radio, just grunted at Luis and walked away.

Fame. It was a lonely place to be.

They were inside the firing area, though the Firenzes had suggested that Luis "stay the hell away from us." Which he'd do for the time being at least. Personally, Luis thought his taped package on the explosion had been pretty good. His live intro had been a little rough, but--

"Jake says to try to get it right this time," Dave said, coming back to where Luis stood near the fence. "Pasquale Firenze is the dead one. Pat Firenze is the son. He's still alive. So far. Tudy's the father of the missing guy, whose name is *Ray*, by the way."

This time it was Luis who waved Dave off and walked away. It wasn't like it was Luis's fault: everybody's name sounded the same. Pasquale, Pat, Ray, Tudy. If you didn't want that kind of confusion, you should name your kid something totally different. Like Ferdinand or something.

But Luis knew what was really eating Dave. He was jealous, and who could blame him? Luis would be jealous, too, if it was Dave reporting and Luis was *his* camera operator.

Yeah, like that would ever happen. Dave didn't have the drive, or the imagination. Case in point: the minute the show started, Luis was heading for the mortars, no matter what the Firenzes said.

And if Dave didn't want to go?

Tough. Luis would take the camera himself. He'd reported and shot tape simultaneously on the barge and that had worked out just fine. Even Jake had said so.

Jake. Luis wasn't sure what the deal with Jake was. She wasn't talking to him any more than she had to, but it wasn't an "I'm mad at you" not-talking.

It was more an "I'm disappointed in you" kind of not-talking. He didn't know if she'd told Gwen yet. And he didn't know if she intended to.

Jake was acting like he stole money or something. If he stole anything, it was what was already his. His "intellectual property," like they say.

So what if he used TV8's equipment? It was the man behind it that mattered. The camera was like a paintbrush and the film was the paint, but he, Luis, was the master painter.

Luis thought about that, wandering down the line of fencing. He had something here, he was sure of it. Something that even Jake and Gwen could understand.

Those little kids on the other side of the fence were watching him, like he was somebody, because he *was* somebody. He was a reporter and an artist, and TV8 no more owned him and his film than Glidden owned the Mona Lisa because Leonardo DiCaprio used their paint.

"Mr. Martin?"

He looked up and saw a kid of about six trying to pass a Lake Days t-shirt and a Sharpie over the fence. "Can I have your autograph?

Now *that* was more like it.

TWENTY-ONE

George: *"Welcome back to the Refresh Yourself Fourth."*

Neal: *"In just a few minutes, we'll be joined by Angela Firenze Guida. As we've reported, Ms. Firenze Guida is the daughter of Pasquale Firenze, who was killed in Friday's explosion."*

George: *"She is also the wife of Ray Guida, who is being sought for questioning in that blast. She's agreed to talk with us about her father and the salute planned at the end of this show, but before that..."*

The papers in front of George blew off the desk. Jake set aside her Croc-questions and her Luis-suspicions for the time being and watched as George peered calmly into the camera. "As you can see, the wind is changing direction a bit here, but as long as the--"

"Shit, Jake, the fog is really getting bad out here." Pete was calling from the boat, and this time he sounded more scared than anxious to get away from Martha. "The Coast Guard has posted a small craft warning. We're going to have to come in."

Shoot. Or maybe <u>not</u> shoot. Maybe the fireworks would be called off. Though postponing at this point might be worse than seeing the thing through tonight. One way or the other, Jake needed to get Pete and Martha safely off the lake. "Get out of there now, Pete."

Behind the anchors, Jake could just make out the running lights as the Coast Guard attempted to warn boaters. Fog horns sounded in the distance.

A wind gust hit the side of the truck, rocking it, and Jake picked up the phone, keeping one eye on the monitor while George and Neal made windblown happy talk and waited for the first salute or, alternatively, the fog.

"Ready Camera Six, take Camera Six." Then, to her tech director: "Get me Brett."

Brett Varich was the station's chief meteorologist. Archie had him on the line in seconds. "Brett, it's Jake. What's your best guess on the fog?"

"The wind is shifting, Jake, and coming off the lake. I'm afraid you're in for some fog."

Nuts. "Okay, Brett. Thanks."

As she hung up the phone there was a perfunctory tap on the door and a blonde woman--a very pretty blonde woman, from what Jake could see of her--stuck her head in the door. "Wendy Jacobus? I'm Dianne Aamot." She climbed in, ignoring Archie, whose mouth was hanging open.

Not only was Simon's ex-wife beautiful, she was very tall. And well-endowed. If this was what Simon had co-habitated with, what in the world did he want with scrawny little Jake?

Scrawny little Jake didn't have time to think about it, because as she took her hand off the phone, it rang. Bryan: "Jake what's it look like there? Are your cameras fogged in?"

Jake dragged her eyes away from Dianne Aamot, and checked the monitors. The stage cameras on the bluff were clear, so was the camera on the Waverly. The lower cameras--Dave's, the seawall and the breakwater-- were all showing fog.

She told Bryan as much, and he hung up. Without even a goodbye.

"I'm terribly sorry I'm late," Dianne Aamot was saying, "but the police wouldn't let me through."

Jake's attention was diverted by Callie's shot, which was a bit off. The crowd was pressing in again. "Kate, get those people back," she radioed to her floor director at the stage. Then to Archie, who was still standing and staring? "Ready, Camera Two, Archie?"

He nodded and turned back to the console, while Jake returned to her guest. "I'm afraid I'm not going to be able to chat right now," she said, politely but firmly.

Dianne Aamot, to her credit, just nodded. "I understand completely. I just wanted to see...meet you, and," she pulled a business card out of her purse, "if you'll give me a call sometime, we can talk about the liability on the microwave van."

Jake blanched and Dianne Aamot saw it. "Don't worry, you're not personally liable, we just have issues to deal with concerning the insurance carrier."

Kate's voice came back over the radio. "Jake, we've got a worse problem than the crowd. Angela Firenze's not here."

Geez, you can stop worrying about one thing for a second, and then another gets dumped in your lap. "What do you mean, she's not there? She's supposed to be on camera in less than ten minutes."

"Sorry, Jake. There was a woman standing just inside the rope--long dark hair, battery-powered fireworks earrings--I thought it was her. It wasn't."

No kidding. Angela Firenze wouldn't be caught dead in battery-operated fireworks earrings. "You have anybody to go looking?"

Callie's camera started to swing back away from the crowd and toward Neal, as Kate crossed in front to move the crowd back. "No, and the fog is rolling in below us and these people are getting nuts. Are we still a go for the fireworks?"

"I'm not sure. Listen, I'm sending Archie over to help find Angela. Tell George and Neal to fill, and I'll see what I can do."

She turned to Archie, who had gone back to ogling Dianne. "Take Camera Two, Archie, and then I hate to ask you to be a gopher, but..."

Her tech director pulled his headset off. "Just call me a friend you can count on."

Dianne Aamot went to follow him. "I'll get out of your way," she said, extending her hand to Jake. Dianne held on just a second too long, studying Jake. If Jake had any doubt the "liability discussion" was an excuse to meet-- or as Dianne put it, "see"--Jake, she didn't anymore.

"Great," Jake said, taking her hand back. "I'll give you a call. Tomorrow, probably."

"Great," Dianne echoed, and climbed out. She stopped outside the door, seeming undecided about something, her face half in shadow and half in the light of the production van. "If that's Angela Firenze you're looking for--"

Jake, who was already back scanning the monitors, looked up, "Yes?" she said, trying to hurry the woman along.

"You might want to check my ex-husband's bed. At least," she leaned forward into the van, so now she was completely in the light, "that's where she was the last time I saw her."

If Simon didn't know better, he would think he'd stumbled on a family reunion instead of a firing site.

Kids were being chased by other kids, Frisbees and footballs were flying in all directions, and people--young, old, and everything in between--were sitting at picnic tables with plates of food in front of them.

All the activity ceased as Simon approached. At first he thought he was the cause, but then he saw the man in blue jeans, dark shirt, and white clerical collar, head bowed and hands folded, at the end of a long table. Simon recognized him from Pasquale's funeral.

"We ask your blessing on this show tonight, Lord. On the workers who fire the display, and on the spectators who enjoy it. We ask that you keep everyone safe in your hand and," the young priest lifted his head and surveyed the fog that was billowing in around them, "we ask that you take a nice big breath and blow this damn fog out of here."

Everyone laughed and calls of "Amen, Father Bill!" came from the crowd. Father Bill sobered again. "One special note tonight, Lord. We lost two men last week--one for certain, and one for whom we are trying to hold out hope. We ask that you bless the soul of Pasquale Firenze, and let this show be, as he would say, the show of his life."

Another chorus of "Amen" followed, and the group seated at the long table stood. It was the fireworks crew, including Tudy, and they were going to work. Father Bill joined them as they headed toward cars parked near the fence. He apparently was one of the crew.

"Simon."

Simon hadn't seen Pat come up. He held a radio in his hand.

"Where's everyone going?" Simon asked, as one after another, the crew got into cars and drove them in a slow caravan around the firing area. If they'd been in the Wild West, Simon would say they were circling the wagons.

"We're ringing the firing area, so we can use the headlights for light. If something happens in this fuckin' fog..." Pat shook the radio at the sky. "They'll just park them and then come back here to the firing console."

Sure enough, each car was turning so its headlights pointed inward toward the mortars and then stopping. It was like synchronized swimming, only with cars. And drier.

Simon was already losing some of the headlights in the fog. "You're really going to shoot?"

Pat shook the radio again. "Williams says it's a go. And the mayor says it's Williams' call."

Simon looked back toward the park where the bulk of the spectators sat. From this distance Shore Park looked like a Jell-o parfait. The cream center layer was the shelf of thickening fog that started about ten feet off the ground and rose almost to the top of the bluff, where it was clear again.

Which was probably the impetus for the guy trying to climb the bluff in his Chevy Blazer.

"Jesus," said Pat, following Simon's gaze.

The Blazer had made it nearly halfway up the side of the bluff, apparently trying to get itself a better view. There was no road and it was a nearly vertical incline, but you can't blame a drunk for trying. As they watched, the SUV backslid. The guy downshifted and gunned the motor. The truck leapt forward and disappeared into the fog shelf. Damned if he wasn't going to make it, Simon thought.

Or not.

The spinning of invisible tires heralded the Blazer's return to earth, as it slipped back down out of the fog bank and then flipped, rolling ever so slowly back down.

The crowd cheered.

"And people say *we're* nuts," Pat muttered.

Dianne Aamot must be a heck of a lawyer, Jake thought. Look at the amount of damage she'd been able to inflict in a short time.

But...Simon and Angela?

Could be, Jake admitted to herself. Jake had even gotten vibes to that effect the night she and Simon had dinner with the Firenzes. But was Dianne saying she'd caught them in the act and that's why the marriage had ended?

If so, it was a very different story than the one Simon had told. But then again, in Jake's experience nothing was ever black and white, just a whole lot of gray.

Like the fog.

On the monitor, George pointed down toward where the lake had been. High on the bluff where the anchors sat, the sky was still clear. Problem was, most of the crowd was below fog level and would never see the show. Might make them a tad miffed.

Jake forced herself to switch gears mentally and then switched frequencies, literally, to the one the Firenzes' radios were set to. One thing they'd learned from the Lake Days disaster was to make sure the radios were compatible.

"TV8 to Pat Firenze. Pat are you there?"

"Pat Firenze here."

"Pat, this is Jake at TV8. What's going on--are you canceling?"

Pat growled, or at least it sounded like a growl over the radio. "Williams says we're a go."

No wonder Pat was growling. "Up here on the bluff, the stars are out," Jake said. "But it looks to me like dense fog is starting to roll in down there."

"You got that right."

"I know the shells will clear the fog so we'll be fine for TV, but there are half a million people in the park who aren't going to be able to see anything."

"No shit," Pat said. "But all Williams cares about is the TV audience. I have to go."

Typical Bryan. He wasn't going to be trapped with 500,000 angry people. He probably was watching the show from someplace cushy and climate-controlled, and with its own bathroom. Sort of like Jake. She looked through the windshield at the TV8 porta-potty. It was swaying in the wind.

She shook her head and flipped the switch on the radio. "Looks like we're a go for the fireworks, Gang. Two, Three, and Dave, you're going to be fogged in, but I want people shots from you. And Luis, we're going to go to you for crowd reaction after the show. They're bound to be upset." Or worse. "Waverly, I'll need a wide shot from you the whole time."

A chorus of "gotchas" answered, but not a single "roger." To Jake's surprise, she missed them. She'd give anything to have Luis back on the right side of the camera. She just wasn't sure which side that would be, given his history.

The van door opened and Jake turned, thinking Archie was back. "Did you--"

But it wasn't her technical director. It was Jenson. Mr. Jenson. Croc Jenson. Jake didn't even know his first name, and here he was in her production van.

"Are you alone?"

No, there are seven dwarfs in the back hiding, Jake thought. What she said, though, was, "What do you want?"

Jenson came in and closed the door behind him. "I'm sorry," he started, coming towards her.

Yikes. Jake was sorry, too, for just about anything the guy wanted her to be sorry for. She flicked the radio transmitter on. "Stay where you are. I'm calling for help."

"No, please, don't. I just want to talk to you."

Norman Bates wanted to talk, too. "You've been watching me all week, and now you want to talk?"

A salute sounded--the signal the show was just minutes away. If getting raped or slaughtered in the production van wasn't bad enough, she was about to miss her cue.

"I've been a little crazy..." Jenson started.

No kidding, Jake thought. Then there was a knock at the door.

Thank heaven, this *had* to be Archie. But of course, it wasn't Archie. Why would he knock? It was Angela. The genuine Angela Firenze. Jake knew that because she wasn't wearing battery-powered fireworks earrings. And, contrary to what Dianne Aamot had said, Simon wasn't attached to her.

"I'm sorry," Angela started.

Everyone's sorry, Jake thought. But she was awfully glad to see Angela, even after what Dianne Aamot had told her.

Jenson turned red and backed out of the door Angela was still holding. "I'll catch up with you later," he said to Jake, and was gone.

Jake's heart was still thumping as Angela crinkled her nose and clutched her Coach Hamptons Carryall to her chest. "That man was looking at my breasts," she said, glancing at Jake's chest and then away.

"I noticed that," Jake said, shaking her head. "Hang on a second, we're coming in from break."

Now Archie burst through the door. "Jake, are you okay? The radio--"

"I am now, Archie, thanks. Can you get Angela over to the stage?"

"You bet," Archie said, surveying yet another treat for the eyes, fortuitously dropped in his lap. "We're out of here."

Angela stopped at the door. "Do you know how long the interview will be?" she asked.

"Just five minutes, though we'd love to have you stay for the entire display," Jake said, knowing the anchors would thank her for giving them something to say besides, "Wow! Look at that one!"

But Angela was apologizing. "I'm sorry, but I must be with Simon at the seawall at nine-fifty, and then with my brother at ten."

That would be one heck of a "quickie," if Jake were to believe Dianne Aamot. Ten minutes, not counting travel time. "Don't worry," she assured Angela, and then Archie eagerly whisked her off.

"Ready Camera One," Jake said, taking a deep breath to calm down. "Take Camera One. Ready Camera Six."

When nothing happened, she realized she would have to "take" Camera One herself, since she'd just sent her technical director off. Duh.

"Jake, it's Pete."

"Pete, aren't you in yet?" She took Camera One as she spoke.

"We just tied up at the old ferry dock, but you're not going to believe what we found."

"Hang on, Pete. Ready Camera Six." On second thought, switching cameras was pretty darn easy when you only had two of them. She could go to a crowd shot, but the view from Camera Three was looking mighty ugly right now. Miffed didn't even come close to what the fogged-in spectators would be feeling once the display started. Jake hoped her crew was all right down there. "Okay, now. What won't I believe?"

"A body," Pete shouted into the phone. "We found a body tangled up on the pilings of the dock. It looks like it's been in the water for awhile."

Jake froze.

"The Coast Guard isn't saying, but it has to be Ray Guida."

The name reverberated though the van, and Jake was reminded of Doug in the fire truck with the bell pealing overhead. Suddenly her head felt like the clanger inside that bell chamber. Thank God Angela had been out of here when Pete called.

Jake turned and looked at the preview monitor, where the widow was being miked.

Neal: *"Despite that fog, the show is still a go in less than...let's see, two minutes now."*

George: *"I understand that the blue stars in the last shell of the night were actually made by your father."*

Angela: *"That's correct. Which is the reason my brother and my mother and I wanted to use them. The 'last shell of the night,' as you call it, will also be my father's final shell. His final work of art."*

"We would not even be having this discussion if you were still 'Wendy Jacobs,' reporter, and not this 'Jake' person you've become," Martha shouted into her microphone.

Jake's voice filtered back through Martha's earpiece. She sounded uncharacteristically sarcastic. "That's right, Martha. I lost my breasts, but grew a conscience. Not a bad trade-off, maybe you should try it."

"I'm very happy with my new implants, you little bitch," Martha screamed, and then realized that the entire crew could hear their conversation.

"Now you listen to me," she said, lowering her voice. "This is what we're going to do. Pete is getting tape right now, and I'm going over to get ready to do a stand-up. You are *not* going to report this to your friend at the ATF--or anybody else, for that matter--until we break the story on the air. You are going to tell George and Neal and then have them turn it over to me. Do you hear me? Jake?"

But all Martha heard was static.

Jake was fuming. She was beyond fuming.

In order to keep her job, she needed to tell George or Neal in his earpiece about Ray's body, with Angela still there for a reaction. That smacked of Jerry Springer to Jake.

If she could just hold off another sixty-five seconds, Angela would be gone. And in the meantime, Jake could call Simon. She picked up her cell phone, still watching the monitor.

"I know we're very close to the start of the show now," Angela was saying, "and I must go to help my brother." She pulled her handbag up onto the table, where it clunked loudly on the audio. The clunk reminded Jake of something and she hesitated, setting down the phone.

"But first," Angela continued, "I'd like to give you something."

As Callie widened the shot, Jake saw that Angela was pulling a bottle from the handbag.

"Champagne?" Neal asked. "To celebrate your father's life?"

"Almost," Angela smiled at him, and Jake could see how Simon could have been smitten. "This is the white wine I make from the grapes that we grow at home. It is my father's favorite wine. And this," she pointed to a scroll of paper attached with a curly ribbon, "this is a tribute to my father that I've written. I'd very much like it, if you would toast him and read the tribute as we fire his final shell."

Jake had the cell again and was punching up Simon's number. First she'd tell him, then--

"Jake!" The voice was Martha's. "Tell George and Neal about the body or patch me through and I will. Now."

Nuts. Either way, one of the anchors would have to be told, and Jake knew which one of them she could trust to exercise some restraint.

"George," Jake said softly into his earpiece, simultaneously pushing "send" on her cell phone. "Pete just called in. A body has been found at the dock. We need to go live to Martha."

As Jake listened to Simon's cell phone ring, she watched George's face go blank. Neal was continuing to talk with Angela, and while they spoke, Jake saw George's expression change from indecision to resolve.

"Excuse me, Neal," George calmly cut in, "but we have breaking news. Apparently, a body has been recovered from Lake Michigan."

The camera was focused on George's face alone now, but the sound of a chair being pushed back on the plywood stage could be heard.

"Callie, go wide," Jake said, feeling badly for Angela, but at the same time needing to look, like when you pass a car wreck on the highway. Funny, having been a car wreck herself, Jake thought she was above that kind of thing.

The monitor showed a white-faced Angela, pulling off the lapel mic and backing away from the anchor desk. "I'm sorry, I'm sorry..." she was saying as she stood up, still clutching the green bottle of wine. Then she disappeared from the shot, leaving her handbag behind.

And that's when Jake put it all together.

She knew how Simon's place had been fire-bombed and by whom.

And maybe even why.

Simon's phone continued to ring.

Simon was walking back from the firing area, toward the seawall, where he was to meet Angela.

His radio wasn't working again, and he was moving fast to get past what he was starting to think of as "The Twilight Zone." Nothing like not being able to communicate in the age of communication, to make a man uneasy.

Except maybe certain women.

Angela was walking toward him. She was early, which figured.

Their affair had been a huge mistake on his part.

Simon could try to minimize it by pointing out it had lasted less than a week. He could even try to justify it by saying that he and Dianne were already separated at the time, physically if not legally...though that sure wasn't the way Dianne had acted when she'd come by the house to pick up some things, and found Angela there.

But Simon's marital status aside, Angela *was* married and Simon was on the job. He should have known better. He *did* know better.

Now, according to Angela, "Ray knows." Presumably about the affair. Which might explain why he had burned down Simon's house--an overreaction if there ever was one--in order to get back the Firenzes' financial records. Maybe it was Ray's way of making sure that Simon and Ray's "widow" didn't live happily ever after when he vanished.

No chance of that.

Angela was perfect, Simon thought as she came toward him, nearly running, with a bottle in her hand. That seemed dangerous, but maybe if your family handles explosives, you don't sweat the lesser hazards, like running with scissors or glass containers.

Overhead, the fireworks display was in full swing. The shells were passing up through the fog bank before breaking, so the crowd in the park below could see nothing but intense flashes of light reflecting on the fog above, like something out of CLOSE ENCOUNTERS OF THE THIRD KIND. Angela was close enough now for Simon to see her face during those flashes.

Yes, Angela was perfect. As exquisite in her darkly exotic good looks as Dianne was in her own porcelain-skinned way.

But Simon had learned not to trust perfection.

Dianne had left him—first in heart and in mind, and then in body. And Angela?

Angela, Simon had found, was a bit of a psycho.

If the meatballs a woman put in her soup had to be flawless, what did she require of the man in her life? Simon had pitied Ray after one rendezvous, but he'd also been fascinated by those eyes, by that body.

It had been worth it for that one week, to put up with her scrunching up her nose when she picked up the smell of smoke that always seemed to cling to him. Or her bringing him Italian cologne to cover the scent. But when she'd been critical of his house and suggested he put Irish outside anytime she was there...well, that was the beginning of the end. The confrontation with Dianne had just hastened it. Along with Angela's distaste for his soft-porn collection.

"Oh, Simon!" Angela said, throwing her arms around him when she reached him and, in the process, thunking him in the back with the bottle in her hand. "Please, please tell me that you still love me. That you will always love me, not matter what."

Psycho, like he said.

As Simon disengaged himself, his radio crackled.

Jake flipped her phone closed. She still wasn't getting through on Simon's cell, though she had managed to contact the Sheriff's Command Center on the grounds to report what the Lake Mist had found.

"I don't care what Neal says, Archie," she to her tech director. "I want to know the contents of that note before the last shell goes off. You understand me?"

Archie assured her he would do her best, and got back on the radio, but Jake wondered whether anything short of walking over and ripping the thing out of Neal's hand on-camera would be enough to keep him from "sharing" it with the audience at the most dramatic moment.

Having "shared" the close-up of Pasquale's death with the audience without screening it, Jake didn't want any more surprises.

The Coast Guard had already cordoned off the dock where Ray's body was, so Martha was in camera-hog heaven with her exclusive. Jake went to Pete live, and then checked the time. 9:41. Simon would be meeting Angela in less than ten minutes.

And Angela was a murderer.

How else could you explain what Martha was now reporting? That the side of Ray Guida's head had been bashed in, and around his waist was a rope with the remnants of a sandbag still attached to the end of it.

The canvas bag probably ripped when Ray was dumped into the water. When enough sand had sloshed out from the motion of the water, the body-- no longer weighted down--had surfaced.

And since Angela had been the only person on the barge with Ray, it wasn't much of a leap to presume he hadn't bashed his own head in.

But there was more: After dinner on Sunday night, Angela's Coach bag had slipped off her shoulder and clunked to the ground when she knelt down to pet Lugosi. Jake had noticed it because Angela and the dog made such an incongruous picture.

Angela had used that same bag tonight to carry the bottle of Pasquale's white "Tribute" wine to the stage. Which meant the Carry-all certainly would have been big enough to conceal an empty bottle of the identical wine on Sunday night.

The recycled champagne bottle--made of thick green glass to withstand the pressure of effervescence--would have been perfect for yet another recycling. To make the Molotov cocktail that had destroyed Simon's house.

Waste not, want not.

Jake would have laughed, if she hadn't been so worried about Simon. If she couldn't get hold of him, could anyone else? Did he even know Ray's body had been found?

She picked up the cell phone, started to dial his number again, and then changed her mind and punched in the Command Center number instead.

She was put on hold.

She checked the clock again: 9:45.

What was she going to do? She couldn't leave the van, or Gwen would certainly have cause for firing her. Heck, Gwen already had cause, but even *Jake* would fire Jake if she abandoned her post now.

Yet in five minutes, Simon would be meeting a woman who had not only murdered her husband and likely her own father, but had done it in a way that brought Simon back into her orbit.

It was brilliant, when you thought about it. Even when Jake's involvement with Simon had thrown a wrench in Angela's plans, she had managed to make double lemonade out of life's lemons: punishing Simon by firebombing his house, while at the same time implicating Ray by leaving his lighter at the scene.

A woman scorned. And ingenious. Not to mention nuts.

And Jake was still on hold.

"Oh, fuck it," Jake said into the phone, and snapped it shut.

Archie turned from the console, his mouth dropping open.

"You're in charge," Jake told him, and slammed out of the van.

The "Star Spangled Banner" was playing on the loudspeakers, but Simon and everyone else in the park had to take the "bombs bursting in air" on faith. They sure couldn't see them. The thunder of the salutes was deafening, though, amplified by the thickening fog.

So deafening, Simon had to reposition his earpiece to be sure what was coming across into his ear was mere static and not words.

"Your radio is not working?" Angela asked.

He shook his head irritably. "I need to be closer to the seawall to get a signal. This conversation will have to wait."

Simon turned and walked away, but Angela trailed after him. "It can't wait," she pleaded.

Simon quickened his pace, but so did Angela. "My father was sick, Simon."

He'd reached the seawall and now he turned, frustrated. "I know that, Angela, you can stop being a drama queen. What I don't know is why you didn't tell me. Why I had to piece it together from what Pat found on Pasquale's computer."

Angela looked down, her dark hair covering her face. "He made me promise. The dementia, it happened so gradually. My father tried everything to make it better. First, simple things, like vitamins and herbs. Then he thought he caught it from aluminum and so he took my mother's pans and gave her cast iron to cook in. He changed deodorants. Started sending money to people to find cures."

She put her hand out to him. "But there *is* no cure, Simon. And he was so frightened. Try to understand."

Simon stepped back. "Are you saying your father committed suicide?"

"I know how he felt, waiting to lose his mind," Angela was saying. "It could happen to me, too. Some types of Alzheimer's are inherited. My uncle had it, my father." She threw herself into his arms. "What about me, Simon? I could get it, too. We must make the most of life, while we have it. Together."

Simon disengaged himself, thinking she'd already lost her mind. "It was one week of our lives, Angela, more than two years ago. Forget it."

Angela shook her head stubbornly. "You're only saying that because of this TV producer."

"Leave Jake out of this," Simon said. "She has nothing to do with it."

"Jake." She spat out the name. "She's disfigured, not even a woman any longer. Look, she even chooses to use a man's name."

"She's as much of a woman as you are," Simon said, losing it. "More."

But Angela didn't react, apparently deciding to switch tactics. She reached out and took his right hand, placing the palm of it against her left breast. Simon felt her nipple harden. "Do you remember, Simon?" she whispered. "Are you willing to never feel this again?"

Jesus. Simon pulled his hand away just as his thumb started to curl instinctively down toward her nipple. "Hell, yes." He shook his hand to make it behave.

Angela stepped back, looking like she'd been slapped. "You're living together, aren't you? I called her number yesterday, and you answered."

The hang-ups on Jake's phone made sense all of a sudden.

As he opened his mouth to reply, his own phone rang.

Luis picked up the camera Dave had just set down by the fence.

"What the hell do you think you're doing?" Dave said, trying to grab it.

Too late. Luis had it, and he also had Dave's number. "I'm doing what a reporter does. What a camera man should do. I'm going after the story."

Luis looked toward the center of the landfill where flashes of light were disappearing into the fog above. "We've already missed most of the show, thanks to you."

"What show? You can't see a thing from down here. What are you going to do? Take shots of fog?"

Luis was disappointed in his former colleague. Then again, it just proved that Luis was right. Dave didn't have what it took to be a reporter. "You don't get it, do you?" Luis yelled, trying to be heard over the thunder of the fireworks. "The story isn't the shells, it's the people."

Dave was looking at him like he hadn't heard him.

Luis tried again. "It's *always* the people, don't you get that? Not the fireworks, not even the explosions. It's the people the audience cares..."

But Dave wasn't listening. He was looking over Luis's right shoulder. Was it a trick? Was Dave trying to distract him? Get him to turn around and then tackle him for the camera?

Nah. Life was never that good.

Luis turned and saw what Dave saw: The ATF guy feeling up the Firenze broad.

Then again, maybe life *was* that good.

Luis shouldered the camera.

Angela checked her watch as Simon moved to stand next to the seawall. She had no need to, though. She knew the call meant time was up. Simon would find out about Ray, find out that she'd killed him and her father.

She watched Simon turn away from her in an effort to hear his cell phone over the sound of the salutes. Angela wrapped her arms around herself.

Nothing was as it should be.

Angela had seen the emptiness in her father's eyes and she knew then, that she couldn't watch it grow each and every day until it swallowed him up. Her father's mind was wasting away. But before it did, she feared he would destroy the company he had worked so hard to build.

Pasquale Firenze had died doing what he loved. Even Simon had said her father hadn't felt a thing. His end had been so much more fitting, so much more peaceful, than...

Angela looked at Simon on the phone, probably hearing about Ray's body. Putting it all together.

As Simon turned back to her, his eyes hard, Angela stepped in and swung hard.

It was the bottle of her father's favorite home-made wine she had in her hand, instead of the flare like it had been with Ray, but as her brother Pat would say, Angela had hit this one out of the park, too.

Simon had gone over the seawall.

Jake had seen it in the flickering light of the fireworks, like something out of an old silent movie:

A flash of Simon and Angela...standing close.

Simon...walking away from her.

Angela...raising the bottle and following.

Simon...turning back.

Jake had shouted a warning as she ran, and had seen Simon try to block the blow with his arm at the last minute. It wasn't enough.

Now Jake ran up the rock seawall and looked over. The light from the fog-obscured fireworks was reflecting on the lapping water some twenty feet below Jake, the motion making her feel queasy as she scanned the water. Jake could swim, but if she couldn't see Simon, she couldn't...

Then a light went on.

Literally.

The light was on Luis's camera, not four feet from her. He was leaning over the seawall, shooting straight into the water.

And there she saw Simon. She couldn't tell if he was moving, or if it was merely the motion of the water she was seeing. She called his name, but got no answer.

"Luis." She grabbed the camera operator's arm, inadvertently making the light bobble around. Luis steadied it.

"Keep the light on him," Jake told him. "So I can find him when I get down there," she said.

But the light was suddenly in her face. "You're going into the water?" the voice behind the camera asked.

"Light, Luis!" Jake screamed, as she climbed up onto the seawall. Not five feet behind Luis, Angela stood watching like she was in a trance. Jake didn't have time to worry about it.

"Light...on...the...water, Luis!" she yelled again. Then she held her nose and jumped. She hadn't been kidding when she told Luis she didn't dive, but going in feet first seemed the prudent thing to do anyway, though probably not as photogenic from Luis's point of view.

Jake had been smart enough to direct her jump so she didn't land on top of Simon, and lucky enough to surface less than ten feet away. She let go of her nose, and then almost plugged it again. The water was cold and black and smelled like fuel oil. It tasted like fuel oil, too.

Spitting a mouthful out, she swam over to Simon and struggled to turn him over so she could tuck the crook of her elbow under his chin like she'd learned in high school swim class.

He seemed semi-conscious and the side of his head was sticky with blood. Jake let out a little whimper as she tried to tread water and hold up Simon's head at the same time. Treading water was another one of those things she'd never quite gotten the hang of, like diving. Moving in the water she was fine. Staying still? Uh-uh. Jake sank like a rock. Boobs probably would have helped. Saline implants. Salt water...wonder if they'd provide extra buoyancy--

"Swim, Jake," Luis urged from above. "Swim to the ladder."

Luis gestured with his light and Jake bobbed and scissor-kicked her way hundred-eighty degrees around, so she could see the corrugated metal that formed the seawall down here in dead-fish-and-floating-garbage country.

Sure enough, there was the ladder that led up to the promised land of cotton candy and porta-potties. It was the same ladder Jake had thought Luis would climb, given half the chance, to get back from the barge with his tape the night of the explosion that had killed Pasquale.

And now it might just save Jake's life and Simon's. If nothing else, they could hang on it until Luis could get help. She side-stroked over to the ladder, towing Simon along. It was slow going--

"Jesus," Simon gurgled, tugging at the crooked arm under his chin. "Let me go. I can't breathe."

Jake let go and he went under. "That's the last time I save your life, Aamot," she said, grabbing the ladder with one hand and pulling him back up by his shirt with the other.

"I sure hope so," he said, spitting out a mouthful of water.

Jake pushed him toward the ladder. "Thank God, I don't have to tote you up this," she said, her heart thumping like crazy now that she had the time. "You go first."

He did, climbing slowly and stopping two-thirds of the way up to rest.

"Luis," Jake called up as she waited behind Simon on the ladder. "Light."

No answer. Simon continued up and over the top of the seawall, then collapsed in a heap next to it. Jake followed.

"You're bleeding," she said, touching his forehead.

He nodded wordlessly and put his hand over hers, bringing it to his mouth so he could kiss it. "Thank...you..." He was still trying to catch his breath.

"How do you feel?" she asked. It was hard to tell in the light, or in the absence of light, but he looked like he was about to pass out.

Didn't stop him from trying to stand up, though.

"You need to stay sitting," she said, as he pushed himself up, and started searching through his pockets for something.

"I have to call in." He had a lights-on-nobody-home kind of look on his face. "We need to find Angela before she does something stupid."

"Stupider than trying to kill you?" Jake asked, still trying to make him sit down.

"All these people here..." Simon stopped suddenly and then looked Jake straight in the face, like she'd just arrived. "I've lost my cell phone. Do you have one?"

Jake pointed at her dripping clothes. "Sorry, buddy, I forgot my purse."

He just stared at her.

Jake sighed. Loopy or not, Simon was right, Angela could do all sorts of damage in the state she was in. Insane.

"Luis has a cell," Jake glanced around for him as she spoke. It was weird that Luis didn't have his lens stuck in their faces, interviewing them for the late news.

But the camera operator was still on the same story--just a different angle. He was turned away from them, his camera trained on Angela, not ten yards away. The woman must have stood there and watched the whole thing, anxious to see how her handiwork turned out.

Bitch.

Angela started, and Jake realized she'd said it out loud.

And it had felt good. Really good. "Bitch!" She was screaming it now as she advanced on Angela. "Bitch, bitch, bitch!"

Confronted with a crazy woman to rival herself, Angela turned and sprinted off across the landfill.

The titanium salutes of the finale were thundering overhead, piercing the fog, and seeming to light Angela's way as she ran. The sound bounced off the glass of the Waverly Apartments--the windows her father had talked about, with Mrs. Fetcher and her little dog behind them.

Angela ran past the firing console and past a flash of Pat's face and then of Tudy's. She ran through the ring of cars and over the wires that criss-crossed the firing area, and along the widening ribbon of finale shells and mortars.

Angela ran like an angel, her father had said, but that was in the past, too, like everything else.

Jake--who smelled of dead fish and gasoline--caught up with her at the final shell in the final mortar.

Pasquale's shell.

The fireworks were getting louder and faster, shells erupting from the line of mortars that multiplied exponentially as they pointed the way to where Angela stood in the center of the ring of headlights, like she was some kind of deity.

The deity was going down.

Jake launched herself. She planned to beat the crap out of Angela and then throw her into the lake like she had thrown Simon. And Ray. And Pasquale.

"You killed them, didn't you?" Jake screamed, forgetting the swim and the run, and moving onto the third part of tonight's triathlon: pummeling Angela in the side with her fists. The woman was scrunched up into the fetal position, so it was all Jake could get to. "Even your own father?"

Jake might have greater upper body strength from swimming, but Angela had the advantage of runner's legs. She kicked out sideways, catching Jake in the knee and toppling her.

Angela stood up, towering over Jake on the ground. "I did my father a favor," she screamed, her foot lashing out at Jake.

Jake grabbed it. "Killing him was a favor? To who, yourself?" The noise and light from the shells going up around them was so intense that Jake was getting disoriented. She managed to get up on her knees.

"My father was sick," Angela protested. "I couldn't let him suffer."

Good thing she hadn't been around when *Jake* was sick. "So you put your father down like you would a dog? Like you tried to do with Lugosi?" She had hold of Angela's whole leg now, wrapping herself around it like it was a tree she was climbing.

"You don't understand. He was going to die anyway." Angela was trying to shake Jake off. "But he would have ruined Firenze Fireworks first."

Now *there* was a motive Jake could believe. "You killed him to protect your company."

Angela had inched back toward the apex of the finale line, Jake clinging to her leg like a bull terrier. Now the fireworks woman stopped and bent down to scream into Jake's face. "No!"

Jake turned her head to avoid the flying spit, thinking that if Angela could see herself in a mirror, she'd probably surrender out of pure mortification. Assuming the witch even had a reflection. Jake held tight to the other woman's leg. "No? Then why?"

"I killed him," Angela's hands closed on Jake's throat, "because it was the only way I could keep him."

Simon had cut directly across the landfill toward the finale, negotiating the cables by the headlights of the Firenzes' vehicles. His head still hurt like hell and he was groggy, but when he'd seen Jake take off, he'd known where she was going.

So Simon had followed, albeit a little slower and a lot more unsteadily than he'd like. And now, he finally caught sight of Angela and Jake in the dead center of the ring of headlights. Jake was on her knees in front of Angela, and Angela had her hands around Jake's throat.

As Simon started for them, the noise from the titanium salutes cut off abruptly. In the sudden eerie silence, he saw Jake drive herself upward, pulling at Angela's thumb with her right hand, while giving her a shove in the stomach with the heel of her left hand.

It was just enough to throw Angela off balance and send her stumbling back. She caught herself, but froze when she saw Simon, almost like she couldn't decide whether to run *to* him or away from him. Then she cocked her head and looked up at the empty sky, like she'd just registered the silence.

Silhouetted in the glow of the headlights, Angela Firenze Guida spread her arms wide and fell backwards.

The last shell of the night broke through the fog bank, climbing high into the sky before finally exploding.

It was the biggest shell, of the clearest, most vibrant blue anyone had ever seen. It seemed to hang in the air forever, sapphire strobes arching slowly down to evaporate into the fog from whence it came.

Pasquale Firenze's True Blue Shell.

At last.

The sea of people making for the parking lots stopped and looked to the landfill as one, when the shell exploded. They could see nothing through the fog, but they looked anyway.

There they stood unmoving--their children, their blankets and their coolers in hand. Like a giant game of Statue Maker.

And when the echo off the Waverly came a second later, they turned in that direction, too.

So when the low, slow CRRRRACK began, when the glass of the Waverly Apartments trembled, when the windows finally shattered and all came tumbling down, they could say--would always say--that they'd been there to see it.

"Don't move."

Jake had no intention of moving. She was enjoying having Simon run his hands over her arms, and legs, and...

Simon?

She opened her eyes, and sat up abruptly, the top of her head colliding with his chin. "How'd you get here?"

Simon rubbed at this jaw. "Ran, sort of. Only to take a head-butt from you, to go with where Angela teed off on me." He pulled her close. "You're okay?"

Jake nodded into his shirt. "You?"

"Yeah."

Jake stayed with her head on Simon's chest, listening to him breathe and trying not to think. Or look, for all the good it did her.

Not twenty feet away from them was a huddled figure on the ground. Jake had seen Angela's body carried up about ten feet on the shell, so she knew the other woman had taken the impact squarely.

Which was why Jake couldn't believe her eyes when the body got up.

When it reached down and picked up what looked like a camera, she believed it.

Luis.

But not just Luis. All around, figures were converging on them, silhouetted against the headlights. It was like a scene from *Night of the Living Dead*.

But, in this version, the living were coming to look for the dead, not the other way around.

And Jake wasn't about to let Luis record it.

She opened her mouth to call him off, but then realized Luis hadn't even seen the Firenzes. He was holding the camera up, still taping as he walked to investigate a small, dark shape on the ground nearby. He stopped and looked down. Then he dropped the camera.

Simon got up and pulled Luis away from Angela's dismembered leg as the shadowy figures approached and then veered away from the other once-human debris scattered on the ground in the ring of light.

186

TWENTY-TWO

George: *"It's nearly five a.m. and we'll be signing off in just a moment, but first we're going to read, once more, the note Angela Firenze Guida left with us. It was meant to be a tribute to her father, who died in last Friday's explosion, but now it seems it's also her epitaph:*

"'My father loved nothing better than to be directly under the shells when they broke. He told me once that the only thing better would be sitting in the sky with them. And now...he is.'"

Neal: *"And now, so too, is Angela Firenze Guida. For TV8..."*

Simon knocked on the production van door at the stroke of five. He was carrying two lattes.

Jake took one like the caffeine-junkie that she was. "Thank you, thank you, thank you. Where in the world did you get these so early?"

"Flattened my face against the front window of That Coffee Place, when they were getting ready to open. I must have looked pretty pathetic because they took pity on me. The coffee wasn't brewed yet, but they made these for me."

"You do look pathetic, but at least you got to change." Jake was looking down at her own clothes, which were now dry, stinky and wrinkled, instead of wet, stinky and wrinkled.

Simon, on the other hand, was wearing a forest green shirt, apparently fresh from the cellophane package, since it still had folding wrinkles and a stick pin in it. "That Henley looks nice on you," she said, removing the pin.

Simon, who was busy taking the lid off his latte, turned red. "Thanks, I just bought it. The bag was still in the Explorer."

"Guess you do have some shopping to do, to replace everything you lost in the fire." She took a sip and shuddered. "Gosh, that's good."

"Are you sure you should be working?" he asked, watching her.

"You are," Jake pointed out.

He tilted his head. "Yeah, but--"

"Yeah, but you're a professional, huh? Used to getting bludgeoned and then coming back for more." She grinned at him. "How's your head?"

"Okay. You probably saved my life, you know." He said it like it hurt a little--not his head, but to admit he'd needed saving.

"So we're even. You saved mine in the fire." Jake's grin got bigger, and then died out. "People here said the blue shell was the most beautiful thing they'd ever seen. They had no idea of the carnage below the fog."

Simon took the latte from her hand and set it on the counter before she could spill it. "I think Angela planned to die," he said after filling her in on what Angela had told him. "That's why she ran for her father's mortar. That's why she stopped and counted before she threw herself on the shell. She was counting down the timing fuse."

Angela planned to die. Planning for the inevitable, Jake understood. Planning to make it *happen*, though, was a whole 'nother other thing.

"When Eagleton said a body had been found," Simon was saying, "Angela knew it was Ray's and that everyone would know she killed him."

"I thought she had killed you, too."

"She could have," Simon said. "If you hadn't yelled so I raised my arm and started to turn away, the blow alone might have killed me."

"She must have been one heck of a softball player," Jake said.

They sat silent for awhile.

"I have something to tell you," Simon said finally.

Jake put her hand on his arm. "I already know about you and Angela."

He looked surprised. "How could you know that?"

"Dianne told me."

"My ex-wife?" He'd moved past surprised, all the way to shocked, with a smidgeon of "suspicious" tossed in. "When did you talk to her?"

"She came here earlier tonight, or make that last night. She said she wanted to talk to me about liability for the microwave van, but..." Jake shrugged.

"But she just happened to mention I'd had an affair?"

"I don't honestly think she came to tell me that, she just was curious about me. The other thing just slipped out when Angela didn't show up for her interview." Jake grinned at Simon. "She told me where I might look."

"I can imagine." He reached out and took her hand, turning it over to trace his fingers in the palm. "It was a stupid thing to do, and it was wrong. Dianne had already moved out, but technically I was still married and, more than technically, Angela was."

"How did it end?" It might be none of Jakes' business, but she was an information-gatherer by trade.

"Dianne found Angela at the house, which gave me the excuse I needed to end it." He shrugged. "Let's face it. Angela didn't like the smell of smoke, didn't like Irish, and didn't like the house."

"Bitch," Jake said. "Wanna go home?"

"Yeah."

Simon had just pulled the Explorer behind Jake's Jaguar in the driveway when his cell phone rang. "Aamot."

"Hi Tex, you coming in?"

What was Kathy doing in the office before six a.m.? He asked her.

"I figured it was going to be one of those days, so I thought I'd best get a jump on it."

"Well, I thought I'd get a couple of hours of sleep before I came in." Simon yawned.

"Okay, but I have Cruise's complete report on my desk."

"On Firenze's financial records? What's the bottom line?"

"Is that an accountant joke? It's about as funny as an accountant joke."

Simon laughed. "Actually, it's a Simon's-too-tired-to-know-he's-clever joke." He hesitated. "How are you doing, Kath?"

"Fine. Now do you want to know what Cruise found?"

"Yes, please." Jake already was waiting at the door.

"Then get your ass in here." And Kathy hung up.

Aamot sighed. Who needed a wife or a mother or even a wicked stepmother? He had Kathy.

He went over to Jake. "I have to go to the office. Cruise found something in Firenze's books."

"Something else?" Jake asked, looking eager.

"I guess," Simon rubbed his stubbly chin, sorry to be leaving her after everything they'd been through. "You'll be okay?" he asked her.

She nodded. "We need to stop asking each other that."

Simon laughed and kissed her. "I'll report back later, Chief," he said, and returned to his truck.

Jake put the key in the door as Simon drove off. Then she pulled it out again. She hated to admit it, but the only reason going home sounded good, was because Simon was going to be there. Even as tired as she was, she wouldn't be able to sleep. She was afraid of who would be in her dreams, and in how many pieces.

So now what? Where does one go at six in the morning if not home?

Not the station. There would be another producer on duty, so Jake would only be in the way there. She'd done what she could, anyway, even talked Luis down when he came back. The kid had really been shook up by what he'd witnessed.

Jake felt badly for him, but she had to admit the experience had been a valuable lesson, sort of a videographer's "Scared Straight." She didn't expect to have any more trouble from him and LB's Hot Video. At least until he'd paid for the camera he'd dropped.

Whether it was orders from the top--in the person of Gwen-- or human decency on the part of the news staff, no one at the station had pumped Jake for information or asked for an interview. Jake figured that would last about twelve hours, so she'd best make the most of them. What she could really use now was a nice relaxing swim, but her swims weren't exactly relaxing any longer.

She thought about that. Yes, Jenson might be there and no, she didn't want to be stupid and put herself in danger.

On the other hand, was Jake going to let the Croc decide her schedule?

Was she going to give up something she loved, just because he threatened her?

Was she going to let him scare her?

Heck, yes. She unlocked the door, went in the house and made a phone call. Then she got in her car and drove to the Y.

It was a little after six when she arrived, but the pool was open. And Doug, bless him, was the lone swimmer.

She sat on the edge of the pool in the lane next to his and waited for him to reach her.

He stopped and stripped off his goggles. "You are so lucky I was already up and planning to come here anyway."

"Thank you."

Doug grinned. "You know I would have leapt out of bed to come and defend you anyway, right?"

"Of course," Jake said donning her cap. "But you know that I really appreciate it, also right?"

"I do. This guy really has you spooked, huh?"

"You bet. Last night he came to the production van, and--" She glanced toward the whirlpool off to the side in a glassed-in area. "Oh, shoot."

"What?" Doug said, looking around.

"He's in there," Jake hissed. "You can't see him unless he pops his head up to look out. Which he just did. Shoot, shoot, shoot."

"So what are you going to do? Run away?"

Well, yeah. "Well, no, of course not." Jake pulled her cap off. "I think...I'm going, yes, I'm going to talk to him. That's what a guy would do, right? I mean you would confront someone who was bothering you. I should do that, too, right? I mean, find out what his problem is?"

Jenson was now standing up and looking over.

"I've never heard you incoherent before," Doug observed. "It sounds sort of...stupid."

Jake got hold of herself. After all, she hadn't hesitated to confront Angela last night. She stood up, vowing to leave this one alive, at least.

"I'm going to go talk to the guy," she told Doug. "You watch in case he tries to drown me." Or me, him, she thought.

"Want me to come with you?"

Jake shook her head. "No, I think that'll put him on the defensive. I don't want him to get embarrassed and do something to save face."

"Like drown me?" Doug asked. "I don't want that either. I'll stay right here." He hiked himself up on the deck to watch, as Jake padded over to the whirlpool area and opened the glass door.

Jenson stood up and all the opening lines Jake had formulated evaporated. "Just what in the heck are you looking at?" she snapped.

Jenson flushed. "Listen, I am really, really sorry." He started to wade across the whirlpool toward her.

"You said that before. Just stay where you are."

Jenson held up his hands and stopped. "I know I must have scared you last night, showing up at your truck, but I wanted to talk to you. I tried to call, but kept losing my nerve. I just wanted to apologize, and I thought it might be easier when no one else was around."

So maybe the hang-ups hadn't been all Angela, as Simon had thought. That made sense, since they'd begun before the night of the fire.

Jenson nodded toward Doug, who was still watching. "You have a lot of friends here, and I know I've been acting odd. I just needed to explain."

Jake glanced back at Doug and thought of Cindy and some of the other people who swam here every day. Gosh, she really did have a lot of friends. Before she lapsed into full Sally-Field mode, though, she asked, "So what do you want to explain?

"Okay, if I sit on the edge?" he asked, his hands still up in the air.

"Yeah, sure, go ahead." She sat, too, but at the other end of the whirlpool.

Jenson looked down at the water and then off across the pool. "My wife had breast cancer surgery two days ago."

Jake thought about the woman she'd seen during Neal's interview with the family. Young, blonde, pretty, with a couple of little kids. What a shame she had to go through it, but why was Jenson telling Jake this? What was she, the mastectomy poster child?

Then again, since she'd opted to go through treatment practically on-air, maybe she had volunteered for the position.

"I'm sorry," she finally said. "How's she doing?"

He looked at her. "She's doing really good, thanks."

"Lumpectomy or mastectomy?"

"Mastectomy. Double."

They were both quiet. A moment of silence for the fallen breasts, Jake thought.

"It was serious," Jenson continued, "still is." He looked down. "Julia was scared for her life, and I was, too. Still am, but..."

"But you were freaked out by the thought of your wife's breasts being lopped off," Jake finished.

"Yes," Jenson said, looking up at her. "I know that's stupid, that it's..."

"Natural," Jake said. "That's what it is: natural. Both for you and for her."

"I don't think it bothered her, really. In fact, she decided against reconstruction."

Aha. "Like me, huh?"

"Yes. She had seen the coverage of your surgery and recovery, and knows people who have had reconstructive surgery, and had to go back a couple of times to get it right. She wanted one surgery and to be done with it. Like you.

"Every time I looked at you here," Jenson continued, "I saw Julia. It made me angry at fate or God, or whatever you want to call it, for doing this to her. And to be honest," he looked Jake in the eye finally, "it made me angry at you for having influence over her, when I didn't. Even worse, I was angry at Julia."

"For not caring if she had breasts, or for getting sick in the first place?"

"Both."

They were quiet again.

Jenson stood up. "After the surgery, I realized what a jerk I'd been."

"I'm sure reconstruction has come a long way in the last couple of years," Jake said, standing up, too. "Maybe she'll change her mind at some point."

Jenson reached across and shook her hand. "Maybe. That's her decision. As far as I'm concerned, her life is the important thing. All the rest is window-dressing."

"I'm not saying that Julia Jenson made the right or the wrong decision," Jake said, "but it scares me that someone would base a medical decision on what I did."

They were sitting on the couch, Jake having just returned from swimming and Simon from the office. Jake had her bare feet tucked underneath her and was drinking a glass of wine.

It was seven-thirty a.m.

Simon didn't understand why someone as logical as Jake would agree to go through cancer treatment with a camera following her, and then be surprised that people paid attention. He said as much. Gently.

She set her glass down. "I was a reporter who had cancer, and the only way I could make sense of that in my own head was to think of it as an assignment. To be the best damned cancer patient there ever was."

"And were you?" He took her hand and rubbed her palm with his thumb.

"You bet! I did my chemo, and I worked. I threw up, and I worked. My hair fell out, and I worked. Eventually, I was done with treatment, and my hair grew back, and I was still working. As far as everybody else was concerned, it was all over."

"And for you?"

"Me?" She smiled. "I crashed and burned. I'd been so busy playing 'the best darn cancer patient' that I hadn't really taken time to figure out what it meant to *me*.

"So there I was scrawny, sans breasts. My hair was now curly and reddish, instead of blonde. But those were just the physical changes. It's hard to describe, but I felt -- still *feel* ...temporary. Do you know what I mean?"

Simon knew. Most people in law enforcement knew. "We're all temporary. The majority of us just have the luxury of forgetting most of the time."

She looked thoughtful, and Simon pulled her over to him. "So what did you do?"

"Got myself a damn good therapist."

That was good to know. Simon thought she might need one, given what had happened last night. "And quit reporting?"

Jake nodded. "I couldn't keep jumping in and out of people's lives. I needed to maintain some distance. Gwen was very good about it, I have to give her that."

"That and the fact she didn't fire you for abandoning your post."

"She got an exclusive with the heroes of the day—you and me. Why should she fire me?"

Simon was quiet. Jake twisted around to look at him. "Something on your mind?"

Simon shifted uncomfortably. "The cancer. You do get check-ups regularly, right? Mammograms or something?"

Jake laughed and flashed her chest at him. "No mamms to gram, I'm afraid."

Wonder of wonders, Simon blushed. But he wasn't going to let her get away without answering. "You do get checked?"

Jake held her hand up oath-like. "Regularly, I swear. I may be flip, but I'm not stupid."

She snuggled back in and Simon sniffed her damp hair. "Is that the bouquet of 'pooly fuisse' I detect?"

Jake grinned. "You're just trying to one-up my 'mamms to gram.'"

"It was way too good," Simon admitted. "I couldn't let you get away with it."

Speaking of getting away. "So why were you called into the office?"

"Cruise had finished going over Firenze's books."

"And?" Jake prompted.

"And it turns out there was a steady drain of funds from their account over the last six months. Small amounts at first, culminating in the fifteen grand from the Refresh Yourself show for a total of nearly fifty thousand dollars."

Jake whistled. "No wonder Angela had her undies in a bundle. What was he doing with it?"

"The tracking numbers lead to all sorts of quasi-medical sites, selling what looks to me like a bunch of questionable remedies and treatments for Alzheimer's. The last payment, the $15,000, went to some research facility in France."

"And in the end, Alzheimer's didn't kill Pasquale after all. His loving daughter killed him."

"Along with Ray," Simon added, "who apparently discovered that crumpled contract Cruise found stuck in the front pocket of the binder and decided Pasquale was stealing from his own company. He showed it to Angela, who suddenly realized the extent of her father's problem and realized he could decimate the company."

"But why kill Ray?"

"He was going to blow the whistle, at least within the family. Angela couldn't have that."

"By why? Pasquale would have gotten help."

"Not the kind of help Pasquale wanted. Or that Angela wanted for him."

"There was something else Angela wanted," Jake ventured.

Simon kissed the top of her head. "That would be me?"

"'t would be. Think about it: Everything in Angela's well-ordered world was falling apart." Jake looked up at Simon. "So she decided to trade it all in for you. Her fantasy knight in shining armor."

Simon kissed her lightly on the cheek. "Her goal may have been understandable, but her methods sucked."

"Big-time," Jake agreed, tucking herself under Simon's chin.

Silence, then: "He was in that blue shell."

Jake pulled back. "Who?"

"Pasquale."

Umm. "In a 'God is everywhere' kind of sense?"

"No. Literally. Pasquale's ashes were in the last shell."

"The one Angela fell on?" Jake was still trying to understand this.

"A devoted daughter," Simon said, dryly.

"Sick. I think I'd rather have a faithful dog."

"Hey, I have a faithful dog. You can share."

Jake tilted her head up and kissed him. "You and that faithful dog of yours are going to need to find a place of your own eventually, you know," she said gently.

"Yup."

And that's all he said.

Jake's head was on Simon's chest so she could feel his heart beating, but that was the only outward sign that he was alive.

They just sat there like that until she finally cleared her throat. "Listen, it's not that I don't--

"You know," Simon interrupted, "this room could use a coat of paint. I'm thinking 'Too Beige, or Not Too Beige' maybe, or..."

ABOUT THE AUTHOR

Sandra Balzo is an award-winning author of crime fiction, including two different mystery series--one set in the High Country of North Carolina and the other outside Milwaukee, Wisconsin.

The Maggy Thorsen Mysteries
Uncommon Grounds
Grounds For Murder
Bean There, Done That
Brewed, Crude And Tattooed
From The Grounds Up
A Cup Of Jo
Triple Shot

The Main Street Mysteries
Running On Empty
Dead Ends

Made in the USA
Middletown, DE
12 June 2021